LITTLE
GIRL
LOST

Also by Brian McGilloway

The Inspector Devlin Series

Borderlands

Gallows Lane

Bleed a River Deep

The Rising

LITTLE GIRL LOST

BRIAN McGILLOWAY

MACMILLAN

First published 2011 by Macmillan
an imprint of Pan Macmillan, a division of Macmillan Publishers Limited
Pan Macmillan, 20 New Wharf Road, London N1 9RR
Basingstoke and Oxford
Associated companies throughout the world
www.panmacmillan.com

ISBN 978-0-230-74765-4 HB
ISBN 978-0-230-75336-5 TPB

1 3 5 7 9 8 6 4 2

A CIP catalogue record for this book is available from
the British Library.

Typeset by CPI Typesetting
Printed in the UK by CPI Mackays, Chatham ME5 8TD

Visit **www.panmacmillan.com** to read more about all our books
and to buy them. You will also find features, author interviews and
news of any author events, and you can sign up for e-newsletters
so that you're always first to hear about our new releases.

For Ben, Tom, David and Lucy

CHAPTER 1

There was definitely something moving between the trees. He'd been aware of it for a few moments now, a flitting movement he'd catch in the corner of his eye, weaving through the black tree trunks set vertical against the snow. At first he had dismissed it as the result of snow hypnosis from staring too long through the windscreen into the unrelenting downdraught of snowflakes.

Michael Mahon shunted the gearstick back into first as he approached the hill leading into Prehen. He knew almost as soon as he had shifted down that it was the wrong thing to do. He felt the wheels of the milk float begin to spin beneath him, could see the nose of the vehicle drift towards the kerb. He eased back on the accelerator, pumped the brakes in an attempt to halt the inexorable movement sideways but to no avail. He knew the wheels had locked and yet still the float shifted sideways, sliding backwards across the road, coming to rest finally against the far kerb.

Cursing, he shut off the engine and dropped down from the cab onto the road. Just behind him lay the edge of the ancient woodland stretching for several miles from Prehen all the way up to Gobnascale. Light from street lamps reflected off the snow, illuminating further into the woods than normal at this time of night. Black branches of the trees sagged in places under the increased weight of snow.

Shivering involuntarily, Michael turned his attention to the milk float again. He picked up the spade he'd left on the back for just such an emergency. As he was bending to clear the snow from the wheels he became aware once more of a movement in the woods, on the periphery of his vision.

It was cold, yet the goosebumps that sprang up along his arms and down his spine caused him to start. Brandishing the spade in both hands, he turned again to face the woods, dread already settling itself in the pit of his stomach.

A child came into the open at the edge of the trees. Her hair, long and black against the white background of the forest floor, looked soaked through, hanging lank onto her shoulders. Her face was rounded and pale. She wore a pair of pyjamas. On the chest of the jacket something was written. Her feet were bare.

When the girl saw him she stopped, staring at the spade he was holding, then looking at him, challengingly, her gaze never leaving his face, her skin almost blue from the luminescence of the snow. It was only as he stepped closer to her, crouching cautiously, his hand outstretched as one might approach an animal, that she turned and ran back into the trees.

CHAPTER 2

Lucy Black sensed someone in her room. She felt groggy as she stretched across to the lamp on the bedside locker, her fingers spidering over her service revolver.

'Are you coming?' her father's voice whispered into the darkness.

She swore softly to herself, fumbling with the switch on the lamp, causing it to fall off the bedside cabinet.

'Get to bed, Daddy,' she said.

The ceiling light sparked into life, dazzling her. She shifted in the bed, pulling at her nightdress to straighten it around her shoulders.

'Are you coming?' the old man repeated. He stood in the bedroom doorway, his hand still resting on the switch. He wore a grey suit over his pyjamas, his good shoes, polished. In his hand he carried a suitcase, empty judging by the ease with which he swung it, its sides thumping against his leg. White dollops of shaving foam flecked one cheek. Along his jaw a thin line of blood trickled from a shaving cut, gathering against a clump of grey stubble he had missed.

'It's half-four in the morning, Daddy,' Lucy said, struggling to get out of bed.

'He's coming at nine, they said. We'll need to get going. Are you not getting dressed?'

'Who's coming?'

'The Pope,' he said with exasperation. 'I told you we were going to see him. You'll make us late.'

'Let's get you back to bed,' Lucy said, moving towards her father, taking his arm.

He snatched away from her quickly, the movement causing the suitcase to swing violently, connecting with her shin.

'We'll be late,' he hissed, his teeth gritted. 'Get dressed.'

Lucy stood in front of him, wiped the blear of sleep from her eyes. 'Where is he? The Pope?'

'Drogheda,' her father said. 'He's saying Mass in Drogheda.'

'The Pope was in Drogheda thirty years ago, Da.'

The old man's jaw clenched, his bird-like chest puffing slightly. 'You're always contradicting me. He's coming today.'

'It was 1979, Daddy,' Lucy said, quietly, pleadingly, hoping the plaintive tone to her voice might somehow penetrate his muddled thoughts.

He looked at her, his mouth quivering, the sound of his denture clacking against his remaining teeth as he considered what she had said. He sniffed and she could see his eyes begin to glisten with tears, as if on some level he was aware of his mistake.

'We're early yet, Daddy,' Lucy said, instead. 'We'll not need to be leaving until later. Why don't you grab a few more hours of sleep?'

The man looked at her a little defiantly. 'Maybe so,' he said finally. 'I'll tell your mother.'

'Don't worry; I'll tell her,' Lucy said, taking her father's arm again, gingerly. 'Let's get you to bed again.'

She led him back into his bedroom. He'd drawn the curtains and, as she went to close them again, she could make out the mountains on the far side of the Foyle valley, draped in snow. The reflection of the city's lights on the water meant she could make out the form of the river itself, snaking in the distance, cutting its way through the city of Derry, splitting it in half.

Her father lay on the bed and allowed her to remove his suit. She pulled the duvet over him, leant and kissed his forehead, the smell of tobacco from his breath returning her affection.

'Goodnight, Janet,' he said to her, turning his head on the pillow in such a way that, in the still light of the room, his cheeks seemed sunken, his skin suddenly taut and waxy-looking.

'Lucy,' she mouthed into the darkness. 'I'm Lucy.'

She had settled back into bed, and was on the cusp of sleep, when her mobile rang. She had to rush to answer the phone lest it woke her father.

'DS Black, Chief Superintendent Travers here.'

'Yes, sir,' she said.

'I need you out. We think we've found Kate McLaughlin. A milkman claims to have seen her in the woodland at Prehen. He's at the bottom entrance, near the hotel. The snow's making access to the area difficult and I understand you're living there. A Response team is on its way.'

'I'll be there as quick as I can, Chief Superintendent,' she said. 'My dad's help doesn't get here till . . .'

'Just get a move on!' Travers snapped.

CHAPTER 3

It took her fifteen minutes just to leave the house. She'd needed to have all the breakfast stuff set out for her father in case he woke before nine when the help, a middle-aged woman called Sarah King, would arrive. Sarah could let herself in; she had a key and her father was used to her.

The snow was still falling heavily. Lucy was wearing a thick jumper over her shirt and had pulled on a heavy black coat. She'd worn her jeans, a pair of tights beneath to keep her warm. Even so, the cold wind bit at her skin and made her lungs ache when she breathed in.

Her gloves were soaked already from having to brush the snow from her windscreen. Then she'd set off at ten miles an hour, vainly using the bare flat of her hand to rub away the fern-like patterns of ice that formed on the inside of the glass from her own expiration.

The tyres on the car began to lose grip and Lucy felt the vehicle drift across the road. Quickly she remembered to steer into the skid to keep the car on track. She tried not to be distracted by the snow beating silently against the windscreen, nor the ominous presence of the woodland itself, standing black behind the orange fluorescence of the street lamps. It ran the entire length of Prehen, extending far beyond the estate, almost to New Buildings in one direction and Gobnascale in the other. There were a number of entrances to the woods, including one at the far end of the street on which Lucy lived, but Travers's comment on the proximity of the hotel narrowed down where the child had been seen.

When she reached the bottom entrance, she realized that despite the slowness of her travel she was there before the Response team. An abandoned milk float sat at an angle, its headlamps ablaze, illuminating the edge of the woods. Long dark shadows from the trees stretched away into blackness.

As she got out of the car, a man struggled down from the cab of the milk float and made his way up towards her.

'There's someone in there!' he shouted up to her. 'I think it's the McLaughlin girl. I've phoned the police.'

'They've arrived,' Lucy responded, waving the torch she held in her hand. 'DS Black. Were you the one who saw her?'

The man had reached her by now, his cheeks flushed with the chill.

'Michael Mahon,' he said, nodding in response to her question. 'She went in there.' He pointed to his right.

'You didn't try to stop her?' Lucy asked, trying not to sound accusatory. Failing.

'Of course I did,' he replied. 'She turned and ran.'

Lucy paused, rephrasing before she spoke again.

'It was safer not to go in alone after her,' she said.

He looked at her a moment, as if searching for offence, then nodded.

'Where're the rest of you?' he asked.

'The rest are on their way. Things are busy tonight, sir.'

Mahon grunted in response, spat on the ground in front of him, ran the tip of his shoe against the snow.

'I was thinking it was her. You know, the wee girl Kate.'

Lucy nodded. 'Was it?'

The man grimaced apologetically, shrugged his shoulders. 'She didn't stand still for long. I couldn't tell with the dark.'

'Understandable, sir,' Lucy said. 'We'll know soon enough.'

She puffed out her cheeks, then began trudging through the snow towards the woodland edge. She knew she should wait for the Response team, but in this weather they could take an hour to arrive. The child would be past helping by then.

'You'll never find her in there on your own!' Mahon shouted from behind her.

'I'm not on my own, though, am I?' Lucy replied.

The surface snow scattered the light from her torch as they moved into the trees. Sweeping the beam from side to side, she scanned the forest floor for footprints, for even the slightest indentation on the snow's crust that might signal the passage of the child the milkman had seen. Even with the falling snow, the air around them seemed unusually chilled and sharp with the scent of decaying leaves.

'Nothing,' she said.

'Uh?' Mahon stooped slightly to avoid the hanging branches of the trees now surrounding them.

'You're sure you saw someone?' Lucy asked, inadvertently turning the torch on the man as she twisted to look at him.

'I swear to God,' he said, his right hand raised slightly in front of his face to shield his eyes. 'I think she came in here; but the whole bloody place looks the same. I definitely saw someone though. A girl.'

Lucy turned again towards the woods. Looking left and right she saw only lines of tree trunks, the snow settling implacably on the ground around her with a whispered hush. Absurdly, it reminded her of her earlier movement as she pulled her father's blanket around his shoulders, whispering him to sleep. Further into the woods the trees disappeared among the deepening gradations of darkness rippling out beyond the light of her torchbeam.

'It might have been down there a bit,' Mahon said, stepping away ahead of her, already having to take exaggerated steps to progress through the thickening drift at their feet. 'She'll freeze to death in this,' he commented, almost to himself.

They walked along the edge of the trees, treading carefully so as not to walk over any prints. Six or seven hundred yards south of their starting point Lucy saw for the first time marks in the snow, slim indentations, the hollows already filling. The prints seemed to be circling around trees, the movements of the child's steps indiscriminate. There was no doubt in her mind that the prints were those of a child.

'I told you,' Mahon said, gesturing towards the marks. 'I knew I saw something.'

Lucy grunted acknowledgement, stamped her feet, the snow crunching beneath her. She followed the trail with her torchbeam, her tongue poking through her teeth in concentration, like a child completing a join-the-dots exercise. The trail twisted back on itself a few times, moved towards the edge of the woodland, where presumably the child had watched the milkman, then moved back again and cut at an angle across to the left.

'This way,' Lucy said, moving off now, walking alongside

the marks in the snow, and taking care to preserve them in case they had to retrace the child's movements again.

The tracks rounded a tree whose lower branches, though leafless, were fanned with thin twigs that had served to hold a deadweight of snow. Something seemed to have disturbed it in some way, probably the child in her passing, for much of the snow had fallen, piled like spilt sugar on the ground.

'Shouldn't you call her or something?' Mahon asked as he trudged behind her.

'It might scare her off,' Lucy said. 'The gentle approach might be better.'

The hush of the falling snow was split with the wailing of sirens as in the distance other police cars approached. For a few seconds, Lucy found herself disorientated by the combination of the snow and the elliptical flickering of blue lights through the trees, like strobe lighting. She considered going back to her colleagues, to Travers, who would no doubt be annoyed at her going into the woods alone. On the other hand, a child alone in such conditions took priority over everything else, she reasoned, and she kept moving deeper into the trees.

Her breath was laboured as she strode through the drifts, eventually having to kick out sideways in order to step forwards. She could not catch a breath, yet was grateful for the heat the struggle to move generated.

She heard the silence resume as the sirens were cut off. Her colleagues must have arrived and would be following her own prints into the woods, just as she had tracked the child's.

She had known these woods once and still remembered them enough to know there were landmarks by which to gauge her whereabouts. She recalled there was a hollow somewhere close by where, rumour had suggested when she was young, an elephant had been buried after dying during a performance by a visiting circus. The hollow had sunken further over the years, making the story seem all the more believable.

But she did not reach that far. Nor was she likely to in the worsening weather. She had been moving for almost five minutes when she heard something above the roaring silence of the falling snow. Moving forwards more slowly, the torch held low to widen the spread of the beam, Lucy found herself holding her breath as she listened. Stertorous gasps seemed to come from upwind. For a moment, Lucy could see little, the torchbeam only serving to highlight the downdraught of snow pounding towards her. Then, gradually, she became aware of a figure sat at the base of a hawthorn tree fifty yards away.

The child sat hunched against the tree trunk, her knees drawn up against her chest, the thin cloth of her pyjama top stretched over her kneecaps. Her hair lay flat against her head, lank strands plastered to the porcelain skin of her face. Her lips were almost blue, her teeth audibly chattering as she attempted to control her breathing. When she realized Lucy had spotted her she shrank back tighter against the tree, clamping her mouth shut.

Lucy lowered the torch a little further, approached the child slowly, her hand outstretched, her body hunched to bring her closer to the child's level.

'You're OK, sweetheart,' she said. 'I'm not going to hurt you. My name's Lucy – what's your name?'

The child eyed her warily, her eyes flashing under the dark furrows of her brow. She wrapped her arms around her knees, tightened her grip, as if trying to make herself even smaller.

'I'm not going to hurt you,' Lucy repeated. She was aware that Mahon was standing back to her right, didn't want to look though, in case it drew the child's attention to him.

'You must be cold,' she said. 'Why not come with me?'

The girl shook her head, her eyes squeezed shut.

Lucy moved closer till she was almost touching the child, could feel the chill of her skin, the crystalline tracks of tears that had frozen on her cheeks.

'Come with me, sweetheart,' she said again, holding out her hand, palm open, in front of the child.

'Take my hand and come with me,' she repeated.

The child did not move, though involuntary shudders seemed to rack her body, the muscles of her neck taut beneath the skin.

At least she could be reasonably certain that she was not Kate McLaughlin. Kate was sixteen, this girl looked closer to eight or nine.

'What's your name?' Lucy asked again.

The child unclamped her mouth as if to speak but seemed unable to form words.

'I'm Lucy,' she said again, inching closer to the girl, moving her hand ever nearer, until finally the tips of her fingers made contact with the girl's frozen arm.

The child initially reacted sharply to the contact, then seemed to relax. She looked at Lucy, then her eyes rolled backwards and she slumped onto the cushion of snow at her feet. Looking down at her, lying prostrate on the ground, Lucy could see clearly for the first time the image on the girl's pyjama top: a teddy bear, clasping a large blood-red heart, beneath which was written the name 'Alice'.

Lucy glanced around her, looking for support. The milkman stood frozen behind the tree where he watched her, open-mouthed. Then she began to shout for Travers.

*

The flickering of torches between the bare trunks of the trees signalled the arrival of the other officers. Chief Superintendent Travers led a group of uniformed constables, pounding his way through the snow seemingly with no regard for preserving the child's prints. When he reached Lucy, he found her crouching in the snow beside a child. Lucy had taken off her coat and wrapped it around the young girl, who was now shuddering convulsively. He shone the torch towards her, not wanting it to glare fully on her face but eager to check her identity.

He scrutinized the features, the dark hair.

'Has she spoken?'

Lucy shook her head, placed an arm around the girl's shoulders, felt the dull tremors running through the body.

Travers lifted his radio, clicked through to the station.

'It's not her,' he said with a hint of disappointment. 'It's not Kate McLaughlin.'

Lucy, without knowing why, found herself hugging the child even tighter because of this, laid her cheek against the child's forehead, wrapped her fingers in the heat of her own hands.

CHAPTER 4

Lucy sat outside the hospital ward where Alice was being examined, listening to the noises of the place, registering their familiarity as she waited for the emergency social worker to arrive. Over the past month since her arrival back in Derry she'd been in and out of this place with her father more often than she cared to remember. He'd fallen getting out of the bath one day and hurt his arm. Then he'd tripped on the stairs. Each incident had required an overnight stay for him and also for Lucy who would keep vigil by his bed.

She tried to shut out the noises, but couldn't; the clattering of instruments, the squeak of the trolley wheels as beds were pushed to and fro across the ward, the soft squelch of the porters' shoes, the echo of their distant voices. And above them all, the intermittent screaming of the girl she had found.

When she had woken, she had clung to Lucy as they'd made their way out of the woods to the ambulance. She wouldn't let anyone else touch her so that, eventually, Lucy had to carry her out through the trees. Only when she had wrapped her arms around Lucy's neck, could see her face, did she allow some of the other officers to help hold her weight. The touch of her arms against Lucy's neck had been chilling. She had not spoken, had not held eye contact with anyone.

Because of this, Travers had suggested that Lucy travel in the ambulance with her. Not that she'd minded. The grip of the child was almost feral. As word had filtered through that this was not Kate McLaughlin after all, some of the other officers seemed to lose interest. Travers had said he'd contact McLaughlin's father. Lucy was to stay with the girl until Social Services took over, then get back to the station; Travers wanted to speak to the CID team working on Kate McLaughlin's abduction.

In the ambulance, Alice had begun to moan, shifting uneasily beneath the blanket that the crew had draped around her after removing Lucy's coat. Then as they'd neared the hospital, the moans had changed in pitch to an inarticulate keening. Now though, they had shifted again: the child screeched in agony, each yell bullying the rest of the ward into silence. Several patients from the rooms further along had wandered dazed into the corridor, squinted under the fluorescent glare, looking for the source of such agonized cries.

Finally, sure that something was wrong, Lucy stood up and pushed her way into the room. The child was hunched in the corner, her knees drawn up in much the same way as when Lucy discovered her. A foil blanket had been wrapped around her and she was trying to remove it, apparently not realizing that she could not because she was sitting on the edges.

The paediatrician was giving orders to one of the nurses who was rattling through the items in the drawers of the pharmacological trolley.

'Why's she screaming like that?' Lucy asked.

The doctor, a harried-looking Indian woman, glanced at her, gauging her right to ask such a question.

'She's warming up,' she explained. 'As her body heats, the blood returns to the extremities again. When she was so cold, her body didn't feel its pain. She's feeling delayed pain now.'

'Is there nothing you can give her?'

The woman nodded towards the nurse who was holding a hypodermic needle aloft, pressing it into a small vial of liquid, and drawing the medicine into the barrel of the syringe. She handed it to the doctor, who nodded to Lucy and the nurse that they should hold the girl still.

Lucy approached Alice from her left-hand side, feeling guilty as the girl stared up at her, her gaze strangely empty, her eyes never quite connecting with her own. She reached around the child's shoulders, as if to hug her tight. For a moment, Alice seemed to relax, as if trusting the affection of Lucy's movement. Then she saw the doctor approaching, the needle in her hand, and she began to writhe, her feet flailing, her arms, barely more than skin and bone, jerking against Lucy's chest. She twisted her head towards Lucy, her eyes wide and bulging.

Lucy wanted to look away, to glance at the floor, but could not. She held her stare now, watching as the eyes widened, then seemed to deaden, the lids, suddenly heavy, began to droop, the wriggling of her limbs settled, and she began to slip onto the floor. Holding her fast around the shoulders, Lucy let the child lean against her.

The doctor brushed her hair back from her face, wiped her brow with the sleeve of her white coat, as if she had been the one engaged in the physical exertion.

'Lift her onto the bed,' she said.

Between them Lucy and the nurse managed to manoeuvre the child from the floor onto the bed. Her face twitched even as she slept, her eyes shifting beneath the thin veils of their lids. Her skin was still chilled to the touch, though her mouth had begun to regain some of its colour.

The doctor approached the bed, pulling on a pair of latex gloves. She checked the girl's head first, combing the hair back against the roots to see if there were scalp injuries. Then she gently followed the lines of her neck, and across her shoulders. She checked her arms and hands next, then feet and legs, before raising the pyjama top and checking her trunk.

'Good and bad news, I'm afraid,' the doctor said when she'd finished her examination. 'The child hasn't suffered any serious physical injury from being outside in the snow.'

'And the bad news?'

The doctor peeled off her gloves as she spoke. 'She's suffering quite severe hypothermia. We'll need to keep her in for a few days. Have you found her parents?'

Lucy shook her head. 'I'd hoped to ask her how to contact them.'

The doctor frowned slightly. 'The sedative we gave her will last a few hours now. She might not be any use to you until later this morning.'

A Scene of Crime Officer arrived on the ward about half an hour later. Because of the involvement of a child and the possibility of abuse, Alice was considered a 'crime scene' and would be subject to the same investigation with the paediatrician in attendance.

Then the duty social worker blundered into the room, a wheezing corpulent woman who announced herself as Sylvia. She dropped a large handbag on the ground near the door and moved over to look at the girl, angling her head slightly to stare at the child face on.

Finally, a little deflated, she shuffled over to Lucy.

'I thought it might have been her. You know.'

Lucy nodded her head. 'It's not.'

'How is she?' Sylvia asked.

'They've sedated her. She was screaming in agony.'

Sylvia nodded her head absent-mindedly. 'I'll not be working on this one. Robbie's starting his rotation at nine. I'm only holding on until he comes.'

'I see,' Lucy said. She was about to leave when she realized that she'd no car with her, having come in the ambulance. She'd need to catch a lift back to the station with the Scene of Crime Officer when he had finished.

Sylvia grunted softly to herself, lifted her bag, then went to sit in one of the armchairs near the bed. She took out a tabloid newspaper and settled herself to read.

The SOCO worked quietly on the girl, only occasionally sharing murmured comments with the paediatrician.

'God love that poor family,' Sylvia commented. Lucy looked across at the picture of Kate McLaughlin on the cover of the paper.

'God love this girl's family too,' she found herself saying, aware that it sounded a little petulant.

'But Kate's still lost. At least this girl's been found,' Sylvia explained, rattling the paper as she turned the page.

Lucy watched the young girl shift fitfully through her sedation. She lay alone, no parents or friends, no name, no voice, no dignity even, as the SOCO and doctor began to remove her clothing.

'She doesn't seem very found to me,' Lucy muttered.

CHAPTER 5

She waited for the SOCO, Tony Clarke, who worked for around twenty minutes with Alice, alongside the doctor. He was a heavyset man, in his mid-thirties, Lucy guessed. When he had finished he seemed more than happy to give Lucy a lift back to the station.

'I've not seen you before,' he commented as they walked out to the car park. 'Newbie?'

'I've been here a month,' she said.

'Sorry,' Clarke said, reading something into her comment she had not intended. 'It's a big place; you don't get to know everyone straight away.'

Lucy felt she should say something, but wasn't sure where to start. 'How's the girl?' she asked instead.

'No obvious signs of abuse,' Clarke said. 'I've brought her clothes for examination, but I reckon she was sleepwalking or something. By the time you get to the station her parents will have phoned to report her missing.'

'I hope so,' Lucy said.

Suddenly, she felt her legs go from beneath her as she skidded on the compacted ice frozen beneath the most recent fall of snow. She reached out to steady herself, or to break her fall, but Clarke grabbed her before she hit the ground. He held her arm in one hand, his other arm wrapped around her trunk. She straightened up and adjusted her coat, thanking him for catching her.

He linked his arm through hers until they made it to his car, then opened the door for her to get in while she struggled to decide if she should be annoyed with him or not.

They drove down through the Waterside and across the Craigavon Bridge. Glancing upriver, she could make out the outlines of the houses in Prehen, just visible through the haze of falling snow. Cracked sheets of ice were forming around the outer edges of the river. At the far end of the bridge there was a bronze sculpture of two men, hands outstretched towards each other, representatives of the two sides of the town, and the two communities who lived there. Some local wag had dressed the pair with football scarves and hats, though had been careful to ensure the tribal rivalries remained, for one wore the colours of Celtic and the other the blue of Rangers.

After going along the Foyle Embankment they went to Strand Road where the CID suite was located. Various members of the CID team had already gathered in the Incident Room by the time Lucy got there. Travers stood at the head of the room. He had changed since she saw him in the woods for he now wore a navy-blue suit with a fresh white shirt and red tie. He stood in front of a large cork noticeboard, which was covered with maps, information sheets and diagrams, among which was pinned the same picture of Kate McLaughlin that Lucy had seen in the paper. Another female detective sergeant on the team, Tara, acknowledged her arrival with a slight tip of her head. A few others glanced at her quickly, then dismissed her from their attentions.

Travers paused for a moment to allow her time to sit, then continued.

'We've managed to piece together the events of Friday night a little more fully now. We know that Kate was at the cinema with her friends until ten thirty. Her father had arranged to collect her at a friend's house – Elaine Grant. As best we can tell, Kate received a text message she assumed to be from her father telling her he would collect her from Victoria Market car park which is four hundred yards from the cinema.' He pointed out the locations on a map on the board.

'Wouldn't she know her father's phone number?' a Uniform beside Lucy asked.

One of the senior CID team twisted round in his seat to see who had asked the question.

'Sorry,' Travers said, raising his hand. 'I should have mentioned that her father's phone went missing on Friday afternoon.'

It was a well-organized pick-up, Lucy thought. Well planned and clearly targeted. One difficulty was that there had, as yet, been no ransom demand. The police had been treating it as a missing persons case until one of the papers got wind of it and, realizing the girl's father was Michael McLaughlin, ran the story as a kidnapping.

McLaughlin was one of Derry's wealthiest businessmen. During the late eighties he had built a reputation through smart investment, buying huge swathes of property in the depths of the last recession, then selling it when the market recovered. His greatest success story had also been, until now, his costliest. He had bought a run-down market building on the docks, at the corner of which was an old sailors' bar. He had planned to convert the entire waterfront, years before anyone else considered developing the dilapidated docklands. However, during one of the more sustained periods of violence in the city during the Troubles, the bar had been destroyed in an explosion targeting a passing British Army convoy. McLaughlin's wife, Carol, had been trapped inside and died in the blast. McLaughlin still owned the prime land, though he had never developed it.

'In the absence of any ransom demand,' Travers began, 'we continue to play down suggestions that this is a kidnapping. Unofficially that continues to be our belief and should inform our investigations. Now might be a good time to start asking around on the streets, especially your more reliable CIs. I've requested Police 44 to do a fly-over the town once the snow lessens sufficiently. The City Centre Initiative has provided us with relevant CCTV footage of Kate leaving the cinema. I want a team to work through it. Footage from the car park where she went missing is unuseable, apparently; both the camera and the lamps above the car park were smashed in the hours before the abduction. We're going to do a reconstruction of Kate's last movements this evening along Strand Road. I'll want everyone out to take statements.'

The comment was greeted with a collective groan; the only thing worse than taking statements from well-meaning members of the public was having to do it in such inclement weather.

'I know,' Travers said, smiling lightly and raising his hands again in placation. 'The ACC has agreed overtime for all working the case.'

This, at least, reduced the groaning, even if it didn't suppress it entirely.

'Your team leaders have been briefed on what I want each of you to focus on for today; we meet back here at 1600 for an update. DS Black, I'd like to see you in my office.'

One or two of the men, as they passed, feigned anxiety,

believing that Lucy would have to explain her lateness at the briefing.

Tara placed her hand on Lucy's arm as she passed and whispered, 'Good luck. Don't let him lock the door.'

CHAPTER 6

Lucy watched Travers's lupine gait as he padded up the corridor towards her. His shirtsleeves were rolled up revealing sinewy forearms marked with blue smudges of tattoos from his time in the forces. His face too was thin and taut, his eyes deep set, the thick greying brows shadowing his eyes. He ran his hand through his hair as he approached, shifted the pace of his step.

'How's the girl?'

'Alice. She's sedated, sir,' Lucy said, standing at his approach.

'Come in,' he said, pushing open his office door, holding it for Lucy so she had to pass by him to get in.

'Sit down,' he said, passing her to get to his side of the desk, touching her shoulder gently to guide her to a seat as he did so.

He placed himself opposite her, joined his hands together on the desk, smiled enough to expose his teeth. Her glance took in his frame, the thinness of his arms, the tight musculature. The tattoos were clear now – a blurred blue anchor, a small red rose with a name, indistinct, beneath it.

'Coffee?' he asked, gesturing towards a small table to his left on which sat a tray with a flask of coffee and cups and saucers.

'No, thank you, sir,' Lucy said.

'It's been quite a first month for you,' Travers began.

'Yes, sir,' she replied, her clasped hands resting on her lap.

His eyes looked at her mouth as she spoke, then drifted to her neckline.

'You've found things different here from Lisburn, I dare say.'

Lucy nodded, unsure whether 'different' was pejorative.

'You'd no problem getting a transfer to D District. Anyone shy of work doesn't want to find themselves here.'

'I'm not shy of work, sir,' Lucy said, smiling. 'I'm ready to muck in.'

'And how is your father?'

The shift in focus unsettled her slightly. Was he implying that her work had been affected by her father's illness?

'He's not good, sir. I needed to be closer to home for him, sir. It's why I applied to come here.'

Travers nodded, smiled with understanding.

'He's lucky to have you.'

'Thank you, sir.'

'You went in without support this morning, Lucy,' he said quickly.

Lucy shifted in her seat. 'I knew I shouldn't have, sir. But I thought it might be best to find the girl as soon as possible.'

Travers waggled a bony finger at her, the backs of his hands covered with grey hair.

'Ah now – you thought it was Kate, didn't you? Maybe you thought it would do you a power of good if you got her yourself. That's OK,' he added, holding up his hand to prevent Lucy's inevitable protestations. 'I'd have done the same. You're ambitious. I like that.'

Lucy smiled as if in acknowledgement of the accuracy of his comment.

'I wish all detective sergeants were as keen to impress.'

'I wanted to get off to a good start, sir,' Lucy said, suspecting it was what he wanted to hear.

For some reason, though, the smile faded slightly, the expression became pained in a pantomime of regret.

'Which makes this move all the more unfortunate,' Travers said.

Lucy's smile froze to a rictus. Was he moving her because she went in for Alice alone? 'What move?'

'The assistant chief constable has instructed that, as you found Alice and she seems to have connected with you, you should be seconded to the Public Protection Unit for the foreseeable future.'

Lucy attempted to speak several times before she was able to formulate her words. 'But I want to be in CID.'

'And I want you here, Lucy. I need bodies like yours on my team.'

'Thank you, sir,' Lucy said, while not entirely sure the comment warranted gratitude.

'It's a pity, now, but it's out of my hands. You'd be perfect CID material.'

'I'd rather be here, sir, if I'm honest. Working with you.' She almost stumbled on the last words. Did Travers sense this? Realize he was being flattered? If he did, he showed little reaction.

'Don't be fretting, now,' Travers continued. 'I'll not let you get too far away. I'll have a chat with the ACC and tell her just how eager I am to have you stay on my team.'

'Thank you, sir,' Lucy said.

'Besides,' he added. 'Tom Fleming runs the Unit there, down at Block 5. He's a decent spud. I'll tell him to keep an eye on you for me. Maybe see if he'll let you throw a hand in with us over here. PPU are involved in the Kate McLaughlin case anyway.'

'Thank you, sir,' Lucy said again.

Travers stood, showing that the meeting was concluded. Still he came towards her, shook her hand, held hers in his for a few seconds, the tips of his fingers rubbing back and forth across the skin of her wrist.

'Don't you be worrying now,' he said. 'I'll do all I can to have you back here in no time.'

CHAPTER 7

Her car still parked at the edge of the woods in Prehen, Lucy had had to get a lift to Maydown station with a Response team who'd got a call out to Strathfoyle.

As a passenger, she had time to look out of the window at the city. It still shocked her how much it had changed since she had left. Then it had seemed on the verge of destroying itself; two banks of the river, two names, two tribes, the schism so great that at one stage a British prime minister had seriously contemplated running the border down the Foyle, bisecting the city with the Cityside in the Republic and the Waterside in the North.

Now, though, the place seemed to have found its feet. Red brick still abounded, but one by one bridges literal and metaphorical were traversing the river, drawing the two sides closer. The city that had been the birthplace of the Troubles was now being used as an example of accommodation in the quest to solve the issue of Orange parades.

Craning her neck as they crested the Foyle Bridge, she could see the city, sprawling either side of the broad sweep of the river, caught in a still grey light. Then, they turned left at the roundabout at the end of the bridge and out towards Maydown.

The Maydown station was an expansive compound, built several miles out of town and housing most of the major units, with the exception of a few CID teams who operated out of the smaller stations around Derry City itself. In addition, it acted as a training college for new recruits. Twenty red-brick blocks were placed around the complex, as well as accommodation units.

After the Response team dropped her at the front of the station, she'd had to ask directions to the PPU block. The officer on duty at the gate had pointed across the yard to Block 5, warning her to mind herself on the slippery roads as she went. He smiled at her as she thanked him, rubbing his hands together then placing them behind his back to benefit from a gas heater behind him. He winked at her as she left and she felt sure he would be watching her the whole way across, perhaps half willing her to fall, if only to enliven the boredom of his morning posting.

She began making her way across to Block 5 which was at the back of the compound. Shuffling across the car parks, trying desperately not to slip on the ice and failing, Lucy twice had to wipe loose snow and ice from the backs of her legs and buttocks while the man at the sentry box made increasingly cursory efforts to hide his amusement at each fall.

She finally reached the main door of the unit. Not yet having the access codes, she buzzed and waited. Shortly, through the mirror foil of the door, she could discern the silhouette of a figure ambling towards her. She regarded herself quickly in the foil, pushed back a strand of hair that had fallen loose from her ponytail when she'd lost her balance. Her face was thinner than it used to be perhaps, but she was small so she was able to carry it.

She heard five electronic beeps then the door opened. The man who stood in the doorway, squinting at her against the light, was about five ten. He wore blue corduroy trousers and a white shirt, tucked in at the waistband which did nothing to hide the roundness of his belly. His hair was cut short, perhaps to disguise the fact that it was receding anyway. His shoulders slumped slightly as he stood, as might one defeated. He held what looked like a sausage bap in one hand.

'I'm here to see Inspector Fleming, sir,' Lucy said, offering her hand.

'You're seeing him,' the man replied. His grip was warm and strong. His melancholic eyes held hers.

She stepped past him, letting him close the door behind her. They stood looking at each other. Lucy smiled expectantly, raised her eyebrows in enquiry as to what she should do.

Fleming smiled lightly in return, still squinting against the glare of the fluorescent lights overhead, their gentle humming the only noise disturbing the quiet of the building.

'Can I help you?'

'I'm Lucy Black,' she said assuming that the name would mean something to him. The blankness of his response suggested this was not the case.

'Yes?' He nodded encouragingly.

'I've been seconded to your unit,' Lucy said, a little irritably.

'Have you indeed?' Fleming asked, raising his eyebrows now, though continuing to smile mildly. 'I wasn't told.'

'Chief Super Travers sent me down. I found the girl in the woods this morning,' she added.

'Ahh,' Fleming said, as if this made perfect sense. 'I'll give the Chief Super a call and see what I'm to do with you, shall I? Come in and have a seat.'

Lucy stopped Fleming before he turned. 'I was wondering, sir, if I might use the phone.'

'Of course,' Fleming said. 'I'll find you an empty office. It won't be hard.'

He led her into a small room on the ground floor. Apart from a desk on which sat a phone and a lamp, and an old swivel chair with the fabric on the seat torn, the room was bare.

'Help yourself,' Fleming said. 'I'll be with you in a moment.'

Lucy sat behind the desk and the chair immediately slopped to one side as the right-hand castor broke from the bottom casing and skittered across the linoleum floor. She lifted the receiver and dialled.

'Daddy?'

There was silence at the other end of the line. Then, listening closely, Lucy could make out the shallow breathing of her father, the scrape of his stubble against the mouthpiece of the receiver.

'Daddy?'

'Who's this?'

'It's Lucy, Daddy. Is Sarah there?'

'Who's Sarah?'

'The lady who helps you. Is she there, Daddy?'

'There's no one here. I'm on my own. Lucy's not here either.'

'I am Lucy,' she said, exasperatedly.

'I've no breakfast,' her father said.

'I left the stuff on the table for you, Daddy,' Lucy said. 'Your cereal is on the table. And your favourite bowl.'

'I can feed myself,' her father snapped, suddenly angry. 'I'm not an imbecile.'

'I know, Daddy,' she said, swallowing back her comment. 'I'll phone Sarah.'

'Who?'

'I love you, Daddy.'

The receiver clicked on the other end first, then Lucy hung

31

up. She called Sarah three times before the woman finally answered. The weather had made access to Prehen difficult, she explained. She'd had to park her car down at the hotel and walk up to the house. She was on the incline of Sandringham Drive as she spoke, and was clearly finding the hill a struggle for her conversation was punctuated with laboured breaths and half-finished words.

Satisfied that her father's help was at least on its way, Lucy hung up, only to realize that Fleming was standing in the doorway watching her. She was unsure how long he had been there, or how much of the conversation he had heard.

'Is everything OK?' he asked.

'My father's not well,' Lucy said.

'I'm very sorry to hear that,' he said. 'I've spoken with Travers and you're to be here for a while, I believe. Tea?'

Lucy followed him from the small office, down the corridor and through a door marked *Interview Room*. She was immediately struck by the size and airiness of the room, afforded by three windows high up on one wall. The furniture consisted of soft seating and, against one wall, an orange sofa. To one side stood a table with a trainset built on top. A beanbag spilled on the floor from beneath it on which were scattered a number of shabby-looking dolls. On a shelf above, separate from the others, were anatomically detailed boy and girl dolls. Below it, Lucy noticed on a tripod, a small video camera.

'Nice room,' Lucy said.

'We deal with children a lot,' Fleming explained, standing at a unit in the corner of the room on which sat a kettle and a few mismatched mugs. 'We interview them here rather than in the main station. Milk and sugar?'

'Both please,' Lucy nodded, looked around the room. She

was aware of Fleming watching her, though not with the same hunger as Travers.

'This used to be the Care unit. Then they mixed a lot of different units together. We deal with domestic abuse, child cases; anything involving vulnerable persons, I suppose.'

'So what have you for me to do?'

Fleming looked at her expectantly. 'Chief Super Travers tells me you're to be involved with the Kate McLaughlin case whenever possible.'

'OK.'

'And, you saved the girl this morning. Well done.'

'There was nothing to it, sir.'

'Well, we need to get an ID for her pronto. So until I'm told different by the Chief Super, you can work on that.'

Lucy raised her eyebrows again. 'So where do I start?'

'Schools and hospitals,' Fleming said. 'Where kids are concerned, always start with schools.'

Lucy was given a small office on the first floor of the building from which to work. One wall showed the bare paint, flakes missing in places where Blu-Tack had been removed without care. A noticeboard on the other wall held nothing but an assortment of drawing pins and an aged poster on the need to destroy ragwort. Two plastic chairs either side of a desk with an old telephone were the only furnishings in the room.

Sitting, she took out the list of local schools Fleming had given her and began to ring each one. She'd worked out a description of the child: four three, a slight frame, about six stone, sharp-featured, brown hair, blue eyes.

She asked to speak to the principal of the first school on her list and, when she answered, explained to her that they had found a child, gave the description, wondered if a child of that description was absent from school, or if she might be able to identify the child. She withheld the fact that her nightshirt had 'Alice' written on it, for so far they had not been able to confirm that was her name.

'Can you send me a picture?' the woman asked.

'Not yet, ma'am,' Lucy said. Pictures would not be released for the first twenty-four hours.

'You're not giving me much to go on,' the woman said.

'It's all we have. Do you have any children matching that description absent today?'

'Have you looked outside?' the woman asked. 'Half the school is off with the snow.'

'Does that description mean anything to you?'

'It could describe any number of our pupils, officer,' the principal replied tersely. 'It doesn't strike me as any one student though. I'll ask our senior teachers to keep an eye out; if anything comes up I'll let you know.'

Lucy thanked her for her help, scored the school off the list, moved on.

By lunchtime, a pattern had developed. She was halfway down the list and the schools she'd contacted were either closed because of the weather, or were poorly attended for the same reason, and no one was able to help her. One or two principals suggested names which, in the absence of any further progress, would have to be checked.

Lucy stood up, stretched and stared out at the snow falling again, marking with damp the metal barricade opposite. Finally, she picked up the phone and dialled the switchboard.

'Assistant Chief Constable Wilson's office, please?'

'One moment.'

A click. Then the phone rang three times.

'ACC Wilson's assistant. Can I help you?'

'This is DS Black,' Lucy said. 'I'd like to come up and speak to ACC Wilson, please?'

Lucy was almost sure she heard a snort of derision from the assistant. Even in Belfast, lower ranks didn't get near the top floor; didn't have the codes to get in; you went through the steps: sergeant to inspector to chief inspector and onwards. A detective sergeant would never get to speak with the assistant chief constable directly.

'Excuse me? Who did you say you were again?' the assistant asked, her tone veering between annoyance and bemusement.

'Tell her it's her daughter,' Lucy said.

The woman's tone changed.

CHAPTER 8

Lucy crossed the yard again, trying to stick to paths cars had taken to prevent a repeat of her earlier slips. The officer at the gate had changed and this one just glanced lazily at her from over the top of his paper before looking down again.

In the main building, she took the lift to the top floor, stepped out into the corridor and waited at the double doors. A security camera above shifted its angle slightly and she could see the lens retract as the focus shifted onto her. She looked up at it, resisting the urge to make some kind of gesture. There was no need for anyone to ask who she wanted to see, only one person had an office on this floor.

Assistant Chief Constable Wilson had kept her own name after she'd married, which, as Lucy had told her more than once, was handy for it meant there had been no need to change it again when she divorced Lucy's father fourteen years earlier. Lucy, who'd been thirteen then, had stayed with her father. At the time, she'd believed it was her choice; now she understood enough about custody cases to know that if her mother had wanted to keep her, she'd have been with her regardless. That she allowed her to stay with her father told her all she needed to know about the woman and their relationship.

The one benefit of having a different surname from her mother was that no one would make the connection between them. She assumed that at some stage someone would find out, and then the news would spread, but at the moment no one realized they were related. She'd told one colleague in Belfast during a drunken evening in the Empire. Then, when she got her promotion to detective sergeant, it had been brought up again. No surprises that she'd got promoted. Wasn't her mother the ACC?

She did not mention that, ironically, her mother was the person least likely to do her any favours.

So, upon moving to Derry, she told no one and was grateful that she did not have to carry her mother's name, nor the attendant weight of expectation that would have brought.

She heard the beeps of the access code being entered on the other side of the door and it swung back to reveal an anteroom. A middle-aged woman with platinum blonde hair and large hoop earrings swished back towards the desk while motioning that Lucy should go on through the heavy oak door facing her.

Inside, her mother's office was almost the size of the complete PPU unit across the yard. The room seemed to have been split into two, then left open plan. As she entered, on her left Lucy could see a large meeting table, around which were placed a dozen leather seats. A water dispenser squatted in one corner. A door near it lay ajar and Lucy guessed it was a toilet.

Her mother sat at a mahogany desk, with two small windows high on the back wall behind her. Such windows were a vestige of the Troubles when stations used small windows, in case of sniper fire, to reduce visibility of targets and also in case of explosion, to ensure less flying glass. As a result, the office was quite dark, not helped by the fact that through the windows, to the west, Lucy could see slate-grey clouds gathering.

'So you've arrived,' her mother said by way of greeting; a statement, not a question.

Unsure where to start, and not trusting herself to express her concerns without losing her temper, Lucy sat in the chair in front of the desk. Her mother had aged since she had last seen her; her hair, once ash blonde, was now growing greyer and she'd cut out her perm and gone for a short, masculine cut. Her cheeks had hollowed slightly, and the deterioration in her eyesight had outstripped her vanity for she wore her glasses now, attached to a chain around her neck. Slight wattles of skin hung at her throat.

She was not soft-featured, like Lucy, who'd inherited her looks from her father. Her mother had always looked sharp, a thin aquiline nose, tight lips, arched eyebrows that required no cosmetic accentuation. The tightness of the skin around her mouth gave her a choleric appearance. But then, as Lucy knew, she had the temperament to match.

'Why did you move me from CID?' It seemed like the best place to start.

'On your application you said you wanted to come to D District; I didn't think it mattered to you which unit you were in.'

'I applied for CID.'

'You're still a detective, Lucy.'

'That's not the point.'

Her mother's skin pinched further. 'Watch your manner, young lady.'

'Because you're my mother?' Lucy scoffed.

Lucy thought she winced, almost imperceptibly. She hoped she did. Regardless, the older woman continued: 'Because I'm your commanding officer. You wanted to come here and I allowed it. Operational needs require someone in PPU at the moment. I thought the experience would be good for you.'

'Inspector Fleming didn't even know I was coming. The place is dead. How is that good for me?' Lucy said.

'You found this girl, I believe. That will be a good first case for you to work on in the city.'

Despite her keenness to stay with the Alice case, if only to find out why the child was allowed out into the snow in her nightclothes, Lucy sensed she was being sidelined.

'I want to work in CID. The Kate McLaughlin case needs everyone working on it.'

'And what expertise would you bring to it that the hundred other officers working the case lack, exactly?' her mother asked, leaning forward.

'You don't think I'm good enough, do you?' Lucy asked.

'I don't think you're CID material. Not in D District anyway.'

'Why?'

Her mother removed her glasses, closed the arms deliberately and set them on the table. 'Look, I know Bill Travers. He's already been on the phone; he has his eye on you. If he knows you're my daughter, well . . .'

'I can take care of myself,' Lucy said. 'That's no reason to block my promotion.'

'I didn't block it. I directed it elsewhere. You're still a DS.'

'But I wanted CID,' Lucy said, her voice rising.

'Look, Lucy, I really don't give a shit what you wanted,' her mother hissed quietly. 'I worked my way through CID here. During the worst years of the Troubles. I made my name there; I made it to behind this desk from there.'

'Are you afraid I'll ruin your reputation?' Lucy said incredulously.

Her mother puckered her lips slightly, as if indicating that she would say nothing further.

'So you think I'm not capable?'

Again, her mother demurred from answering.

'As you pointed out, I am a DS.'

'Appointed by me,' her mother said. 'Because you wanted to look after your father.'

'As if you cared.'

Her mother's tone softened slightly. 'How is he now?'

'He's not well.'

'I'm sorry to hear that.'

'No, you're not,' Lucy muttered.

'Didn't I bring you closer to home?'

'Because someone needed to look after Dad.'

'Your father has other helpers, other people to look out for him,' she replied, a little bitterly.

'He deserves better than *other* people.'

'Don't deify him just because he's sick,' her mother replied darkly. 'No one's perfect.'

Lucy glared across at her mother, aware that there were layers to the conversation she couldn't grasp.

'You've been placed in PPU, Lucy. Work with Tom Fleming. He's a good man and a decent cop. He worked with your father, actually.'

'Does he know who I am?' Lucy asked.

'I haven't told him. It's your choice whether or not you want to.'

Lucy stood, pushed the chair in against the desk.

'But don't ever come blustering in here again, Lucy.'

Lucy stared at her mother who had already put on her glasses and bowed her head to the paperwork on her desk.

'Yes, ma'am,' she said, then turned and left the room.

Lucy was picking her way carefully back to Block 5 when her mobile phone rang.

'DS Black? Tony Clarke here.'

'Who?'

'I was at the hospital with you, this morning, with the wee girl. I've found something you might want to see.'

CHAPTER 9

Clarke was waiting to buzz Lucy in at the door to the Forensics suite, wearing the light-blue paper suit of his trade. As he led her through a series of small labs, he explained his concerns.

'I was trying to find you,' he said over his shoulder as he walked. 'I called CID but they said you weren't there. It took me a while to find you were at PPU.'

'I've only found out myself today.'

'Oh, right,' he said, clearly unsure how to respond. 'Well, I took the girl's clothes. I've found something interesting.'

As he spoke he keyed a code into the panel at the door leading into a darkened room, pushing the door open with his behind and stepping back to allow her past.

Inside, the room was in semi-darkness save for the dim purple glow of a UV lamp. On a board on the worktop against the back wall, the girl's pyjama top had been pinned up. A fine mist of luminous purple spots covered the front of it; so fine against the glow the UV light created from the white material that Lucy had to squint closely to see exactly what it was.

'Blood,' Clarke said. 'Her pyjamas are covered in blood.'

'Is it hers? The doctor said she wasn't injured this morning.'

'It doesn't seem to be,' Clarke said. 'I've typed this as O positive. I called the doctor in the hospital and had him check the tests they ran this morning. She's O minus, apparently. I've sent it to be DNA tested, along with a few hairs I got from the girl's head.'

'Will those not just belong to her?' Lucy asked.

Clarke laughed at her confusion. 'I combed out a few hairs that weren't hers – blonde hairs.'

Lucy peered more closely at the pattern on the pyjama top; the minuscule bubbles of purple gathered in the fibres of the cotton, each a part of a larger fluorescent arc that crossed her chest.

'So whose is it?'

'That's what you need to find out,' Clarke said, raising his eyebrows. In the light of the lamp his skin appeared scarlet red, his teeth flashed yellow as he spoke. 'And you need to do it fast, too.'

'Why?' Lucy turned her head to look at Clarke and was a little disconcerted to find him closer to her than she had thought, with his face turned towards her, his eyes holding her gaze, despite the fact that the shirt was the focus of their conversation.

'Whoever owns this is injured,' he said, smiling lightly. 'The misting pattern.'

Lucy deliberately turned her gaze to the shirt again, pointed unnecessarily to the arc of the pattern to draw his attention back to it.

'What caused it?'

Finally Clarke shifted his position, took a pencil from his desk and gestured towards the blood spatter, following the direction of travel as he spoke.

'Misting is caused by three things. Blow-back from a shooting, which seems unlikely in this case. I'll have to residue test the girl's hands as procedure. The second reason is blunt force trauma. Someone cracks you on the head with a bar or something, you'll get a mist of blood as well as thicker spurts.'

'But there are no thicker spurts here,' Lucy said.

'Which leads me to the third and, in this case, most likely cause. Expirated blood.'

'But not her own?'

Clarke shook his head. 'Someone was breathing close to her and blood droplets were in their breath like a mist. This area,' he added, pointing to a rainbow-shaped pattern close to the hem, 'this pattern is probably continued on her legs. I need to check her for blood again.'

'Wouldn't you have seen it this morning?' Lucy said. 'I didn't see any blood.'

'The girl was walking through snow. There's no reason why the surface blood wouldn't be washed from her skin. You wouldn't necessarily see it; but a luminol test will highlight it, if it's there.'

'I'll take you up,' Lucy said, then realized that her car was still in Prehen. 'Or maybe I could cadge a lift with you.'

Clarke smiled again, more broadly this time. 'Gladly, DS Black.'

'So, why would someone be breathing blood?' she asked, shifting in her seat, clasping her knees together as Clarke took another bend and the rear tyres of the car briefly lost their grip.

'Could be any number of reasons: someone with lung disease would do it, as well as coughing up blood; someone who's been injured in an accident or through a beating to the face and head, causing bubbling from the nose or mouth; or a stab wound to the lungs. Any range of things. Whatever causes it, it's not good news for whoever owns the blood.'

Lucy nodded, glanced out the window at the dirtied snow piled to the sides of the road.

'It might explain what she was doing wandering in the woods.'

'It might,' Clarke said.

The girl was curled in a ball when they came onto the ward. A man and woman were in the room with her; the man, youngish, in jeans and a checked shirt, wore a pair of Converse trainers, the other, an older woman, was dressed in a charcoal suit.

'I'm DS Black,' Lucy said when she entered, in response to the looks they gave her.

The man in the jeans smiled. 'Robbie McManus,' he said.

The woman glanced at her irritably, then turned her attention again to the girl. For her part, Alice seemed desperate to keep away from her.

Robbie nodded towards the door and moved towards it, taking Lucy by the elbow and guiding her out as he did so.

'Dr Matthews is trying to get her to speak,' he explained quietly as he closed the door, holding the handle until it clicked into place, wincing at the barely audible click of the lock.

'And who are you?'

'I'm the assigned social worker,' the young man explained. Lucy examined him in more detail now. His face was thin, tanned, lined in a way that revealed his age more clearly than the youthful clothes he wore. 'Sylvia told me you're in charge. We'll be working together.'

Lucy nodded. 'This is one of our Forensics team, Tony Clarke.'

Clarke raised his chin in greeting, lifted his hand to show that the bags of equipment he carried precluded shaking hands.

'He needs to check the girl over again,' Lucy explained. 'We've found blood on her clothes.'

Robbie smiled affably, put his hands in his back pockets. 'Was she not checked over this morning?'

'We found blood on her clothes,' Lucy repeated.

Robbie nodded. 'I understand that. We try to limit the number of medical examinations a child has to endure.'

'And I understand that,' Lucy said. 'We have reason to believe that the blood is not her own. Which means she has been in contact with another injured party. So PC Clarke will examine her again. Now.'

Robbie smiled against the glare of the overhead lighting and glanced at Clarke.

'You'll have to wait until Dr Matthews is finished. If she can get her to talk, she might tell you what you need without any further tests being done.'

They sat outside the room in hostile silence for the next twenty minutes while they waited for Matthews to finish and for a female doctor to arrive who would assist Clarke with his tests. Periodically, Lucy glanced in through the glass pane of the door. Matthews seemed to be talking a lot. The girl was not. Finally the woman stood up and stalked out to them.

'Nothing,' she said, shaking her head at Robbie.

'DS Black,' Lucy said, extending her hand.

Matthews took it, shook it lightly. 'Your interruption probably didn't help,' she said.

Lucy swallowed back a response. Her encounters with psychiatrists dealing with her father had eroded any residual respect she had for them simply by virtue of their profession. Still, there was no point in antagonizing Matthews unnecessarily.

'What's your opinion?' Lucy asked.

'I avoid labelling patients,' Matthews said, wrinkling her nose slightly as if to convey her distaste at Lucy's request. 'Still, the child seems to be suffering selective mutism.'

'Why?'

'I suspect she's been through some form of an ordeal,' Matthews said. 'Something which has caused her to choose not to talk. There's no physical impediment to speech.'

'Some form of an ordeal?' Lucy echoed.

'Yes,' Matthews said. 'Selective mutism often signifies trauma.'

'Would her experience of being lost in the woods be enough to trigger it?' Robbie asked.

Matthews considered this, nodded. 'Possibly. Everyone has different thresholds,' she explained. 'What one person could handle, another won't.'

'We believe the girl has blood on her,' Lucy said. 'We think she might have been in contact with someone who had been injured in some way. Would that qualify as an ordeal?'

'I think it's safe to assume that it would,' Matthews said.

The Indian doctor Lucy had seen earlier arrived and Lucy nodded at Clarke, who excused himself and moved into the room. Alice eyed him warily from the bed as he approached.

'So,' Lucy said, turning her attention again to Matthews. 'How do you get her out of it?'

'I don't,' she said, a little sharply. 'She'll come out of it herself when she's ready.'

'Can you at least speed it up?'

The woman looked at Lucy, her glance sliding across her face wordlessly. 'When she trusts me, she'll speak. We can't rush her recovery.'

Behind her, Clarke was gesturing to Lucy that he wanted her to come in.

'We might need to,' she replied, then passed Matthews and entered the room.

Clarke was removing his gloves as she approached. He manoeuvred her away from the girl's bed before speaking.

'She's had blood all over her hands,' he whispered.

'How did you not see it earlier?' Lucy asked. Despite her instinctive dislike of Matthews, she agreed that they should keep the number of tests to a minimum.

'It's not visible now. The snow must have washed it off as she came through the woods, if she fell or something. You can see traces of it under luminol; more than just misting this time, too. She was in contact with someone who was bleeding fairly profusely.'

Lucy glanced back to where the girl was hunched on top of the bed.

'So, who and where are they now?'

CHAPTER 10

Lucy spent the next hour checking the records of those who had been brought into the hospital over the previous twelve hours with bleeding injuries. None of them were connected with the girl. She then joined Robbie, who had been contacting other Social Services agencies from his office on the ground floor, to prepare a press release for the local media.

That done, and with little reason to stay in the hospital, Lucy made her way back to the station with Tony Clarke. She had only just got back to the unit, and was busy warming her hands against the radiator in the room she'd been given, when Tom Fleming came in with a yellow Post-It note in his hand.

'Message for you,' he said. 'The principal at St Mary's Primary School phoned.'

When Lucy heard the woman's voice on the phone, she remembered speaking to her earlier. She'd promised to keep an eye on the attendance lists for the day and to let Lucy know if anyone fitting the description Lucy had given her was absent.

'I have one pupil I'm concerned about,' the woman explained. 'Mary Quigg.'

'What's your concern, ma'am?' Lucy asked, jotting the girl's name on the pad in front of her.

'Mary's a small child. She's eleven but looks about nine. Tall and thin, brown hair.'

'She does fit the description,' Lucy agreed. 'And she hasn't turned in for school today?'

'No,' the woman replied. 'She missed days last week too. I was away in London at an ICT award ceremony, so I hadn't been informed. Mary's a lovely girl but . . .'

Lucy said nothing, knowing the woman would continue anyway.

'I'm not being snobbish, but Mary often isn't very . . . well, there have been hygiene issues,' she said finally. 'Her shirts are always grubby, her hands and face aren't washed in the morning. Her PE teacher has spoken to her about personal hygiene, but even when she has sports she never brings soap or a towel to school.'

'Have you informed Social Services?' Lucy asked.

'No,' the woman said. 'No, I haven't. We've mentioned her to the Education Welfare officer a few times, but you can't call a child at risk just because she's untidy.'

'Give me her address and I'll call at her house and see if it's the girl in question.'

'Please . . .' the woman began, then hesitated.

'I won't mention your concerns, ma'am,' Lucy said.

The house was the end of a terraced row in one of the warren-like estates running off Foyle Springs. The air was sharp when Lucy got out of the borrowed squad car, her breath misting before her. The snow had eased slightly, the odd flake swirling in the wind. Tom Fleming, who had driven with her, slammed his own door, leaned on the car roof and scanned the street. To their left was a group of teenagers huddled at the corner of one of the terraces, football scarves wrapped around the lower halves of their faces. They returned Fleming's stare, shuffled against the cold, but said nothing. Lucy knew that by the time they came back out of the house, the crew would have a stock of snowballs ready for their departure.

The garden to the house was flat and bare in the snow. Rusted handlebars of a discarded bike poked through the hedge. A small bird exploded out into the clear air with a burst of its wings, scattering the snow that had settled on the outer leaves.

Fleming thumped on the door with a gloved fist, stepped back off the step, slipping slightly as he did so. Lucy gripped his elbow, helped to steady him, smelt the staleness of damp off his jacket.

'Thanks,' he said, coughing to cover his embarrassment. The lock on the front door shunted open and the door swung back. A tall man, probably in his early thirties, stood in the doorway. He wore black denim jeans and a black T-shirt with the name of a rock band emblazoned on the chest.

'What?' he snapped angrily.

'Mr Quigg?' Lucy asked.

The man glanced in her direction and scoffed, then turned and walked back up the hall, away from them, leaving the door ajar.

Fleming looked at Lucy, eyebrows raised, then stepped across the threshold as she followed.

The room to the left was the living area of the house. It was small and stuffy, the air heady with the smell of gas being given off from the gas heater blazing in the corner. An ironing board was set up against the opposite wall, on which was piled wrinkled laundry. At the tip of the board sat a child's school exercise book, held open by a pencil.

The man who had come to the door flopped into an old arm-chair in front of the TV, twisting out a cigarette in the ashtray that balanced on the armrest. He grunted as he shifted in the seat, using his foot to move to one side an open beer can that had been sitting in front of the chair.

Beside him, on an equally threadbare sofa, a woman lay snoring heavily. She wore her nightdress, though was lying in such a way that the garment was pulled up around her legs. Lucy glanced at her, resisting the urge to pull the hem of the nightdress back down over her legs, threaded with varicose veins, the outer thigh yellowed and purple with bruises.

'Are you Mr Quigg?' Fleming repeated.

The man stared up at him a little stupidly. 'She's Quigg,' he said, nodding towards the prone figure on the sofa, then twisting his head sharply to flick his hair from his face.

'And you are?'

'Her partner.'

'What's your name, sir?' Lucy asked.

'Cunningham. Alan Cunningham.'

'We're looking for Mary Quigg, Mr Cunningham. Is she here?'

The man squinted at her, his eyes almost disappearing into red-rimmed slits.

'What for?'

'We've found a missing child who fits her description.'

'Mary's not missing,' Cunningham said. 'She's upstairs.'

'Can I go up to her?' Lucy asked.

Cunningham shrugged, turning his attention once more to the chat show on TV. 'Do what you like,' he said.

Fleming remained in the living room while Lucy made her way up the stairs. Somewhere, higher up in the house, a baby started crying.

'Hello? Mary?'

Lucy took the corner at the top of the stairs, glancing into the bathroom which lay empty. Cardboard tubes were littered on the floor. Dirty nappies were piled in a wastebin beside the toilet bowl, the smell of faeces strong enough to make Lucy recoil, and move away from the door out into the hallway.

She heard something behind her and turned. It sounded like tapping at the door facing her. As she approached it, Lucy realized that a small shiny brass bolt had been newly fitted to the top of the door, effectively locking the occupant of the room inside.

She slid back the bolt and pushed the door open. A small child stood in the doorway. From her appearance, Lucy could understand why the principal had thought of her; the child was thin-framed, her hair, brown and lank, hanging over her shoulders, her bony arms jutting at angles from her side, her nightdress so long it reached her ankles.

'I need to pee,' she said, pushing past Lucy and making her way to the toilet, as if a stranger standing in her doorway was not an unusual event.

Lucy stepped into the room and was immediately hit both by the smell of a dirty nappy and the shrill keening of the baby in the cot against the far wall. She went to the child and lifted it. The baby bunched its fists against its face, scrunched its features in preparation for another cry. Lucy could feel her hand wet at the child's bottom where the urine had soaked through the sodden nappy.

Laying the reluctant child back in the cot, Lucy noticed that the area around the clasp of the white vest was dark with stains.

53

Pulling on a pair of blue latex gloves, she began to change the child, removing the old nappy before realizing that she didn't have a clean one in exchange.

Holding the wriggling child in place with one hand, she began hunting under the cot in the hope that she might find something.

'I have them,' a reedy voice said. Lucy turned to see Mary Quigg standing in the doorway again. 'I keep them in the cupboard. I only have one left. I wanted to make it last,' the girl said simply, the plaintive nature of her voice more a trick of her accent than an expression of regret.

'Can you get it for me, please?'

The child went to the cupboard at the end of the room and opened it. A few desultory pieces of clothing hung limply from hangers. A single nappy lay on the floor and Mary Quigg reached in and took it out, before bringing it to Lucy.

'I need wipes too,' Lucy said.

The girl squinted up at her. 'I haven't got any,' she said.

Leaving the child with the girl, Lucy ran back across to the bathroom. A grubby towel hung over the radiator and she lifted it and held it beneath the running tap. Wringing out the excess water, she returned to the room and began gently to wipe around the baby boy's bottom – for she could see now that he was a boy. The soft skin of his buttocks was red and blistering in places.

'You'll need Sudocrem,' Mary said. 'But we don't have any.'

'We'll do without, eh?' Lucy said as she worked. 'Are you Mary?'

Mary Quigg nodded silently as she watched Lucy, as if committing what she was doing to memory. 'And he's Joe,' she added.

'Do you look after him?'

Mary nodded her head, her small teeth worrying her bottom lip.

'Only when Mummy's friend stays over. Most of the time Mummy looks after us. When her friend comes, she gets too tired.'

'How often does that happen?' Lucy asked, trying to make the question sound conversational.

'A few days a week,' Mary said.

Lucy glanced at the girl, but her attention was focused on Lucy changing her brother's nappy. Lucy realized with a pang that the child wasn't watching her to see how it was done; she was watching to make sure Lucy was doing it right. Indeed when, having never had to change a nappy before, Lucy struggled with the tape tabs, Mary reached her thin arms through the bars of the cot to help her.

'Shouldn't you be at school?' Lucy asked.

Mary Quigg looked at her blankly, her head a little to one side, her bright eyes glinting momentarily. 'I stay here in case Mummy needs me.'

As she fitted the baby's vest back on, having wiped at the stains with a clean edge of the wet towel as best she could, she thought of something.

'Why would your mummy need you, when her friend is here?' she asked.

Mary's voice lowered to barely a whisper. 'Sometimes he shouts at her,' she confided. 'Sometimes he leaves her crying.'

'Does he ever make you cry?' Lucy asked, keeping her voice even.

'He hurts my mummy,' Mary repeated. 'In bed. I went in one night so they had to put a lock on my door. In case I got hurt too.'

'Does he hit you or your mummy?' Lucy asked, but the girl had thought of something else.

'I don't like him,' she stated. 'I like you.'

'Thank you, Mary. I like you too,' Lucy said, hefting the baby up against her chest, his head resting on her shoulder.

'I think Joe likes you as well,' Mary Quigg added with a smile.

By the time they made it downstairs, Mary's mother had woken and was sitting on the edge of the sofa, a cigarette in one hand, her other tugging at the hem of her nightdress to cover the bruises on her legs.

Lucy was surprised, and a little disappointed, when the baby she was holding – upon seeing his mother – began struggling and reached out his two arms for her to take him.

Handing him down to her, Lucy added: 'I changed his nappy.'

'I didn't ask you to,' the woman said, shifting the baby from her left-hand side to her right.

Riled, Lucy opened her mouth to speak, but Tom Fleming interrupted. 'As I was explaining to Ms Quigg and her part-ner, we're following up on a missing child. Mary is obviously all right, so we'll be on our way. I'd like a word with you, Ms Quigg, before we go.'

Fleming led the woman out to the hall leaving Lucy stand-ing in the middle of the room. She assumed he'd felt the woman might be more amenable to whatever he had to say without Lucy being there, but she couldn't help being annoyed at being ex-cluded. Cunningham, meanwhile, had turned his attention from the TV screen to her and was openly looking her up and down. He realized she was watching him and smiled good-naturedly.

'All right,' he said.

'Mary needs to be at school,' Lucy said to Cunningham.

'I tell her mother that,' Cunningham said. 'I'd be glad to have her out of the way for a bit – a bit of privacy, you know, but her mother keeps her off.'

'I'll have to contact Social Services and arrange for someone to visit you here,' Lucy continued, hoping for a reaction.

'You do what you have to do, love,' Cunningham said.

Mary herself was standing on the threshold of the living room, clearly trying to listen to both conversations at once.

Lucy bent down a little towards her. 'If you need anything, you contact me,' Lucy said, handing the girl her card. 'Any time. Just ask for Lucy.'

The girl took the offered card and clasped it in her hand.

'Any time, Mary,' Lucy repeated, as Fleming gestured to her from the hallway that it was time to leave.

'What a shithole,' Lucy said as they made their way down the path towards the car.

'There's no point antagonizing people, though,' Fleming said. 'If we ever have to go back there, you'll want that woman on your side.'

'We shouldn't leave those children in there.'

Fleming shook his head. 'Old Alan won't hang around long. Still, we'll refer it to Social Services, have them pay a visit.'

Lucy was about to speak when something exploded off the roof of their car with a dull thud. A second bang, this time on the window.

Looking across the street, the gang of youths they had seen earlier had grown significantly. Fifteen or twenty now stood in the shadows of the houses, faces obscured. Buckets in front of them seemed to be filled with snowballs. As a third exploded near her, before skittering across the pavement and exploding off the wall and exposing a rock inside it, Lucy realized that the gang had compacted the snow into ice around stones.

One rose in an arc above them, then dropped at an angle towards Fleming. He ducked out of the way with only partial success and the missile cracked him on the left cheek, causing him to fall to the ground. A cheer rose from the youths and more snowballs began flying towards them. Lucy struggled to keep her own balance as she pulled Fleming towards the shelter of the car. A lump of ice exploded against the bonnet, splintering into her face as she bent towards Fleming. Another cheer.

Looking back at Quigg's house, Lucy saw Cunningham silhouetted in the window, the curtains pulled back enough for him to see out. He stood, his hands in his pockets and Lucy could discern, even without seeing his features, his head as he laughed soundlessly before turning and speaking to someone in the room.

Finally the barrage ended, and Lucy, glancing over the top of the car, could see the youths scrambling in the gardens of the houses, scooping up more snow to restock. Using the lull to their advantage, she and Fleming bundled into the car and drove off, their departure marked with the occasional dull thud of rocks exploding off the reinforced glass of the rear windscreen.

CHAPTER 11

The wound on Fleming's face was being attended to. They'd cut straight back to the station before finishing for the day. Lucy had suggested taking him to the hospital but the cut, while still bleeding profusely, was superficial. Three paper stitches should hold it, the first aider advised him.

Lucy had headed back up to the office to call Robbie, recalling that he finished at 5.30 p.m.

'I was waiting to hear from you,' he said when she called.

'I was out on a call,' Lucy said, feeling a little riled that she should have to explain herself. 'A school principal suggested a possible ID for Alice.'

'Any luck?'

'None,' Lucy said, shaking her head despite the fact she was on the phone. 'Though the girl we went out to needs help too.'

'I'll get the details from you later and pass it up the chain,' he said, clearly eager to get home. 'There's been no word back on the alerts I sent. No one has reported a child missing who fits Alice's description.'

'Has she spoken yet?'

'No. Nor has she eaten. They're talking about fitting a drip tomorrow if she doesn't eat.'

'The press releases should throw something up soon, hopefully,' Lucy said.

'Mmm,' Robbie replied, non-committally.

She had to take a taxi back to Prehen so she could collect her car. It took her a while to get the car started and even then it skidded and slid as she made her way up the hill into Prehen again.

She knew as soon as she pulled up outside the house that something was wrong. Despite the encroaching gloom, the house lay in darkness, the front door yawning open. Using the fence running the length of the sloping driveway for support, she made her way up to the house. When she went in, she noticed her father's coat still hung at the end of the banister, as usual.

'Sarah? Dad?'

No response.

She heard a clicking noise in the kitchen, then the humming of the central heating boiler firing up.

The living room was to the rear of the house and she checked there first. A mug of tea sat on the small coffee table next to his chair, the antimacassar from the back of the seat lying on the floor. A box lay open on the carpet. Lucy recognized it as one of the two dozen or more that lined the wall of the spare room she was using for her bedroom. Her father had, several weeks earlier, begun sorting through his old notebooks, so as to free up room for Lucy. Instead of dumping the notebooks, though, he was reorganizing them according to some system he had devised. She had watched him doing so over a series of nights, bending to the task with a compulsive intensity that frightened her, his pursuit of order depressing in its futility.

Stepping over the opened box, she saw a small folded scrap of paper on the mantelpiece, the spidery font of her father's handwriting instantly recognizable.

'Gone to the shop. Back soon.'

Lucy shouted again for her father, despite already feeling the inexorable dread that he had gone out, in the snow, without his coat, to look for a shop that had closed fifteen years earlier.

Even if his footprints were not clear in the snow, she'd have known where to check. For years, when she was a child, there had been a small corner shop at the top of Sunningdale Drive. Her father would go every day for his paper and a bag of buns. He would carry her on his shoulders. They would always stop at the house on the corner; they had a fountain in the centre of their garden but the six foot wall around its perimeter meant that none of the kids ever saw it, except, Lucy believed, her, atop her father's shoulders, her chin resting on the coarseness of his scalp, the smell of his tobacco clinging to her clothes for the rest of the day. At night, sometimes, in her bed, she'd lift her dress from the bundle of discarded clothes at the foot of her bed and try once again to inhale his smell.

There was little point taking a car now; the roads were so bad that she'd be quicker on foot. Besides, to access the street with the shop, her father would have gone along an alleyway that lay between two houses on Knoxhill.

In fact, it was there that she found him, standing staring up at the swirls of snow falling through the halo of a street light. He raised his fists ineffectually against the flakes, shouted indistinctly. His shoulders were slumped, his frame thinner than she remembered, accentuated by the fact that his damp shirt clung to his chest and the softness of his belly.

'Dad?' Lucy ran to him, slipping as she did so, righting herself and continuing.

Her father turned to look at her, his eyes red, the tears shining on his face beneath the street lamps. His nose, reddened through his years of drinking following his divorce, looked scarlet and swollen under the glare of the lamp.

'Janet,' he called. 'I'm sorry, Janet.' He began to blub, bringing his fists up to his face, his shoulders shuddering with his tears.

'Janet, love. I'm sorry.'

'Dad,' Lucy said. 'It's me. Lucy.'

'Lucy?' Her father's expression hardened.

'Come home, Dad,' she said, moving towards him, her hand outstretched.

'I've to go to the shop,' her father said, raising his own hand in a placatory manner, out of her reach.

'The shop's closed, Dad.'

'Don't talk rubbish.'

'The shop's long gone, Dad,' she said. 'It's been closed for years. Come home.'

He turned his face towards her, his eyes narrowed. 'Don't you treat me like I'm stupid,' he growled, his anger rising at her having contradicted him.

'I'm not, Daddy,' she said, stepping gingerly towards him, trying not to lose her balance. She could see the quivering in his jawline from the chill.

'I'm not stupid,' he said, more venomously now, his teeth gritted.

'I didn't say that, Daddy. Come with me.'

She was beside him now, could smell the fresh cigarette

smoke coming from his clothes. His skin was pale, his teeth chattering slightly. She reached out, placed her hand on his back to draw him towards her. It was only then that she felt something hard and cold beneath his shirt.

'What is that, Daddy?' she said, reaching for the object she had felt.

Her father twisted from her, reached around and drew out a revolver, which he had tucked into his waistband.

'Jesus, Daddy, give me the gun,' Lucy said, moving towards him.

'No,' her father said, clasping it to himself. 'It's not safe.'

Lucy raised her hands, placating him, even as she inched towards him. She could see the gun clearly beneath the street lamp – an old-style Ruger Speed Six. It must have been her father's personal protection weapon when he served in the RUC. The Glock 17 had replaced the gun in 2002 as standard issue for officers.

'You don't need the gun, Daddy,' she said. 'I'm here to protect you. You can give it to me.'

Her father glanced at her sceptically, gripped the revolver tighter.

'You can trust me, Daddy,' she said, reaching out to him. 'Just give me the gun.' Her hand inched closer, her fingertips just connecting with the blue metal of the barrel.

'No,' he screamed, flailing his arm out of her reach; in doing so he caught her a blow to the side of the head, knocking her to the ground, then stumbling and falling awkwardly himself. The gun fell from his grip, landing with a soft thud on the snow-covered pavement.

Lucy heard the soft groan that escaped him as he fell. Struggling to her feet she retrieved the gun quickly, checking to see if it was loaded, but each of the chambers was empty. She pocketed it then slid towards her father to help him get up. He lay like a dead weight, the gash on his temple clear where he had struck it against a half-covered piece of discarded red brick. In the illumination of the street lamp, his blood appeared as black as tar against the snow.

CHAPTER 12

She stood again in the corridor of a hospital ward, watching the bustling of the nursing staff, the slow shuffling of the elderly patients, their slippers squeaking against the yellow linoleum floor as they walked. Some used IV stands for support as they moved. One man, his pyjama top opened to reveal grey wisps of hair matting his chest, passed her four times on his way up and down the corridor, his false teeth clacking in his mouth as he muttered to himself.

Her father had been taken into the treatment room and had the cut stitched. The triage nurse who stayed with him was a stout woman in her mid-forties.

'You've not been getting yourself into fights now, have you?' she asked, winking at Lucy.

Her father swore at her, his aggression only building as she laughed off Lucy's apology for his behaviour.

'I've heard worse,' she said.

'Bitch,' her father spat. 'She has the devil in her, that bitch.'

'Not much worse, mind you,' she conceded, pulling the thread through and tightening the knot at the edge of his wound.

*

The doctor who examined her father was a young, fresh-faced man who introduced himself as 'Josh'. Lucy put him at no more than twenty-five. He smiled when he spoke to her, held eye contact, laid a hand on her arm as he explained why he thought it best to keep her father in overnight.

'He's a little unsettled,' Josh said. 'Between the cold and the fall and that, we'd like to keep an eye on him.'

'I can watch him at home,' Lucy said. She knew her father would not react well to being told he was being admitted to hospital again.

'I'm sure you're very capable,' Josh said, smiling. 'But you can't be expected to watch him all by yourself. We all need some respite once in a while, don't we?'

'He can be a little difficult,' Lucy found herself saying, despite feeling that in so doing, she had somehow betrayed her father to this stranger.

'We can handle it,' Josh said. 'Why don't you grab a coffee and we'll get him settled? The older ones, sometimes it helps if family stay clear for an hour or two.'

'I'll stay with him, thanks,' Lucy said.

'Of course,' Josh said, as if that had been his hope all along.

Fifteen minutes later, she relented and left the ward, her father screaming from the bed, his arms restrained after he had hit Josh.

Lucy sat in her car in the car park. The snow fell in light flurries now, coating the windscreen of her car. As it thickened, she felt both that absurd claustrophobia she always felt inside a car in bad weather, and deep gratitude that the covering would prevent anyone from seeing her crying.

Her father's gun was locked in her glove compartment now,

but she knew she could not keep it there; she would have to mention it to her mother when next they spoke. She rested her hands, red raw, on the steering wheel, turned it lightly back and forth despite the fact she had not turned the key in the ignition. Depressing the accelerator, she toyed with the key ring, unsure where she was going.

Finally, decisively, she took the keys out and got out of the car. Back in the hospital, she stopped at the shop for a bottle of lemonade. Then she made her way back into the belly of the building, past the corridor leading down to the geriatric ward where her father was being kept, and instead took the stairs up to Ward 6.

Alice lay alone in her room. Her dinner sat untouched on the tray beside her bed. Lucy asked at the nurse's station for Robbie.

'He only works to five thirty,' the young nurse reminded her. 'He said he'll be back in the morning though,' she added, smiling.

'I'm just going to sit with Alice for a few minutes if that's OK?'

The nurse nodded. 'Go on ahead. Just be careful. Visiting time's over, so Sister Hall might ask you to leave,' she added conspiratorially.

'It's OK. I'm a policewoman,' Lucy said. 'I was the one who found her.'

The nurse nodded with understanding, but repeated, 'Sister might still tell you to leave.'

Alice's room was silent, but for the gentle humming of the radiator, its heat heavy with the smell of fresh paint. She lay on her side, her hands clasped, pillowing her cheek. She did not turn to look at Lucy when she came in, her only acknowledgement of Lucy's presence in the room a slight shifting of her position.

'I brought you something to drink,' Lucy said, holding the bag aloft.

Nothing.

'I thought you might like company,' Lucy explained, sitting down by the bed. Again, there was no response.

'I thought I might like company too,' she added.

The door opened and an older nurse backed in, using her bottom to prevent the door swinging closed again. When she turned she had in front of her a plastic storage box containing a few old toys and some books. She seemed embarrassed to find Lucy sitting there.

'I was just going,' Lucy said, half standing. She could see by the woman's badge that this was Sister Hall.

The sister glanced out at the ward. 'Sit where you are, love,' she said. 'These are some old things lying around the ward,' the woman explained, placing the box by Lucy's feet. 'Alice,' she said loudly. 'I've brought you some toys, love.'

She waited a moment to see if this would elicit some reaction, but to no avail.

'That's very kind of you, Sister,' Lucy said.

'Margaret,' the woman said, glancing at Alice before she turned to leave.

Lucy waited until the door closed, then spoke to Alice again. 'She's a lovely woman, isn't she?'

The child did not move, and showed no signs of having heard.

'Do you mind if I sit with you?' Lucy asked, then continued before the child could answer. 'I'm on my own, too, you see. I thought I might sit here with you for a while. You can keep me company.'

Somewhere down the corridor a child began to scream, the sudden intrusion of sound making Lucy jump in her seat. Alice jumped too, then clutched the bedclothes tighter in her joined hands.

'Would you like a drink?' Lucy asked. She stood and poured some lemonade into the glass by the bed.

'Come on, Alice. Sit up and have a drink.'

Slowly, the blankets shifted as the girl turned towards her. She sat up timidly in the bed, her elbows jutting at angles as she leaned back on them.

Lucy held the glass to her mouth. The child took the smallest sip, some of the liquid spilling down the sides of her mouth. Lucy lifted a tissue and wiped the girl's chin, then offered her the glass again. She drank more deeply this time, smacking her lips when she'd had her fill, then turning again in the bed, so that her back was to Lucy once more.

'You got her to take something then,' the nurse said. Lucy had not heard her coming in. 'Good for you. Sister Hall said to tell you we've made tea if you want some.'

Lucy sat for the next half-hour in the sister's office with Margaret and the two staff nurses who were on duty for the night. As one cup of tea followed another, Lucy felt herself begin to relax and realized that, in the weeks since she had moved to Derry, this was the most companionable half-hour she'd spent.

Finally, one of the nurses asked her how she liked the police.

'It's great,' she said instinctively, knowing it was the thing to say. 'Well,' she added, 'it's OK. It's a job.'

'What made you do it?' Margaret asked.

'I don't know,' Lucy said. 'I was a fitness instructor for a while, but got bored.'

The three women regarded her, smiling encouragingly, but not speaking. Lucy felt she needed to continue to fill thes silence. 'My father used to be in the force, during the Troubles. He retired early.'

The three other women watched her, nodding.

'He was kind of forced into leaving. We were put out of our house one night. We moved into barracks in Antrim. Daddy stuck it a few more weeks, then resigned.'

'What happened?'

Lucy wondered how to respond. Did she tell them the truth: that they hadn't been welcome in the Catholic areas because her father was a cop; nor welcome in the Protestant areas because they were Catholics. In the end, they'd settled into an estate in the Waterside where, one night, their windows had been smashed in and petrol poured through the letter box and set alight.

'The usual,' she said instead.

'What about your mum?'

'She . . . they split up soon after. She's in the police too.'

'They must be very proud of you, following in their footsteps,' Margaret said.

'Yes,' Lucy said, forcing herself to smile. She stood up. 'Thanks for the tea. I'll check on Alice.'

'Tell her to keep the noise down,' one of the younger nurses said.

When she went back into the room, Lucy saw that Alice appeared not to have moved and remained buried beneath the bundle of blankets. However, one of the books Margaret had brought in now lay open on the bed beside her.

'Were you reading this?' Lucy asked, picking up the book. It was a collection of fairy tales, the cover depicting a child in a red cloak smiling gaily as she strode down a woodland pathway, a basket hanging from the crook of her arm. Just to her right, peeping out from behind a thick tree trunk, was the hairy face of the wolf. In the distance behind her, three pigs, arm in arm, danced up the pathway.

'Would you like me to read one of them to you?' Lucy asked, opening the book to the contents list and scanning the titles. Choosing one she thought the girl might like, she began to read.

'Once upon a time, there was a little girl called Goldilocks . . .'

CHAPTER 13

Lucy woke with a crick in her neck, her cheek wet with her own drool, and the pattern of the stitching at the edge of the chair impressed into the skin of her face. The ward was coming to life, the clatter of the breakfast trolley merging with the noises of the nurses beginning the day's work. The sharp swish of bed curtains being drawn, the clanging of instruments and trays; somewhere, towards the end of the corridor, a television played SpongeBob SquarePants.

Alice lay curled in a ball beneath the covers, her face pressed against the wall. She'd woken Lucy on several occasions during the night with her screaming. At 4.30 she'd wet the bed and Lucy had had to hold her while the staff changed the sheets. The girl had sat on Lucy's lap, unresponsive. Her hands rested lightly on Lucy's but applied no pressure.

Margaret, the sister, had suggested Lucy sleep in the parents' room, but she'd not felt right doing so. For a start, she wasn't a parent. Besides, if Alice woke in the night from her nightmares, she'd want someone there, Lucy reasoned.

She'd managed to drift off before six. By that stage, the coldness of the night had passed and the ward was beginning to warm up. Lucy had taken off her coat, but used it to blanket herself in the seat. She'd laid her head back against the cool of the seat, then must have dozed off.

Margaret came in to see her before her shift finished.

'She's settled then,' she asked, nodding towards Alice.

'Eventually,' Lucy said, standing and moving towards the window, both to allow room for Margaret to work, but also to allow her to stretch out the cramps in her muscles.

'You should go and get breakfast,' Margaret said. 'Use the staff canteen on the second floor. I'll stay near here until you come back up. Get yourself a decent fry-up.'

'Sound's healthy.'

She winked good-naturedly. 'Add an orange juice to balance it out, sure.'

Lucy's father was still sleeping when she went down to check on him. He'd had a peaceful night, the nurse said. Considering the sedation they'd given him, it was hardly surprising, she added.

Lucy stood at the end of the bed and watched him sleep. He'd aged a lot over the past year, ironically since he had stopped drinking. Lucy remembered him at her graduation in the Police College three years previously. She'd been surprised he'd come. Her mother was there, obviously, though in her role as ACC. She barely acknowledged Lucy's presence and made sure that she did not come into contact with her father. But her dad was still raw about the police, even after almost two decades. He'd never said as much, but Lucy suspected that he regretted having to leave. She could only assume that he had done so for her.

She recalled the night of the attack. Her father had come home from work as normal. They'd been having dinner. She remembered that she was eating spaghetti hoops; she'd never been able to eat them since.

The first brick had come through the kitchen window at the side of the house. The glass pane cracked and collapsed into the room in a few large shards and a multitude of smaller splinters. A heavy grey block landed with a dull thud on the table in front of her, leaving a divot of white wood exposed beneath the mahogany veneer of the table surface.

Immediately her father grabbed her around the waist and flung her out into the hallway. The corridor was already dark with the onset of evening. She lay on the carpet and watched with terror as the large window above the sink shattered and another brick clattered onto the kitchen floor. Her mother was under the table, reaching out to Lucy to come to her while her father crawled across the floor, through the broken glass, to the locked cabinet under the sink where he kept his service revolver.

Just then, she heard creaking behind her and turned to see a pair of eyes looking in through the small letter box cut in the front door. The face was young and the eyes wide. They regarded her with hatred.

'Pig bitch,' their owner spat.

The letter box clattered shut again and Lucy glanced back at her father. More creaking forced her to turn back again and this time she saw fingers holding the letter box open while liquid poured in through the gap. It sloshed heavily onto the carpet of the hall. The empty plastic bottle was forced through as well. Lucy smelt the fumes of the petrol even as the hands outside the door struck a batch of matches and dropped them in through the letter box. They hit the floor and instantly a stream of flame rushed up the door towards the shutting letter box, while a second ran across the carpet towards her.

'Daddy!' she screamed.

She felt his hands on her legs, dragging her back towards the kitchen. She saw, from the floor, his feet rush past, back and forth, as he filled pans with water and threw them on the flames. Her mother had come from beneath the table now and was soaking towels at the sink and giving them to her dad to fight the fire.

Ten minutes later, a Land Rover load of her parents' colleagues screeched to a stop outside their house. Several burst in through the front door and took Lucy out to where their vehicle waited, back door ajar, at the foot of the drive. She saw beyond, a number of other officers, supported by the army, standing in the centre of the road, guns raised at the crowd gathered at the end of the street. She heard, before the Land Rover's heavy plated rear door shut, the absurd popping of rubber bullet rounds being launched into the air above the heads of the crowd, and the clattering of rocks off the riot shields the soldiers brandished before them.

She was taken to a hotel on the outskirts of the town where her parents joined her. Half an hour later, her father's boss, a heavy man with red cheeks and a thick moustache, arrived at the door. She was in the room next door where soldiers were unloading some of their belongings recovered from the house, while her mum and dad talked with him. She'd sat with her cheek pressed against the adjoining door between the two rooms, as much to hear the reassurance of her parents' voices, to feel their proximity, as anything else. There were raised voices, her mother's mostly, dulled by the closed door. Twenty minutes later, her father's boss had left. She'd opened the door and peeped out at him leaving. He'd stopped in the corridor, shook hands with her father and wished him well. Then he'd spotted her watching. He'd saluted her, stiffly, then winked and smiled at her. She'd returned the salute, even as her mother pushed past her into her room.

When she followed her in, her mother was already filling black bags with the belongings the soldiers had brought from their house, stuffing them in unceremoniously.

'Where are we going?' Lucy asked.

Her mother continued working, pausing only to push back a stray strand of hair from her face. She glared at the girl for a moment.

'Away,' she replied.

Within an hour, a black transit van, the windows tinted out, pulled up outside the hotel. By ten o'clock that night, the family were on their way to Antrim. Only as the lights of Derry receded in the distance, did anyone explain to Lucy that, after the attack, bad men had threatened to hurt her daddy.

He did not see Derry again until well after the ceasefire. In some personal act of defiance to those who had driven him out of his home, he moved back to the same area again. Lucy, on the other hand, had not been able to return until just a month earlier.

CHAPTER 14

The road out to Maydown from the hospital was still treacherous. The snow overnight had not been quite as severe as the previous night, but the dip in temperature refroze the slush from the previous day, with the new fall going on top.

Lucy called Robbie as she drove to check for any progress with the Social Services alert, but nothing had been flagged up. The next step, he said, was for her to release a picture of Alice to the press.

Tom Fleming was already in the office when she arrived, filling the coffee-maker with water.

'Morning,' he said. 'Do you want a cup?'

She nodded. 'Please.'

After leaving her coat in her room, she went back into the kitchenette. 'Who do I speak to about organizing a search?'

Fleming smiled at her. 'Me. What do you have in mind?'

'I was thinking of searching the woods where we found Alice. There's been no response from her parents. I thought maybe we could get a Tactical Support Unit and a few dogs in.'

Fleming nodded. 'I'll put in a request through the Chief Super. It might be worth getting Police 44 to do a fly-over too.'

'That would be great, sir,' Lucy said. 'Thank you.'

Forty minutes later, the responses to the press release began to filter through. Lucy had deliberately withheld a description of Alice's pyjama top to help filter out crank callers. Still, there were a few callers who suggested that the girl might be a neighbour's daughter, which she had to follow up.

She was working at her desk when Tom Fleming knocked at the door and came in.

'Good and bad news,' he said, frowning. 'The Chief Super thinks sending in Tactical would be a waste of time at the moment. We don't know what we're looking for and the girl's tracks will be long covered. He also says that the Dog Unit tells him the dogs would struggle to follow a scent with it being so cold and the snow so heavy. They think we should leave a dog search for a day or two.'

'Is there good news?' Lucy asked.

'Travers agreed to Police 44 doing a thorough aerial search of the woods. If they spot anything from the helicopter, we can send in Tactical Support then.'

'That makes sense, I suppose,' Lucy said.

'Plus, Michael McLaughlin is doing a press conference today at three. Travers asked him if you could make an appeal at the end of the conference for information about Alice. It'll get a load of coverage.'

'That's brilliant, sir.'

'In return, Travers wants us to interview Elaine Grant, the girl with Kate McLaughlin on the night of her disappearance.'

'Why us?' Lucy asked.

'Officially, because she's fifteen, she falls under our remit. That doesn't usually mean we get involved though. I think Travers is keen to keep you involved with the case. He asked for you specifically. I think my attendance will be optional. She's coming in at eleven,' Fleming continued. 'That should give you plenty of time before the press conference.'

'Thanks for your help, sir,' Lucy said.

Fleming waved away the comment. 'If we don't get a response from some of her family after that, we'll have to accept that they don't want her.'

Elaine Grant arrived just before eleven, accompanied by her mother. Lucy had spent the morning thinking about how she would approach the interview, how best to lead the girl through the events on the evening of Kate's disappearance. The girl looked older than her fifteen years; her small ear lobes carried several piercings while her hair, ginger at the roots, was dyed black. She glanced around at the objects on the floor, the toy box and bookcases and raised an eyebrow. Her mother stood beside her, her hand on the girl's shoulder, likewise glancing around the room, her eyes narrowed behind her glasses.

'Please, sit,' Tom Fleming said.

The Grants sat side by side on the small sofa while Fleming lifted the box of toys from beside Mrs Grant's legs and placed them in the corner.

'We normally interview young children in here,' he said by way of explanation.

Mrs Grant smiled nervously.

'First time inside a police station?' Fleming asked.

Both nodded.

'It's very simple today,' he continued. 'DS Black will ask you a few questions about your recollection of the night Kate went missing. I'm setting up a camera just to record your statement. Is that OK?'

Elaine attempted to say yes then simply nodded.

'So, you were at the pictures?' Lucy began as Fleming worked with the video camera.

'Is that the first question?' Elaine asked.

'Well, yes, I suppose . . .' Lucy said.

'Yes.'

'What was the film?'

'*Avatar*.'

'Was it any good?'

'S'all right.'

Lucy glanced at Fleming. One-word answers wouldn't yield them too much information.

Fleming frowned. 'Elaine, it might help not to think about this as an interview. We know you are a friend of Kate's and we just want to know about the night you last saw her. There's no right or wrong thing to say. Just tell us about your night, who you spoke with, who did Kate see, anything that springs to mind really. We'll decide what might be helpful from all that.'

Elaine swallowed, clasped her hands together, pressed between her legs. Her mother sat towards the edge of the sofa, straight-backed, watching her daughter.

'So the film wasn't great?'

'The boys liked it.'

'Which boys?' Lucy asked, as she noticed Mrs Grant's lips purse. Elaine obviously hadn't told her mother there were boys with them.

'Some college boys. One of them liked Kate. I told her that, but she didn't believe me. I think he wanted to ask her to the Formal.'

'Does he have a name?'

'Busty,' she replied, then realized from the expression of the others in the room that the nickname meant nothing. 'Barry

Watson. You can't speak to him though; he'll go mental if he thinks I said anything.'

'Did you see Kate with anyone else that night? Anyone stand out?'

The girl shook her head. 'We watched the film then headed down the Strand. We'd been asked to a party by one of the boys, but I wasn't allowed to go.' The final statement was muttered towards her mother.

'I think she's too young for boys,' the woman said, directing her answer towards her daughter even as she addressed Lucy and Fleming.

'So what happened?' Lucy asked. 'You were walking down Strand Road . . .'

'Kate got a text from her dad. He'd told her he'd collect her from mine at eleven, so she was surprised when the message came through.'

'What did it say?'

'Something had come up and he needed to pick her up early. He was parked in Victoria Market car park, up the road from the cinema.'

'What did Kate say?'

'She wasn't happy,' Elaine responded diplomatically. 'She wanted to go to the park.'

'What park?'

Elaine glanced at her mother quickly. 'I meant the party.'

'You said park, though,' Lucy said. Mrs Grant shifted her body on the sofa towards her daughter. 'Where was the party?'

'Joanne's,' Elaine said irritably. 'I told you already.'

'So Kate wasn't happy,' Fleming asked.

'No,' Elaine responded, petulant now.

'What did she do?'

'She phoned her dad,' Elaine said. 'To see if she could stay out.'

'Did she speak to him?'

'No,' Elaine said, though she smiled lightly at the memory of it.

'What?' Lucy asked, sharing the smile.

'It's stupid,' Elaine said. 'Silly stuff.'

'What was it?' Lucy asked again. Fleming was watching intently, careful not to break Elaine's flow.

'It was nothing. She said she was going to phone her dad and give him hell and we all stopped to listen. At the same time she phoned her dad, this gimpy guy walking up the street's phone rang. We all told Kate he was her dad. It was just silly.' Still, Elaine smiled fondly at the thought even as her eyes moistened.

'Kate walked up to the car park. I offered to go with her but she said she was OK; she didn't want me to miss the party.'

'The man whose phone rang,' Fleming said. 'Do you remember anything about him?'

'Nothing,' Elaine said.

'Why did you call him gimpy?' Lucy asked. 'You said a gimpy guy.'

'He was, you know . . .' She struggled to find the word. 'He walked funny, you know. Like a limp. Like he was a spastic or something.'

'Elaine!' her mother snapped.

'What? I'm just saying. He limped.'

Fleming glanced at Lucy.

'Anything else you remember? What was he wearing? What height was he? Colour of hair. Anything?'

The girl narrowed her eyes as she concentrated. 'It was too dark to see the colour of anything. He was just normal, I guess. He had on a puffy coat, I think.'

'Did you see his face?'

Elaine shook her head. 'He was walking in the other direction when his phone rang.'

'Did he not pass you then as he went by?'

Elaine considered the question for a moment. 'I don't remember. I don't think so. I'd remember his limp more clearly if he'd come past us. He was behind us when his phone rang.'

'Did you see where he went then?'

'I'm not sure. I think he crossed the road away from us, heading into town.'

She held her hands out, palms open, glancing from Lucy to Fleming. Neither could think of anything more to ask and a moment later Lucy thanked the Grants for coming and concluded the interview.

'You think he was following the girls, then when she called the phone he had to turn and go the other way?' Lucy asked Fleming after the girl had signed her statement and left.

'It's possible. We know McLaughlin's phone was missing. It makes sense that whoever texted her would want to be close by to see if she took the bait. We'll check what time *Avatar* finished in the cinema, then we'll ask Travers to place a request with the City Centre Initiative for the CCTV footage for the street outside.'

'Why can't we get it ourselves?' Lucy asked.

'The CCTV in the city centre is run by the CCI. They monitor it. Any requests for footage have to be made through the Chief Super. They send a feed to the Strand Road station and, if we see anything we need, they'll make a copy.'

'Why all the hassle?'

'It was the only way the people in the city would accept

CCTV in the centre. They were worried it was another form of RUC surveillance. This way it's run by a local group and people don't feel like they're being spied on.'

'Does it work?'

Fleming nodded. 'Surprisingly well.'

CHAPTER 15

The press conference was to be held in Strand Road station at three, so Fleming asked that Travers request the feed to be patched through to there immediately beforehand.

As they crossed over the Foyle Bridge, Fleming pointed out the spires of the two cathedrals. 'One Catholic and one Protestant,' he explained. 'There's a point on the east bank of the city where the two appear to lie in a line. There's a painting of it back in the station.'

Lucy had seen the picture on the way into the canteen. She'd actually thought that the painter had moved one of the buildings to make them fit into the same image.

They moved up Strand Road at a crawl. The area to the left of the road, along the riverbank, was fenced off, though Lucy could see that almost an entire block was missing from the docks, the brickwork of the building piled in rubble against the fence.

'Was that not where the old docks building was?' Lucy asked.

Fleming glanced at her. 'How did you know that?'

'I grew up in Derry,' she said.

'You should have said. I've been droning on about cathedrals and you know the place better than me.'

'I was young when I left,' Lucy said.

'Not that young if you remember the docks building,' Fleming countered.

'I just remember it was a beautiful big place, even if it was run down.'

'One of the splinter paramilitary groups blew it up.'

'What?' It was an absurd idea.

'They planted a bomb along the road. We think it was meant to go off when a convoy went past or something, but it must have gone off early. Took the whole front of the building down. McLaughlin had a pub attached to it that was destroyed in the blast.'

'Was that where his wife was killed?'

Fleming glanced at her again. 'That's right.'

'How did he afford to buy the docks building in the first place?' Even though she'd been a child when last she'd seen it, she could remember the site stretching a considerable distance along the river. She used to see it when she and her parents would come back into Derry on the train. Coming along the far bank of the river on the approach to the station, the train provided a panoramic view of the Cityside.

'He built himself a fortune in property. And, if rumours are to be believed, he's about to earn even more. One of the local rags ran a story a few weeks back saying he was close to selling that site for £25 million. Rumour also suggests he's going to relieve himself of some of it at this conference and offer a reward.'

'Is that wise? It'll bring out every crackpot in the city.'

'He's hoping the cash will encourage someone to grass. He's not even interested in arrests apparently. He just wants his daughter back.'

They arrived earlier at the station than they had expected and Fleming asked the desk sergeant to rustle them up tea before the CCTV feed started.

He brought them into a small anteroom off the main reception area where a monitor sat on a Formica desk beside an intercom system.

They chatted for a few moments while they waited for the feed to begin. The screen flickered into life and they saw a paused image of the Strand Road area immediately outside the cinema. The image was clearly taken at night and the time and date on the screen confirmed that it was the feed from the night of Kate's disappearance.

A voice echoed tinnily through the small speaker on the intercom. 'Hello?'

'Hello?' Lucy said.

'Who is this?'

'DS Lucy Black. And DI Tom Fleming,' she said.

'You're looking for footage from Strand Road for the 12th, is that right?'

'Yes,' Lucy said, aware that she was speaking too loudly into the microphone. 'We know a group of girls left the cinema at around 9.30. They came down the Strand Road, away from the city. A man with a limp was behind them. He crossed the road, we think.'

The image fast-forwarded on the screen, the groups of people shuffling quickly past. Finally, the image slowed again at 9.30 and played at normal speed. After three minutes, a group of girls could be seen making their way from the cinema.

'Watch behind them,' Fleming said to Lucy.

A number of people were strolling behind the group, many of whom had left the cinema at the same time. However, from the edge of the screen, as the girls passed the Chinese restaurant to their left, a lone figure stepped out into the street and began to follow them. A few seconds later the group stopped and the figure, about twenty feet behind them, stopped too. Suddenly he turned and made his way out onto the road in front of a taxi which slowed to allow him to cross, then drove on again.

'Can you focus on the man crossing the street?' Lucy asked.

The image rewound a little on the screen then resumed again. This time, the image enhanced as it focused on the man. The man's face was difficult to see.

'Can you make his face clearer?' Fleming asked.

The image paused and zoomed in further, but the man's face was still partly obscured.

'That's the best I can do,' the voice at the other end of the line said.

'Can we see where he goes?'

The image resumed again and they focused on the man as he made his way across the road. Sure enough, as Elaine Grant had commented, he seemed to limp slightly as he walked. The quicker he moved, the more pronounced the limp became.

Finally the man disappeared out of the range of the camera, though he seemed to slow to a halt just at the edge of the frame.

'Can you pick up on another feed to see where he is?' Fleming asked.

'Wait a second,' the voice replied.

Fleming looked at Lucy and raised his eyebrows. There was silence for a few seconds, then the voice spoke again.

'I'm sorry. The feed at the top of the street is the one that covers the car park where the girl was taken from. We've checked it already for your Chief Super. The camera was disabled about half an hour before the girl vanished.'

'Thanks anyway,' Fleming said, before Lucy had a chance to express her frustration.

'No problem,' the voice said, then the line went dead.

'That was a waste of time,' Lucy said.

'Not necessarily,' Fleming commented. 'We know the man was there, we know he had a limp. We know that he stopped at the top of Strand Road too.'

'And?'

'Was it just me or did he look like he'd joined a queue?'

Lucy glanced again at the screen but the final image had already gone.

'I guess.'

'There's a restaurant at that corner, but you wouldn't need to queue outside it. The only other thing there is an ATM.'

'You think he used the cash machine?'

'It's a possibility,' Fleming said. 'Maybe he used it as cover so he could keep watching the girl. Contact the bank and ask them for a list of details for all those who used the machine around 9.35 p.m. on the 12th. You might get lucky.'

CHAPTER 16

Lucy had seen Michael McLaughlin's picture in the newspapers over the past few days, but the grainy images had done little to reproduce how handsome the man looked in real life. He stood over six feet tall, with dark hair brushed back on his scalp, his sideburns touched with grey. He wore a charcoal, pin-striped suit for the conference, with a pale-blue shirt and navy tie. He shook hands with Lucy when Travers introduced her to him, his hands soft, his shake warm and firm. She smelt a hint of cologne on her own skin afterwards.

Lucy stood at the back of the room while the press took their seats. A long table had been placed at the front of the room, covered in a green velvet cloth on which was stitched the Police Service of Northern Ireland logo. Behind the table an enlarged version of the Missing Persons poster was taped to the wall. In the picture Kate McLaughlin was smiling. It was clearly a studio shot; her hair was tied back away from her face. Her eyes were crinkled as though she were laughing at something the photographer had said. She was posed, resting her chin on her hand, a gold charm bracelet visible around her wrist.

Michael McLaughlin sat in front of the picture, next to

Travers. The two men leaned their heads together as they discussed the final details of what role each would play. Travers had dressed in a navy suit with a dark-red tie for the occasion. His hair was brushed to the side, still impressively thick despite his age.

Travers spoke first, welcoming the press then reading a statement regarding the disappearance of the girl. The room flickered with flashing, the solemnity of Travers's tone underscored by the whirring of cameras as the gathered reporters huddled forward slightly, focusing on McLaughlin. He stared ahead the whole time Travers was speaking. Once, his eyes caught Lucy's where she sat and she smiled with encouragement. If he saw the gesture he did not respond.

When Travers finished reading the statement, McLaughlin raised his voice to be heard above the constant soundtrack of the cameras. He seemed composed but, as he spoke, his hands fidgeted with the cable of his microphone.

'I'd like to speak to the person or people who have taken Kate from me. Kate is the most important thing in my life . . .' He paused for a moment.

'Since . . .' The word seemed to catch in his throat. Taking a sip of water from the glass in front of him, he cleared his throat and spoke again.

'Since my wife's death, Kate is the only family I have. She's a beautiful child, a lovely girl; if you have her you'll know this. Please don't hurt her. Please let her come home to me.'

His eyes glistened as he spoke. The silence grew in the room; even the cameramen seemed to have stopped shooting. Someone to Lucy's left sneezed, then immediately raised a hand in apology.

The distraction seemed enough to cause a shift in

McLaughlin's demeanour. He straightened himself in his seat and laid his hands lightly on the desk. 'I have received no ransom demand yet for Kate's return,' he stated. 'However, I would like to make it clear that I am prepared to pay for my daughter's return. Not to her abductors, but to any member of the public who provides the police with information which leads to my daughter's safe return. Therefore I am offering a reward of one million pounds to anyone with information which leads directly to Kate's recovery.'

The gathered reporters sprang to life, raising hands and shouting questions both at McLaughlin and Travers.

'If there's been no ransom demand, how do you know she's been abducted?'

Travers leaned forward without waiting for McLaughlin. 'Without revealing too much, the circumstances surrounding her disappearance suggest that someone targeted Kate specifically. Considering her father's status within the community, we suspect that this is an abduction.'

'Why do you think your family has been targeted?'

McLaughlin shrugged lightly. 'I'm not sure.'

'Do you think it's linked to the rumoured sale of the docklands site?'

'I can't . . . I can't answer that. I have no idea.'

'How does the PSNI feel about the offer of a reward?' one voice shouted.

'We understand that Mr McLaughlin is prepared to take any steps to help us find his daughter. I would appeal for anyone with information, which might help us reunite this family, to contact us as soon as possible. I would also appeal to those who have taken Kate to reconsider their actions. It's not too late to let her come back home.'

As he spoke, he looked over to Lucy and beckoned her with his finger.

'Mr McLaughlin has also kindly agreed to allow one of our officers to make a further appeal regarding another child. DS Black will brief you, if you'll allow her a moment.'

Lucy made her way through the crowd of reporters. She carried a sheaf of leaflets that she'd made using the press release she and Robbie had composed the previous day, with an image which Tony Clarke had provided of Alice.

At the top table, Michael McLaughlin stood and allowed Lucy to take his seat.

She tapped on the microphone, despite the fact that both McLaughlin and Travers had used it a moment earlier, then felt immediately foolish for having done so.

'Ladies and gentlemen. I will distribute flyers regarding the child, Alice, who was found in Prehen woods yesterday morning. The child in question is aged between eight and ten, has brown hair and blue eyes. She is four foot eight and weighs eighty-four pounds. We have reason to believe that she may have come into contact with an injured party prior to her discovery. Anyone who knows this child, or believes they may know someone related to her, please contact the Public Protection Unit at 71555999.'

Lucy held up the photograph Clarke had given her. Automatically, the room was illuminated with flashes. One of the reporters lifted a handful of the leaflets from the table, took one and passed the sheaf back to those nearest him.

Michael McLaughlin approached Lucy after they had left the podium.

'The child that you found? Alice? Was she hurt?'

'No, sir,' Lucy said, feeling that she should offer her sympathies to the man but was unsure whether it would be appropriate.

'We believe that she was in contact with someone who was hurt though; we found traces of blood on her clothes.'

'And no word of her family?'

Lucy shook her head. 'Even if her parents are hurt, you'd think a grandparent or aunt or uncle would know her.'

'It's strange; I'd do anything to recover my daughter. You'd imagine everyone would feel the same way about their own.'

'You'd think so, sir,' Lucy agreed.

A small, thin-featured man approached them. He stepped lightly as he walked, as if walking on the tips of his toes.

'Will I bring the car around, sir?' he said, glancing at Lucy but offering no apology for interrupting their conversation.

'That would be fine, William,' McLaughlin said. 'I'll be ready in a few moments.'

'Sir.' The man nodded curtly to Lucy, then left.

'You have a chauffeur,' Lucy said. 'Nice.'

McLaughlin laughed. 'William's not really a chauffeur. He's an old friend who needed a helping hand. At his age he can't do anything else so he drives for me occasionally and gets a weekly wage for it. I've been lucky; it seemed only fair to share it around a little.'

'That's very decent of you, sir.'

'It's only money, Sergeant. Good luck with the child you found.'

'Thank you, sir,' Lucy said. 'And I hope you get some good news soon.'

McLaughlin smiled briefly, then turned to leave.

94

CHAPTER 17

Travers was sitting behind his desk when Lucy went into his office following the press conference. His suit jacket hung from a hook on the back of the door.

'You did well,' he said. 'You did very well. Sit down.'

'Thank you, sir.'

'You looked very professional. It'll raise your profile no end,' he added, rubbing his hands together lightly.

Lucy wasn't sure if that was meant to be the purpose of such exercises, but there seemed little point in arguing with him.

'We followed up on the interview with Elaine Grant, sir. She said they saw a man with a limp behind them. His phone rang when Kate tried phoning her own father. We thought perhaps he had her father's phone.'

Travers puckered his lips as he considered what she had said. 'Anything on CCTV?'

'Not much,' she admitted. 'Though we think he stopped at the ATM machine at the top of Strand Road.'

'I'll contact the bank and see what they can do.'

'Thank you, sir,' Lucy said, standing.

'How's old Tom Fleming?'

'He's very nice, sir. He's very supportive.'

'Tom's one of the old guard. He was a DS with me when I was first made Inspector. He worked on Michael McLaughlin's wife's killing actually. Hard to believe that was nearly sixteen years ago. Just after the girl was born.'

'The family has had a lot of bad luck, sir,' Lucy said. She silently considered that Tom Fleming hadn't been too lucky career wise, either; he'd been a detective sergeant sixteen years ago and hadn't made it past detective inspector. Travers, by contrast, had moved from inspector to chief superintendent in the same period.

'Police 44 did a fly-over of the woodland where Alice was found. Nothing to report; a couple of walkers spotted in the woods, but no sign of accidents or that sort of thing. I'm not sure sending Tactical into the woods in this weather would be a productive use of resources. The McLaughlin case overrides everything else, I'm afraid. Maybe when the snow shifts a bit we could send in a dog team.'

'Of course, sir,' Lucy said.

'I did promise I'd keep you on the case,' Travers said, standing and moving around his desk towards her. She was unsure whether this meant she was to stand also, but he settled at the edge of his desk, rested one buttock on the corner and stood looking down at her where she sat.

'It's always good to have someone to look out for you when you're starting out,' he said, shifting towards her.

Lucy felt her insides constrict. He's making a move on me in his office, she thought, crossing her legs and shifting in her seat.

'But you already know that, don't you?'

Lucy swallowed drily. 'Yes, sir,' she said, standing.

Travers stood with her, only a foot from her, so that she could feel the heat radiate from his body, could smell the musky smell of his sweat, mingling with the aftershave he'd worn for the press conference. She tried to move backwards, but the chair thudded against her calves and she realized she couldn't easily move.

'You should have told me, Lucy,' he said, leaning a little closer to her.

'Told you what, sir?' she asked, confused.

'About the ACC.'

'What . . .?' Lucy began, but Travers's expression halted her pretence. 'I didn't think it was important, sir.'

Travers laughed lightly. 'I'd say being the daughter of the ACC is important. Though I have to say,' he added, waggling his finger, 'I respect you not wanting people to know. Wanting to stand on your own two feet. It's our little secret.' He winked at her, smiling.

'Thank you, sir,' Lucy said, reaching down and pushing the chair away from her legs, freeing up a little space for her to leave.

'Your mum's an impressive officer, Lucy. I can see why you'd want to follow in her footsteps.'

Lucy looked at him, wondering what to say: that she'd become a police officer in spite of her mother, not because of her? That sometimes she wasn't even sure she wanted to be in the police at all, but couldn't think of anything else to do?

'Thank you, sir,' she said simply, then left the room.

It was only as she made her way down the corridor from Travers's room that it struck her: if Travers knew who her mother was, he should also have known her father, yet he made no mention of the man.

Lucy spent the rest of the afternoon following up leads that had come through following the press appeal from the previous day but all were dead ends. The news report on the TV would not run until the six o'clock news. Despite this, the afternoon bulletins ran the main story of McLaughlin's reward for information about his daughter's whereabouts. Alice would be an addendum in the evening news; she was, after all, not lost but found.

She got a call from Travers's office before five, telling her that the bank was drawing up a list of all those who had used the ATM between 9.15 and 9.45 on the night of Kate's abduction. The list arrived by fax just as Lucy was leaving. She lifted the sheaf of names and glanced down it quickly, half suspecting that a name would stand out that might present the solution to Kate McLaughlin's abduction. Instead she saw over forty names, none of which seemed spectacular enough to warrant immediate attention.

She went to the hospital to see Alice before 5.30, hoping to catch Robbie for an update on his side of things. He was standing outside Alice's room, chatting with one of the nurses. Lucy recognized him from the far end of the corridor by his now familiar posture of standing with his hands in his back pockets as he spoke. A young nurse was holding a patient's file in front of her, twisting a strand of her hair in her free hand as she smiled at him. She was not pleased when Lucy interrupted.

'I saw you on the tele,' Robbie said. 'It was just on the early bulletin. You looked very well.'

The nurse scowled at Lucy, then, touching Robbie's arm lightly as she left, promised to see him later.

'Your adoring public?' Lucy said, watching her leave.

'I'm not the TV star,' he countered. 'You were very impressive.'

'As long as it makes a difference. How has she been since?'

'The shrink has been in with her all afternoon. Nothing. She won't say a word. She brought her colouring stuff; crayons and paper. Wait till you see this.'

They walked into Alice's room.

'Hi, Alice,' Lucy said brightly.

The girl lay on the bed, her back to them, her eyes open, staring at the wall. Her head shifted towards Lucy when she came in, then turned away again. On the desk at the end of her bed were three pictures. One was a page coloured red. The colouring was inconsistent. Some of the lines were thick and heavy, as if the child had leaned on the crayon. Other lines were lighter, swirls of colour. But all were blood red.

The second picture was a matchstick drawing in black of a person. A triangle above the legs suggested the figure was female, small. Whoever had drawn the figure had included eyes and a nose, but no mouth. Then the face had been scrawled out with red.

'The doc drew the figure, left out the mouth and asked Lucy to draw how she imagined the little girl felt – a smile, a frown, whatever. This was what she did.'

The scrawls now were deep, in one place actually tearing the paper. To one side of the desk the stump of the red crayon laid, its edges sharp where the child had pressed it against the pages as she drew.

'What's her take?'

Robbie nodded towards the door, suggesting they should step out again.

'She reckons the child has a lot of anger. Self-loathing. The red might represent blood.'

'Does she? Seven years at medical school paid off dividends there.'

Robbie feigned a frown. 'She's a good psychiatrist. It takes time.'

'What about the scrawling on the face?'

'She suggested abuse – certainly a sense of self-loathing and guilt on Alice's behalf. As if she's trying to erase her own identity.'

The third picture was different from the first two. At the centre of the page was a rectangle, coloured in with deep scrawls of red, but the artist had deliberately stayed within the lines. This time, in the middle of the rectangle, Alice had drawn an animal of some sort.

'A dog?' Lucy muttered, pointing to the creature.

'Maybe. Or a wolf? The psych wondered about the framing in the rectangle. She thought it might be a window. Maybe Alice is looking out.'

'Windows tend to be square, you'd think. The red's only on the inside. Maybe she's outside looking in.'

'Or inside looking out.'

Lucy glanced in through the door to the figure lying on the bed.

'Maybe it's a door frame. Like she's looking through a doorway.'

'Maybe,' Robbie agreed, angling the picture as if so doing would make its meaning more apparent.

'Regardless, God love her.'

Her father initially appeared to have improved from the previous night. He recognized her when she came in and kissed her on the cheek as she hugged him on the bed.

'How are you feeling today?'

'Fine, love.'

'Are the nurses being good to you?'

He nodded.

'Any pretty ones?'

Her father laughed gently, took her hand in his own.

'Are *you* all right, love?'

'Fine. Great. Worried about you.'

'Don't be. I'll be out of here in no time.'

'So long as you're fit to get out.'

'I'm fine,' he said, waving away her concern. 'Never better.'

'Do you want me to bring you anything? Have you had your tea?'

'Aye. Bloody boiled eggs. How's a man of my age meant to live on a boiled egg? I'd kill a nice bit of steak.'

He laughed lightly.

'What date's today?' he asked suddenly, his eyes glinting, his expression sharp.

'The 15th. Why?'

He repeated the number over and over, silently, the words working on his lips.

'Why Daddy?'

'Who's the prime minister?'

'David Cameron,' Lucy said. 'Why, Daddy?'

He quietly mouthed the name a few times, committing it to memory.

'Daddy, what's wrong?'

'That wee shit of a doctor asked me the date and the prime minister. As if I was stupid. If I remember them he might let me go home. You know?'

'What did you tell him when he asked?'

He looked at her blankly, his eyes wet.

'I . . . I'm not sure, Janet.'

Lucy sat for another thirty minutes, as her father drifted further and further away from her. Finally, unable to trust herself not to cry in front of him, she kissed him goodbye and left.

The house was chilled when she got home, the rooms dark and cold, the whole place carrying the smell of her father, the scent of his tobacco. She realized that she had not had a chance to speak to her mother about her father's gun. She checked beneath the sink; sure enough, her father kept his gun locker there, just as he had in their previous house when she was a child. It was empty now save for a small box of bullets. She retrieved the gun from her glove compartment and returned it to the small metal cabinet, then locked it and put the key in her pocket.

That done, she went straight up to shower, glad to have a chance to do so having spent the night in the hospital with Alice. She washed quickly, got changed and padded downstairs again to fix dinner.

In the kitchen she rooted through the fridge for something to eat. An almost empty bread packet lay on one shelf, a hardened slice and a crust the only contents. Her father had told her that the home help, Sarah, normally brought his groceries for him but, since he was in hospital, Lucy had phoned her and told her not to come.

Her search proving unsuccessful, she decided to brave the roads to get a burger and chips. With her hair still damp she took her father's old woollen hat that he used to wear to Derry FC soccer matches and his overcoat, which was hanging on the banister, and went out.

On her way to the chip shop her mobile rang. The desk sergeant from Maydown introduced himself, told her that someone had phoned to speak to her. She had asked for Lucy by name, insisted that she could speak to no one else. Her name was Annie Bryce.

CHAPTER 18

Annie Bryce sat perched at the edge of the armchair in her living room as she spoke to Lucy. Her hands, thick knots of veins criss-crossing the backs, rested uneasily on her knees which bobbed up and down as she spoke. Her eyes were flushed, her nostrils red and flaring. Unconsciously she rubbed at her upper arm at various points during the interview and scratched the skin at the crook of her elbow.

'You're the one offering the reward, isn't that right?' she said after Lucy had introduced herself at the front door.

'No, that's the—'

Bryce laughed conspiratorially before she could explain the woman's mistake. 'Ah, I saw you on the TV. You offered a reward for news about that wee McLaughlin girl. Come in.'

Bryce's house was small, the living room all the more cramped due to the mismatched armchairs and sofa taking up much of the floor space. A fire blazed in the grate, broken sticks and lumps of coal lying on the hearth, which Bryce threw onto the fire as it dipped during their discussion. The heat was such a contrast to the chill outside that Lucy felt light-headed, and had to remove her overcoat and jacket.

A reality television show played silently in the background. The camera shifted from a stern-faced judge to a teenage boy, his hair tipped and dyed, who burst into tears at whatever harsh critique had been offered.

'God love him,' Bryce commented, sitting down. 'They're hard on them young ones, too, aren't they?'

'Look, I'm afraid you've got the wrong person, Ms Bryce,' Lucy began. 'I'm investigating the young girl who was found in Prehen woods. The reward was for Kate McLaughlin.'

Bryce rubbed the back of her hand across her nose, her knee jittering more forcefully now.

'Don't be holding back on me. I heard them say it – one million. I want my fair share, is all. That bitch isn't getting everything.'

'What bitch, Ms Bryce?' Lucy asked.

Bryce lowered her voice and leaned further forward, forcing Lucy to do likewise to hear her.

'That shit Billy thinks he can do me over. He's been bumming for weeks he had a big score coming. When he'd a bit in him, like. "We're getting what's ours," says he. Like he earned it or something.'

'Billy who?'

'My Billy. Leastways he was my Billy till that slapper waved her arse at him. I stuck by him through his whole stretch. He comes out and says, "We're going to get what's ours." Then the bastard dumps me. Takes up with that Duffy tart.'

'What's Billy's name, Ms Bryce?'

'Billy Quinn. Everyone knows my Billy.'

'Why do you think it's something to do with Kate McLaughlin?'

'I went to him last week. I says, "You owe me, Billy Quinn.

Four years smuggling your shit into Magherberry down my knickers and you think you can dump me." That whore standing at the window, her arms crossed, smirking like she's Queen Bee.'

Bryce sniffed again, rubbed her nose between her thumb and forefinger a few times.

'I'm not sure I get you,' Lucy said.

'Are you deaf?'

Lucy bit her tongue, tried a different approach instead. 'So, Billy Quinn did time and you stood by him?'

'Aye, like a bloody saint. No one else would put up with him.'

'What did he do time for?'

Bryce muttered something, lifted a packet of cigarettes from the armrest and took one. 'You smoke?'

'No thanks,' Lucy said. 'But you stood by him.'

'Aye,' Bryce replied, winking against the smoke drifting in front of her face when she lit the cigarette. 'That's what I'm telling you.'

'And he left you for someone else when he got out?'

'It's no wonder you're in the police. He told me he'd see me right, he had a big payday coming. Bumming his load when he got out; him and his mates had a big plan. He was going to take me away.'

'You'd deserve it, standing by him,' Lucy said.

'I know, love,' Bryce replied, smiling. 'I know that. I told him he could take me to Rome. I always wanted to go to Rome. Them Italian men.' She reached across, pushed Lucy's knee playfully with her fist. 'Eh?' Her laugh dissolved into a throaty cough.

'And he didn't take you?'

'No. I knew something was up. I wanted to book it. Hold

out, says he; I've not the money yet. I shoulda knew he was up to no good. He arrived in here rolling drunk one night, a packet of rubbers in his coat pocket.'

'You used . . .?' Lucy struggled to word the question appropriately.

'No love, no need. I've had it out, you know.' She gestured towards her groin with the hand holding her cigarette. 'Cyst on my ovaries.'

'I'm sorry to hear that.'

Bryce laughed forcefully. 'Sure I've had two wains already; I wouldn't be looking for more at my age.'

'So you thought Billy was cheating on you?'

'That slapper Dolores Duffy. She picked him up one night in the pub. Him and her at it in the alleyway up behind the shops. My sister came across them. Phoned me. I had his stuff in bags by the time he got home.'

'What happened?'

'Says he wasn't staying anyway. Dolores was taking him in. Do you know what the lousy bastard says as he's standing in the doorway?'

'What?'

'I'll take Dolores to Rome. She wants to see the Vatican. *The Vatican?* The Pope would chase her if he knew the type of her. There's only one thing that blade's ever on her knees for.'

A sweat had broken on Bryce's forehead now, her eyes glazing. Whatever she had taken before Lucy arrived was beginning to wear off. If Lucy was going to get anything relevant out of her, she needed to keep her talking before she came down completely and lost whatever train of thought she was following.

'So what makes you think Billy was involved in the Kate McLaughlin abduction?'

Bryce nodded, acknowledging that she had yet to explain the link. 'I went down to him last night. He took a hundred pound off me before we split and I needed it back to pay for my heating oil. "We've booked to Rome," says he. "Me and Dolores."'

'Did he say where he'd got the money?'

'No, he did not. And he wouldn't give me my ton either. I waited till they had gone back into the house and went into his car. He used to leave his stash, his wallet, in the car, like.'

Bryce glanced nervously at Lucy to see if she had caught the slip.

'Had he?'

'No,' she continued, releasing her breath slowly, picking her words more carefully now. 'But I found something on the back seat. Your man that was on with you today.'

'What?'

Bryce held up one finger, flicked her cigarette into the fire and stood up. 'Wait here.'

She left the room and Lucy heard her footfalls thudding up the stairs, across the room above her, then back down again. Bryce came into the room a little out of breath. In her hand she held a tiny gold object, shaped like a locket but so small it seemed more likely to be part of a charm bracelet.

'Wait till you see,' she said, working clumsily at the catch. 'I thought it might be worth pawning, if things got tight, you know. Then I saw this.'

Eventually she opened it and handed it to Lucy. Inside the piece were two tiny photographs.

'I just want what's mine, you know. I want my share. Why should that bitch get to Rome and me get nothing? When I heard about the reward, well, you know.'

Lucy blocked out Bryce's chatter as she studied the pictures, holding it close to her face for a better look at the people in the two images. The one on the left was an attractive young woman, the style of her hair and clothes suggesting that the picture was a few years old. The picture on the other side was that of a man; he was younger-looking than Lucy had seen him, but it was unmistakably Michael McLaughlin.

CHAPTER 19

She called Tom Fleming as soon as she made it to her car and explained what had happened. As they spoke she hunted through the assorted papers lying on the back seat for the list of ATM users the bank had faxed. Sure enough, the name of 'Billy Quinn' appeared on the second page at 21.37.

'You went out alone to interview someone?' Fleming said. 'That's bloody dangerous, Lucy.'

'I got the message on my way to the chippie. I stopped off on my way. I . . . I didn't think.'

'Look, I'll contact the Chief Super. We'll need a Response team. Did you get Quinn's address?'

'Apparently he's living with someone called Dolores Duffy. She lives on Bishop Street.'

'I'll get Travers. Good work, Lucy. Just don't go out alone again.'

As she drove towards the bridge, Lucy knew she should continue on the Victoria Road towards her father's house. She could not, however, ignore the irritation she felt that, having managed to get the first tangible lead in the Kate McLaughlin abduction, Tom Fleming had effectively sidelined her.

As she drove off the upper deck of the Craigavon Bridge and turned right, towards Prehen, she made a quick decision and cut left again, crossing the path of an oncoming lorry, and went down onto the bridge's lower deck, and headed over towards the city side again.

A sharp left took her past where the darkened Foyle Railway Museum squatted by the river and onto the Foyle Road, running parallel to Bishop Street. She cut up Brook Street, the car sliding a little on the incline, so that she had to shift up in gear, even as she slowed to gain more traction.

The poor driving conditions suited her, for it meant she was forced to crawl along the road, allowing her time to peer at each house she passed, looking for one with the house number prominently displayed, without the action appearing suspicious to any onlookers.

Lucy pulled up across the street from Duffy's and killed the engine. The lights in the front room of the house blazed brightly, the blinds on the main window open. She sat for a moment, watching the house, then scanned the street for any sign of the Response team which Fleming had said he would call. Finally, aware that her sitting in the car might arouse suspicion, she got out and walked back down the street a distance to a corner shop, which still provided an unrestricted view of Dolores Duffy's.

The young girl serving behind the counter raised her gaze momentarily above a copy of *Heat* magazine. She blew a bubble from the chewing gum she was eating, which burst with a dull plop, then returned her attention to her reading.

Lucy smiled at her, then went to the magazine stand, which was placed in front of the main window of the shop. Pretending to browse, she was able to watch Duffy's house from above the upper shelf.

A woman appeared at the window of Duffy's, heavy-bodied, with platinum-blonde hair fashioned into a loose beehive. Laying one hand on the windowsill for support, she stretched up and attempted to pull on a roller blind at the top of the window. Lucy could see that the small toggle flicked from her reach several times. Finally she turned and addressed someone behind her. A man appeared at the window, his mouth open as he laughed. He reached up and grabbed the toggle, before pulling down the blind.

He'd been five ten at most, thin, his hair cropped close, no more than a crescent of shadow across his scalp. He'd worn a denim jacket and a dark shirt. From the fleeting glimpse, she'd have said his features were pinched and sharp. It only took her a moment to place where she had seen him before: Michael McLaughlin's driver 'William' from the press conference.

'Are you going to buy that or are you just going to read the whole thing here?'

Lucy looked around. The girl behind the till had stood up now and was staring at her, the heavy black eye make-up she wore making her seem all the more menacing.

Lucy glanced at the magazine in her hand, not even aware of what she had picked up and was relieved to find it was a copy of *Vogue*. *Nuts* might have been harder to explain.

'Sorry,' Lucy said. 'I was daydreaming.'

Taking the magazine with her, she went over and took a can of Diet Coke and a Bounty, then approached the till. As she did so, the shop bell chimed as the door gusted open and a figure stepped in.

'Twenty Bensons, Molly love,' Billy Quinn said as he came towards the counter. He paused when he saw Lucy. 'Sorry, you first.'

'That's OK,' Lucy said. 'Go ahead.'

He winked at her, smiling broadly enough to reveal his tar-stained teeth. 'Cold one, eh? You're well wrapped up.'

Lucy nodded, wordlessly, glancing down at her father's coat. She knew that, even with her father's hat and coat on, it would only be a matter of time before Quinn recognized her.

'That's a fiver, Billy,' the girl behind the counter said.

'How's your mother, Molly?' he replied, handing her a ten-pound note which she took.

'Great. The ol' boy's getting out next week so she's up to high doe.'

'Tell him I said hello,' Quinn said, taking back his change. He turned to leave. 'All right,' he said to Lucy.

Just as he approached the door of the shop, Lucy became aware of a blue flickering reflected from the snow lying outside. Quinn must have registered it too for he swore lightly and shut the door. Outside a Land Rover pulled to a halt just beyond the shop, the strobing blue light pulsating along the silent road. They had approached without sirens, but had used their lights.

Quinn glanced nervously at Lucy, and she knew he had placed her. Moving quickly towards the back of the shop, his strides uneven, he shoved open the door marked 'Staff Only'.

Lucy dropped her purchases and dashed to the front door. Flinging it open she shouted out, 'He's gone through the back here!'

Turning, she raced towards the door through which Quinn had gone while Molly shouted after her from behind the counter.

As she pushed through the door into the stock room, Lucy was presented with two choices. To her left a set of stairs led up to above the shop, while to her right was a fire door. She guessed Quinn would not trap himself inside so she shoved the bar down, and went out through the fire exit into the yard at the back of the shop.

The yard was small, entirely concrete, with lemonade crates full of empty bottles stacked close to the door. Beyond that a number of bins stood, flattened cardboard boxes beside them on the ground, soggy beneath a weight of snow. The area was enclosed by a six foot wall. Initially, Lucy guessed that Quinn would have used the bins to help him scale the wall on that side, but as she looked she realized that on two of the three sides, the coping stones had shards of broken glass cemented onto them. Only to her right was the top of the wall clear. As she scaled it herself and looked over the top, Lucy realized why. The neighbouring building to that side was a residential home for the elderly.

Looking across the grounds, Lucy could see the tracks Quinn had left in the snow. She pulled herself up onto the wall to swing her leg over then jumped. Skidding as she fell, she landed face down in the snow, but pushed herself to her feet and took off after Quinn. As she rounded the corner she realized she was running alongside the windows of the small chapel in the home. Two nuns stood at the window looking out at her, illuminated from the lights inside. She pointed in the direction Quinn had gone in the hope that they might understand her intrusion on their property, then raced on, sliding as she tried to keep her balance.

At the end of the garden was an old gardening shed. From the light thrown down from the upper windows of the house she could make out the darkened figure of Quinn pulling himself onto the roof of the shed and then limping towards the alleyway beyond.

He seemed to lose his footing as he neared the edge of the shed and fell off into the alleyway, the dull thud of his landing audible to Lucy even as she built up speed to give herself a running jump at the shed.

She gripped the edge of the roof, the grit in the tar digging into her fingers even through the snow, and using the padlocked bolt as a foothold she pushed herself up to lie on her belly on the roof. She then scrambled to her feet and ran to the other edge from which Quinn had fallen. Looking down, she saw him gather himself as he got to his feet. The snow on the ground beneath him was caked to the front of his clothes. He looked up at her, his laboured breaths misting before his face, then he turned and ran again. His limp, which she had noticed earlier, was even more pronounced now.

He ran out into Foyle Park, slipping off the pavement onto the road as he took a corner too fast. Lucy lowered herself down then dropped to the alleyway. Each breath burning within her as she inhaled, she set off in pursuit. Somewhere to her right she thought she could hear the raised voices of the other police officers. She tried to shout to them to alert them to Quinn's escape route, but her voice failed her.

Quinn crossed Foyle Park, hurdling over a low fence at the front of a property towards the end of the street and cut along the pathway to the side of the house. Lucy was gaining on him now, feeling confident enough to vault the closed gate herself, though regretted it when she slid upon landing and thudded against the front of a car parked in the driveway, setting off the alarm. The squealing was unnaturally loud against the sound of her own breaths and the crunching of the snow under her feet as she picked up speed again.

She went into the back garden of a house. The snow-covered lawn was enclosed by large fir trees, their dense branches appearing black in the meagre illumination thrown by the street lamps outside. Quinn's footprints led to the edge of the trees, then vanished as the ground beneath the branches was mostly free from snow. Unsure whether Quinn had shoved through the trees and out the other side, or had hidden somewhere in the shadows provided by the low hanging foliage, Lucy paused, using the opportunity to take a few deep breaths through pursed lips. Then she held her breath and listened.

Somewhere nearby she could hear the slow rumble of traffic along the Foyle Road, one of the main arterial routes into Derry from Donegal. A dog barked a street or two across, only to have its chorus taken up by another in one of the adjacent gardens.

As her eyes grew accustomed to the gloom she scanned the trees and caught sight of Quinn, half hidden from her view, his legs visible.

'He's here!' she shouted moving towards him.

He cursed angrily, lurching out of the trees at her and knocking her to the ground. She screamed as he lifted his arm as if to strike, then heard a reciprocal shout from the front of the house. The other officers had caught up with them. Quinn heard it too; he spat at her, then turning, elbowed his way through the trees again.

Lucy forced herself up, called to the officers outside, then pushed into the trees herself, their branches springing back in Quinn's wake, cutting across her eyes, causing them to water. Wiping the tears away with the back of her hand, she climbed over the low fence at the other side of the trees and followed Quinn into Brook Street.

He had regained some of his distance from her, and was hobbling downhill, towards the Embankment and the River Foyle. To reach the Embankment and the cover it offered, however, he would have to cross the Foyle Road when he got to the bottom of Brook Street. Lucy followed, trying to keep pace with him. She struggled to stay on her feet; even without a limp she knew they were running downhill too fast; how Quinn would stop himself before he came to the busy road was unclear.

As he came closer to the bottom of the hill, he clearly began trying to slow down, angling himself to try to gain purchase on the pavement. Instead he slid further forward. Arms flailing, he grabbed at the lamp post on the bottom corner, hoping to use it to stop himself. He just managed to grip it, but his feet went from under him and the momentum he had built up in his descent pulled him with it. His feet slid off the edge of the pavement into the gutter and he fell head first into the road, straight into the path of an oncoming car.

Even from halfway down the hill, Lucy saw the terror on his face caught momentarily in the headlamps. The car's driver tried to brake quickly, which only served to make the car go into a skid. The front bumper caught the side of Quinn's head as he struggled to move from its path. With Quinn caught on its front, the car spun on the road, mounted the kerb and crashed against the gable-end wall of the corner house.

Lucy slid down towards the wreck as the driver stumbled out of the still running car, screaming as he did so.

'He just fell in front of me!' he shouted to Lucy, his hands covering his mouth as if he were going to be sick.

'Police,' Lucy said breathlessly.

'Is he—?' The man, his face drawn, turned towards Lucy. 'Sweet Jesus. I tried to stop. I—'

Lucy nodded, placed her hand on the man's shoulder as his body began to shudder with shock.

'It wasn't your fault,' she managed, taking out her mobile. 'Call an ambulance.'

She moved towards Quinn. Despite asking the driver to call for medical help, there could be little doubt that Quinn was beyond their help. He lay partially beneath the car, his head and shoulders visible at the front end of the car, his neck clearly broken, his forehead split where he'd been struck, the blood a black halo in the snow round his head, glistening beneath the orange of the street lamps.

CHAPTER 20

The snow meant that it took almost twenty minutes for the ambulance to make its way across the river to where Quinn's body remained pinned beneath the car. The dead man's eyes had lost their focus, the pupils wide and unshifting beneath the flakes of snow that had begun to fall again.

Not long after, a fire tender arrived to support the paramedics in removing the body. By this stage, Travers had taken control of the scene. Uniforms had established a cordon at the bottom of Bishop Street, closing off the Foyle Road. Already, despite the cold, a group of onlookers had gathered, craning their necks to see the ghoulish sight of Billy Quinn's broken body.

Travers quizzed Lucy about how she had come to be on the scene in the first place. He understood, he said, that Fleming had told her to go home. If she had expected any praise for following the suspect in the manner she had, she was to be disappointed, he said. Quinn was dead and with him the only real lead in the Kate McLaughlin abduction.

Soon after, the ACC arrived; her arrival heralded a significant change in the pace of those assembled. Even the Uniforms handling the cordon became more active in discouraging spectators from staying too long.

Lucy sat on the corner wall and watched while Travers and her mother engaged in a brief conversation as they regarded the efforts to free Quinn from under the car.

Her mother glanced over at her once, then said something to Travers and left. Lucy could just imagine the timbre of the discussion. And could guess the likely outcome too.

Travers approached her, his face flushed, clearly angered by whatever had been said to him.

'The ACC wants to see us. You're to return to base immediately.'

'Did she . . .?' Lucy began, then thought better of it. 'Yes, sir.'

There was no secretary in the anteroom this time, the administrative staff had gone home long ago. Lucy knocked on the heavy door to her mother's office and, thinking she heard a muffled response, opened the door and peered in.

'Come in, Lucy.' Her mother sat at the meeting table she had seen earlier, a half-eaten sandwich in her hand, a can of diet cola at her elbow.

'Sit down,' she said through a mouthful of bread, nodding to the free seats beside her. 'There's tea in a flask there if you want a cup. Do you want half a sandwich?'

Lucy was going to refuse, then realized that she had yet to eat herself, having been directed to Bryce's house on her way to get food.

'Thank you,' Lucy said. 'I've not eaten yet,' she added, as if she needed to explain this to her mother.

'You shouldn't miss meals.'

Lucy arched an eyebrow at the crusts her mother had just laid on the cellophane packet in front of her.

'Do as I say, not as I do.' She wiped her mouth with a paper napkin, drank deeply from the cola can. 'Are you OK?'

'Fine,' Lucy said, half covering her mouth with her hand as she ate.

'Do you need to speak to someone about what you witnessed tonight?'

'You mean apart from you?'

Her mother inhaled, held the breath as if considering her response carefully. 'You saw a man killed, Lucy. That's not an easy thing to witness. If you need time off, that would be understandable.'

Lucy smirked, laid down the sandwich. 'I was waiting for it.'

Her mother looked confused. 'Waiting for what?'

'I saw Travers talking to you. You want me out and now you've the perfect excuse for it.'

Her mother's expression hardened, her upper lip tightening. 'If I wanted to get you out, I wouldn't need an excuse. I'm offering you a breather if you need it.'

'I'm fine,' Lucy said, a little sullenly.

'Good. Bill Travers was complaining that you drove the only lead in the case to his death. Is that right?'

'He was McLaughlin's driver. I chased him on foot. I went to keep an eye on the house till Response got there. He came into the shop where I was standing and saw the team arrive. They had the flasher on.'

Her mother tutted disapprovingly.

'He went out the back of the shop. I called to the Response team and followed him on foot. He ran too fast down that hill; he couldn't stop at the bottom and went out into the road.'

Her mother watched her for a second. 'You'll need to write up an incident report.'

'Yes, ma'am,' Lucy said.

'Finish your sandwich too.'

Lucy smiled despite herself. 'Yes, ma'am.'

'You shouldn't have gone after Quinn on your own. Nor should you have gone to Bryce on your own either; Tom Fleming told me about that.'

Lucy tried to speak through a mouthful of food, but her mother silenced her with an upraised hand.

'That said, I did point out to Travers that you were the only one to date to have created a lead in the Kate McLaughlin kidnapping. If Travers can link Quinn directly to the girl's abduction, it should give the investigation a sense of direction. You didn't kill Quinn, any more than the moron who turned on the blue light outside his house did.'

'Thank you,' Lucy said quietly.

'But you are PPU, Lucy, and that's where you stay for now.'

Lucy nodded.

'Anything more on the girl you found?'

'Nothing.'

'Is it true that you spent the night in the hospital with her?' her mother asked. Lucy could not discern if her tone was one of admiration or admonition.

She took a mouthful of tea and chose not to answer.

'How's Jim?'

The shift put Lucy on guard. 'They've kept him in. He's got very confused. He doesn't always know who I am.'

Her mother nodded, crumpled up the packet, gathering up the bread crusts in it as she did so. She stood, wiped the crumbs into her hand. Lucy, taking the gesture as a sign that she should leave, stood and did likewise.

'Thanks for the sandwich.'

'You're welcome. Go home and sleep in your own bed tonight,' her mother said, moving back behind her desk and opening a folder that lay there.

Lucy stopped at the door. 'Who's Janet?'

Her mother blanched momentarily, then used the act of putting on her spectacles to cover her expression.

'Why?'

'Dad keeps calling me Janet. Who was she?'

'No one. He must be confused.'

'The name meant something to you when I said it. I'm not a child any more. Who was Janet?'

'She was someone your father knew when he was a DS.'

'Why would he still be thinking about her now?'

Her mother's expression told her all she needed to know. 'You'll need to ask your father that.'

'Well, I can't, can I?' she snapped, then regretted doing so. 'What was she called?'

'Janet.'

'You don't know her surname?'

Her mother shook her head curtly, forcing herself to look at the folder before her rather than at Lucy.

'Where did she live?'

'Derry somewhere. She was in care, I believe.' She looked up at Lucy, her features pinched, her lips tightened again. 'She was one of your father's informants before the attack on our house. Before . . . everything fell apart.'

Lucy could have sworn that, in that final statement, she saw a glimmer of pain in her mother's eyes.

'I have work to do, Lucy. Go home.'

CHAPTER 21

Her father was dozing when she dropped in to see him. In addition to the cut he'd suffered when he fell in the alley, the skin beneath his right eye now carried a livid bruise, at the centre of which were two stitches. Lucy drew back the blankets, noticing thick bruising on his forearms too.

She went into the corridor, checking each room as she passed until she found the nurse, a tall, muscular man she reckoned to be in his thirties.

'What happened to my father?' she demanded.

The man shushed her, indicating with a nod the elderly lady lying in the bed in the room.

'Wait at the desk, please,' he said, pointing to the corridor.

A few moments later he came out to the corridor, paused at the hand sanitizer, then approached her, rubbing alcohol gel into his hands.

'I'd rather you didn't disturb the patients when we're trying to get them settled,' he said tersely.

'What happened to my father?' Lucy said, leaning her hand on the counter of the reception, struggling hard to hide her mounting anger.

'Who are you?'

'Jim Black is my father. He has a bloody great black eye. What happened to him?'

'He fell out of bed earlier today. He needed stitches.'

'So I see. No one thought to contact me?'

'He only needed two stitches, Janet.'

'My name's not Janet,' Lucy managed through gritted teeth.

'My mistake. He's been talking about Janet all day. I guessed you were her.'

Lucy could think of nothing suitable in reply. She could hardly tell him that her father was asking for a tout from almost two decades ago. Nor did she want to acknowledge the pang of jealousy she felt at his having done so.

'It's part of his condition,' Margaret said to her over tea in the sister's office later when she went up to see Alice. 'He doesn't mean what he's saying. You need to learn not to take it personally.'

'I know,' Lucy said, leaning forward, resting her elbows on her knees and allowing her head to sink down, her hair hanging over her face. She straightened up, rubbed her face, shrugged her shoulders a few times to dissipate the tension.

'So, who is Janet?' Margaret asked, blowing on the surface of her tea. There were just the two of them this evening. One of the staff nurses who had been sitting with them had been called out when an alarm had sounded further down the ward.

'Someone my father knew when he was working,' Lucy said.

'Not a girlfriend, then?' Margaret smiled gently, watching Lucy's reaction.

'God, no,' Lucy said.

'You said your parents were divorced. Maybe Janet was someone your father dated.'

'I don't think so,' Lucy said. 'Though she must have been important enough for him to think of her all these years later.'

'Maybe not,' Margaret said. 'It could just be random fragments of memory firing off. Maybe he's living in the past. Let's face it, it's the national condition in this country.' When Lucy did not share her smile at the comment she added, 'Don't let it bother you.'

'I'm sorry,' Lucy said. 'I've had a shit night. I was contacted with a lead about Alice, but it turned out to be about Kate McLaughlin. I ended up chasing a suspect to his death.'

'What?'

'He ran into the path of a car.'

Margaret's eyes widened with recognition. 'I heard about that on the radio. You were there? I'm sorry to hear that. No wonder you're feeling rotten.'

'It goes with the job, I suppose,' Lucy said.

'I saw you on TV earlier, by the way,' Margaret said. 'My hubby saw it on the news. He was talking about Mickey McLaughlin's reward and I saw you. I made him shut up and turn the volume up instead. You did very well.'

'The reward was something, wasn't it?'

'It looks like he'd planned on more. My husband works for his accountant.' She leaned a little closer to Lucy. 'He wanted them to free him up ten million. They couldn't do it; Ian doesn't even know where he's going to get one million. He's almost broke.'

'He's getting twenty-five million for the docklands,' Lucy said incredulously.

'No, he's not. He can't sell it,' Margaret said, warming to the gossip. 'Apparently he put out feelers a few years back and was offered forty-five million for it then.'

'I wish I was that broke.'

'But the bubble burst,' Margaret continued. 'The value of the place collapsed, according to my Ian. McLaughlin's been offered five million for it, not twenty-five. He leaked that story himself in the hope that it would push the investors into offering more. But they're sticking at five. He paid more than that when he first bought it. Ian was saying it'll be a miracle if he has the cash to pay a reward, never mind a ransom for that poor wee girl if they ever ask for one.'

'Are you sure?'

'According to my Ian,' Margaret said, lifting another jamring from the plate on her desk and dunking it in her cup.

Alice was lying staring at the ceiling when Lucy went to her. She watched her approach and turned her head slightly as Lucy sat on the chair beside her bed.

'How are we tonight?' Lucy said, taking off her coat and bunching it up into a cushion that she placed behind her head, then sat back in the chair.

Alice stared at her, her big eyes blinking several times.

'Was anyone in with you today?' Lucy asked.

The girl continued to watch her, her eyes following the words on Lucy's lips.

'Can you hear me, Alice?'

Lucy expected no response, so was shocked into sitting forward when Alice's head seemed to nod almost imperceptibly.

'Did you just nod?'

Nothing.

'Alice? Did you just nod at me?' she asked again.

The child continued to stare, her head unmoving.

'Do you want me to read to you?' Lucy asked, picking up the

book of fairy tales from the bedside cabinet, not taking her eyes off Alice.

Lucy opened the book to the next story. Perhaps she had imagined that nod.

'How about Hansel and Gretel?'

CHAPTER 22

When Lucy awoke, her muscles ached with stiffness. She was slouched in the seat beside Alice with her feet up level with the bed. Someone had placed a blanket over her while she slept. Stretching her neck, she noticed that Alice lay facing her, moaning gently in her sleep. Her arms were wrapped around one of Lucy's legs, her cheek pillowed by the softness of a thigh muscle.

Lucy tried to move without disturbing her too much, using her hand to cushion the girl's head while she moved her leg. Alice half opened her eyes and glanced at Lucy. The briefest smile ghosted her lips, then disappeared. The child closed her eyes again and her breathing evened as she went back to sleep.

Lucy gathered her stuff and headed into the bathroom to wash. She checked on her father, then went for breakfast in the staff canteen. By the time she made it upstairs again Robbie was already in. Lucy glanced at her watch: 8.15 a.m.

He evidently caught the gesture. 'You're not the only one who works out of hours occasionally,' he said smiling.

Lucy returned his smirk.

'So, you stayed here again last night, did you?'

Before Lucy had a chance to reply he continued, 'Do you not

have a life outside of the police? You're never tempted to go out for dinner or a drink?'

Lucy smiled. 'Rarely,' she said. 'I look after my father.'

'You need to make time for yourself too. Spend a night at home. Alice isn't going anywhere.'

'I'll bear that in mind,' she said, feeling increasingly uncomfortable.

'No, you won't.'

'I was wondering if you'd do me a favour,' she said, keen to change the topic of conversation.

Robbie arched an eyebrow. 'Personal or professional?'

'I'm looking to locate a girl who was in care in the early nineties. Her name's Janet.'

'Janet what?' Robbie asked.

'I don't know,' Lucy said. 'I know she was called Janet. She was in care in Derry in 1993. She'd have been in her teens.'

'That's it?'

'I'm afraid so.'

'What's the connection with Alice?'

Lucy stumbled over her answer. 'She's . . . it's connected to something else I'm investigating.'

'Personal or professional?'

'Will you do it?'

'Personal or professional?' he persisted, folding his arms.

'Personal,' Lucy said.

He held up one placatory hand. 'I'll do my very best. I can't promise anything though.'

'Thanks,' Lucy said. 'I appreciate it.'

She had only managed to pour herself a cup of coffee and was making her way into her office when her mobile rang.

'Tony Clarke here, Lucy.'

Lucy mumbled a greeting, trying to clamp the phone between her shoulder and cheek as she carried a coffee mug in one hand and lifted a bunch of Post-It notes with the other.

'You need to come over here.'

Before Lucy had a chance to answer, Clarke hung up.

Clarke was the only one in the lab when she went up to him. She was a little annoyed both at him calling her Lucy and then hanging up the phone. Still, his excitement was so obvious when she went in that she could not remain angry for long.

'I wanted to give you heads up,' Clarke said.

Lucy went across to the computer where he stood. He tapped a few keys, then stepped back to allow Lucy to see the screen. On it was displayed a graph of some sort.

'What am I looking at?' she asked.

'I put through the stuff from Alice as part of the Kate McLaughlin caseload,' Clarke said. 'It meant it got fast-tracked, otherwise you'd have been waiting weeks.'

'OK,' Lucy said, still unsure where he was going.

'This is an analysis of the blood we found on Alice's clothes,' Clarke said, unnecessarily tracing the direction of the graph on the screen with the tip of his finger.

'Anything of interest?' Lucy asked, assuming this to be the case as he had called her up to the lab. She understood that lab technicians liked to build up their work, to almost mystify the job in case they were not being fully appreciated. Clarke was no exception.

'It belongs to a family member,' Clarke said. 'A parent specifically.'

'That's useful, Tony,' Lucy said. 'Thank you.'

She began to move away from him when Clarke placed a hand on her arm. His face was flushed in the light from the VDU.

'That's not the important bit. I also got the hairs I took from her typed; the root material contains DNA.'

Lucy nodded.

'They're Kate McLaughlin's,' Clarke said quickly, nodding encouragingly for Lucy to react.

'What?'

His nodding grew more vigorous. 'The hairs belong to Kate McLaughlin.'

'Are you sure? They might have mixed up samples if you sent this stuff in with the McLaughlin case work?'

Clarke shook his head. 'The chain of evidence is completely intact. They are definitely the samples from Alice; I found three.'

'Have you told Travers yet?'

Clarke shook his head more slowly now. 'I thought you should know first. It's your case.'

CHAPTER 23

'You're sure about this?' Travers said.

Lucy glanced at Tom Fleming; she'd asked him to come along for support. As her senior officer, it made sense that she should report first to him. Fleming nodded. 'The Forensics people confirmed it.'

'And the girl hasn't spoken yet?'

'No, sir,' Lucy said.

'But she has been in contact with Kate McLaughlin.'

'Or at the very least they've been in the same place,' Lucy agreed.

'You need to get her to talk,' he said, assuming his spot perched at the edge of his desk.

'The hospital psychiatrist is trying, sir, but she's not had much luck.'

'You seem determined to stay part of this case, DS Black,' Travers said. 'Even the evidence is conspiring to keep you here.'

'Might it be a serial abductor, sir?' Fleming said, keen to keep Travers on focus.

Travers glanced at him, then stood and moved behind his desk. 'It's a bit early to say something like that.'

'If two girls have gone missing and we suspect they've been in contact, sir,' Fleming continued.

'As I say, Tom, it's a little premature to make comments like that. We don't even know for a fact that they have been in direct contact.'

'It might explain the lack of a ransom demand,' Fleming reasoned.

'At the minute, all we have is that your case met my case. If the girl won't talk, we need to look at some other way of finding where their paths crossed.'

'Sir?'

'We trace back your girl's steps. If we move backwards, we should eventually reach a point where they had contact.'

'The woods?' Lucy asked.

'Indeed,' Travers replied. 'You can take us to where you found her and we'll work back from there.'

An hour later, three search teams assembled in the Everglades Hotel car park. Most were part of the uniformed Response team. Lucy was accompanied by Fleming. They all stood about, waiting for Travers to arrive and begin proceedings. When he arrived, he was dressed for the search; he had borrowed a blue bodysuit from the Tactical Support team. He stood in the car park with a map of the woods, dividing up sectors between each team of four. They were to enter the woods where Lucy had been on the night Alice was found, then to fan out, moving through the woods in a line, checking the undergrowth for evidence that Kate may have passed through. They were not, however, conducting a forensic search at the moment; the priority was locating Kate McLaughlin. He had chosen the word care-fully: 'finding' offered some hope she might be alive, whereas, realistically, if she had spent the past few nights in the woods without cover, the chances of her surviving were negligible. The teams began moving slowly through the trees, aware that there was not, perhaps, the same urgency in this search as in others they had conducted.

Fleming and Lucy walked side by side, chatting as they moved.

'How do you feel about being back home?'

Lucy considered the question. 'I'm not sure if it is home.'

'Didn't you tell me you grew up in Derry? I thought you might be glad to be back.'

Lucy shook her head lightly. 'I love the city, but . . . my only memory of this place is being put out of our house by our own neighbours. I'm not so sure the place has changed.'

Fleming laughed mirthlessly. 'Places can't change,' he said. 'Only the people who live in them. You might be surprised.'

Lucy glanced over at him and smiled lightly.

Half an hour into the search, the team came to the lip of a quarry near the centre of the woods. The upper edge was overgrown with bushes, proliferating in the one spot where trees had been unable to find roothold in the rocky ground. Lucy remembered the quarry as a child, remembered scrabbling down the sheer rock face to search in the marshland of the quarry basin for newts and tadpoles. The basin, almost fifty feet beneath them, was overgrown now, some of the trees so tall their upper branches reached almost halfway up the rock.

Fleming stepped back from the edge and leaned his upper body to get a better look.

'I used to slide down there,' Lucy observed, glancing over at the drop. It was only now, as an adult, that she felt any fear in so doing. She felt a retrospective tightening in her stomach at what could have happened to her twenty years ago.

'Nowadays you'd be calling Social Services on someone who let their kid do that.'

Travers had stopped and was standing poring over the map, four of the Tactical Support Unit holding it at each corner while he followed with his finger the paths they had taken. Finally he called the teams to gather around.

'We'll skirt round the top of the quarry first, keeping to our lines. The bottom entrance to the quarry looks more accessible. We'll meet at the opposite point from here, at the bottom, then move down into the basin of the quarry itself. Possibly the girl came to the edge and, in the dark, didn't see where she was going. Best if we prepare for the worst, people.'

Fleming and Lucy moved off east of their position with a number of the TSU officers while Travers and the rest moved off to the west. The pathway, running parallel with the edge of the quarry, sloped downwards, the gradient deceptively steep beneath the thin coat of snow on the rock edge.

Lucy and Fleming followed a path veering to the left. The path dropped sharply for twenty yards, then levelled out. To their right, only a few feet above them, they could see an alcove cut into the rock.

'I didn't even know this place existed,' Fleming observed.

'The stone here was used for the old American naval base at Lisahally docks after the Second World War,' Lucy said, picking her way through the rocks that were now jutting through the snow.

'That's fascinating,' Fleming remarked drily. 'And how did you learn that little snippet?'

'My dad brought me here sometimes when I was a child,' she said.

Her foot skidded on the edge of one of the rocks and she

staggered. Fleming gripped her hand in his and held her steady until she found her footing.

'Thank you, sir,' she said, brushing her hair from her face. The TSU officers alongside them continued on their way, chatting quietly to themselves.

The path began to slope again more sharply until they had come about halfway down. Above them, the rock face rose for about thirty feet. Below them the floor of the quarry basin was thick with snow. As they glanced over, a large brown rat scampered between two bushes, pausing for a moment to raise its snout in the air and sniff the scent off the winter wind.

Lucy shivered involuntarily and moved onwards. Across the way they could see that Travers, who had taken the gentler path down, had already rounded the quarry and was headed towards them along the bottom edge.

Glancing over to her left, she spotted the corrugated metal sheeting of an old shed, set back in the trees. As they came further down the path, the front section of the hut became visible, the door ajar, its bottom edge lodged against a rock.

Fleming nudged Lucy. 'What's that?'

They went towards the hut. The building was around eight feet high.

'Hello,' Fleming called out, entering the hut itself, Lucy following behind. Along the left-hand wall were a number of old kitchen cabinets and a small metal sink. Two opened cans of tinned fruit lay discarded on the worktop. Against the opposite wall was a mouldy old camp bed. A back section of the hut was curtained off. From where they stood, they could see the shape of something lying on the floor just behind the curtain.

'Hello,' Fleming repeated, treading forwards carefully. He reached out and pulled aside the faded material. A crumpled form lay on the floor and Lucy could see blood spots on it. She released her breath only when Fleming stepped to one side and she realized it was an old sheet, bundled up and lying in front of a small metal toilet bolted into the back wall.

To the right of the toilet bowl, on the floor, lay an old penknife, the blade broken. A hole about two feet in diameter had been sawn into the rusting metal of the back wall, as if someone had tried to cut their way out.

Fleming, pulling on his gloves, began to open the cabinets, one by one. The first held old tins of food, similar in age and style to the two empty cans lying on the counter. The next cabinet contained a handful of old tools. The lower shelf held circular lengths of copper wiring and a number of small lengths of copper piping. The next held several glass jars, the bottom quarter of each filled with small nails. A large torch battery lay on its side on the upper shelf, the contacts coated in white powder.

Fleming bent down and opened the cabinets below the sink. Most were empty save for a large plastic container of clear liquid in one and an empty fertilizer bag in the other.

'You know what this looks like?' Fleming said, closing the final cabinet door. He did not get a chance to finish his sentence though, for Travers had entered the hut, his team having made it around the quarry.

'What have you found?' he asked, puffing out his cheeks to catch his breath after the exertion of the walk down.

'It's hard to tell, sir,' Fleming said.

Lucy moved to the back of the shed, taking in the broken knife, the sawn metal of the wall where a flap had been cut and pushed out. She saw a small gold item lying on the floor by the toilet and bent to pick it up.

'Look at this, sir,' she said.

Travers approached, holding out his hand. Lucy laid the object on the flat of his palm – a small golden charm shaped like a penguin.

'Kate McLaughlin's?' Lucy asked. 'From the same bracelet as the locket found in Billy Quinn's car, maybe.'

'We need to get a SOCO up here, pronto,' Travers said, ushering them outside, taking out his phone.

CHAPTER 24

When Tony Clarke finally lumbered down the incline to work on the scene, the search teams continued moving up through the woods. The air grew increasingly chilled as the morning wore on. Even by noon, the watery winter sun still hung low in the sky, barely managing to raise itself above the treetops.

Finally the path they followed brought them to the edge of the trees, not at the top of the woods, but to the east. The path became more pronounced, where walkers, bringing their dogs into the edge of the woodland for a brief walk, had worn the snow smooth.

They came out of the trees at a small gate. Lucy realized with a start that they were standing at the end of her road.

'I live just up there a bit,' she said to Fleming, pointing towards the house.

'You think you'd have us all back for a cuppa then,' he commented.

'I would have if you'd bought biscuits,' Lucy joked. Just then her mobile rang. She looked at the display: *Strand Road station*.

The desk sergeant who spoke when she answered explained curtly that he had been taking calls for her all morning. One man in particular was keen to speak with her: Charles Graham, manager of Clarendon Shirts. He said he knew who Alice was; her mother worked for him.

Clarendon Shirts operated out of an industrial estate on the Buncrana Road, the back windows of the offices facing across the road at the low red-brick buildings of the local school. Lucy could see a number of the pupils, black shapes against the snow, slip-sliding through a lunchtime soccer game in the playing fields before afternoon class began.

Charles Graham sat opposite her, his hands before him, his pudgy fingers entwined.

'I saw it on breakfast TV,' he explained. 'The picture of the girl.'

'I see,' Lucy said, impatient for him to get to the point. She had come alone, Fleming staying in the woods while forensics were carried out on the shed.

He licked his lips drily. 'I thought I'd seen her before.'

He reached out one hand, straightening a sheet of paper on the desk.

'Is her mother here?' Lucy asked, shifting in her seat.

'We got her through a temping agency; she only started a while back,' Graham continued as if Lucy had not spoken. 'That's why I wasn't sure. But when I saw the picture, I knew I'd seen her somewhere before.' He waggled one thick digit to emphasize his point.

'Is the mother here?' Lucy repeated.

'No. She's on leave; she'd booked it before she started with us. I'll show you her desk.'

Graham led her down a narrow corridor to an open-plan office. Six cubicles were partitioned off by freestanding grey boards. Several of the cubicles were occupied. A soundtrack of keyboard keys clacking backed hushed phone conversations.

'Where do you make the shirts?' Lucy asked. Derry had once been famous for its shirt industry, but over the past decades the factories had shut one by one.

'India,' Graham replied. 'We simply handle orders here. All manufacturing has been transferred out. Here we go.'

He rounded into the final cubicle. A single desk, PC monitor, desk tidy with a few biros. Sheets of figures lay in a plastic tray to one side of the desk. On the soft baize of the facing wall of the partition, a few postcards and cartoons were pinned up. In the middle was a single photograph of a woman and a child. The woman had a puffy, aged face, her hair a dirty blonde, tied back from her face. The child next to her beamed for the camera, her cheek pressed against her mother's. There could be no doubt that the girl in the picture was indeed Alice.

Lucy read over the details Graham had given her as she walked out to her car. The woman, Melanie Kent, lived in Church View in Strabane, a good twenty miles from Derry. Alice may well have been in a bad state when Lucy found her, but there was nothing to suggest that she had travelled twenty miles barefoot in the snow.

As she approached the traffic lights at the end of Spencer Road, she cut right, towards Prehen, then continued past it and on up Victoria Road to Strabane. She vaguely knew the town, though certainly not well enough to be able to locate Church View. Instead she phoned through to Maydown and asked them to transfer her to Strabane station.

The desk sergeant who answered sounded young, his accent carrying a rural lilt. She explained the case background and that she had an address for Alice's mother in Strabane. The man knew the case, commented on having seen it in bulletins and on the TV. He promised to have an inspector meet Lucy at the 'Tinnies' on the roundabout.

'How will I know where the Tinnies is?'

'You'll know them,' he said, laughing lightly. 'They're twenty-odd-feet high and made of metal.'

Twenty minutes later, he was proven right. The weak winter sunlight caught on the bands of metal from which the giant sculptures were constructed. The road to Strabane had been salted and Lucy felt the slush beneath her tyres, heard the distinctive sloshing of the watery ice inside the wheel arches as she drove.

She saw the PSNI car parked in the lay-by, just as the desk sergeant had promised. Pulling up in front of it, she got out of her own car and walked back, just as the driver of the first also exited his car. He was a tall man, mid-forties at best, his frame thin and wiry. He had sandy hair, thinning on top and brushed to one side. He smoothed down his moustache with his finger and thumb as he walked, then extended his hand.

'Inspector . . .?' Lucy began.

'DS Black? Good to meet you. Call me Jim.'

CHAPTER 25

She drove with Jim in his car up to Church View, leaving her own vehicle parked in the lay-by. He drove one-handed, his left hand resting on his leg, unless he needed it to change gear. He smiled as he talked, his eyes shifting across her face.

'So what's the story with Melanie Kent, then?' he asked.

'I think I found her daughter in the woods a few nights ago.'

'You think you found her?'

'Well, I did find a girl. We think Melanie Kent is the mother. Her boss called us this morning, after recognizing a picture of the child on the news.'

He nodded. 'I saw the piece. What has the child said about it?'

'Nothing,' Lucy said. 'She hasn't spoken to anyone since we found her. The hospital shrink has been trying all week, but nothing yet. Selective mutism, she calls it.'

'Bloody smart, if you ask me, refusing to speak to a shrink. Maybe the wee girl's not so stupid, eh?'

He winked at her and smiled.

*

The house was the end of a terrace on the hill running up from the town centre. Despite the salting, the incline was still difficult and the car slid on the road a few times, before Jim finally pulled it in to the kerb and suggested they walk the rest of the way.

The house looked neat from the outside, the exterior woodwork all freshly painted. A new-style Ford Fiesta sat in the drive.

He leaned against the car, placed a gloved hand against the glass to reduce glare as he peered inside.

'A few kids' toys lying on the floor,' he observed. 'No booster seat though.'

Lucy knocked at the door, then stood back, scanning the windows for any sign of life inside.

After a moment she knocked a second time, but again with no response. She rattled the door handle, but it was locked. She moved across to the hedge separating the neighbouring house and glanced in the front window there.

'Doesn't seem to be anyone home in either house,' she said.

She glanced over at Jim who was kneeling on the front doorstep, working at the lock. After a few deft movements, he stood and tested the door handle.

'It's open,' he said. 'Who'd have thought it? We'd best check the place hasn't been burgled or something.'

'I checked that door,' Lucy said. 'It was—'

'Open,' Jim said. 'You're absolutely right, DS Black. Very careless in this day and age. After you.'

He held the door open, gestured that Lucy should go in first.

'That's a handy trick, Inspector,' she said as she passed him.

Immediately they were inside, they were struck by the cold dampness of the air in the hallway.

'No heating on for a few days,' Jim said, laying his hand against the cold metal of the radiator beside him for confirmation.

'Hello,' Lucy called. 'Police.'

No response.

The hallway had three doorways, with a set of stairs to the left of the front door. They tried the first door, which opened onto a sitting room. The room was tidy, the TV in the corner unplugged. On the wall above the sofa was a large framed colour print of Alice. It was clearly a studio piece, the girl lying on her front, leaning up on her elbows, her chin resting on the flat of her hands. It reminded Lucy of the image of Kate McLaughlin on the Missing Persons poster.

'It's her house all right,' Lucy said, nodding at the image.

'Lovely looking wee girl,' Jim said.

The next room seemed to be a den of some sorts. One wall was lined with wide shelving on which sat plastic storage boxes containing assorted toys. A portable TV sat on a corner unit, beneath it a games console. Again, both were unplugged.

The final room at the end of the hallway was the kitchen. It was similarly tidied, though on the draining board beside the sink sat an upturned mug and cereal bowl, both dry. A small puddle of water lay beneath the bowl, where the drips had collected as it dried.

Jim opened the fridge. Apart from a few jars of jam and a tub of margarine, the fridge was empty.

'It looks as though they have gone on holidays,' Lucy said. 'As her boss indicated.'

He nodded. 'Looks that way. Check the rooms above.'

The two bedrooms above were neat and tidy. The bathroom, likewise, had clearly been cleaned before Melanie Kent had left.

'Do you think she abandoned her to look after herself?' Lucy said.

Jim stood in the doorway to the bathroom. He pointed to a soap-scummed glass that stood empty on the windowsill.

'Looks like she took their toothbrushes and so on with her.'

Lucy followed him into the room. Assorted toiletries sat on a white cabinet beside the bath.

'All very flowery,' Jim said. 'Nothing masculine.'

'No husband or partner then?'

He nodded. 'I've not seen pictures of any, have you?'

Now he mentioned it, Lucy realized that the photographs she had seen had been of Alice and her mother.

Jim moved into the next room. 'Must be the girl's room,' he called. The bed was made with a Dora the Explorer duvet and pillow set. Resting on the pillow were two teddy bears.

Lucy picked up one of them, the more battered-looking of the two. 'For Alice,' she explained in response to Jim's enquiring look.

To the left of the bed was a chest of drawers. A small goldfish bowl sat on top of it, the fish circling the bowl then surfacing to gulp at the air.

'They can't have been gone too long, the fish is still alive,' Lucy observed.

Behind the bowl was a varnished wooden jewellery box, about six inches long. Lucy flipped the lid open. A tinny version of 'Clair de Lune' began to play for a moment, then ran out of steam and tinkled to a stop.

Inside the box were a handful of photographs. Lucy lifted them and glanced through them. Most seemed to be of Alice and friends from school. They wore a burgundy uniform.

'Is that a local school?' Lucy asked, handing Jim one of the images.

'Don't think so,' he said. 'I've never seen that uniform before.'

Other images included Alice and an elderly couple who Lucy assumed to be her grandparents.

At the back of the photos was an envelope. Lucy glanced at the postmark: Kilmainham, Ireland.

The paper on which the letter was written was thin and flimsy. The letter itself was short.

Dear Alice,

I'm so sorry I'm not there for your big day, sweetheart. Mummy wrote me that you liked the present I sent.

I can't wait to see you when I get out. Knowing that you will be there when I get out makes these final few months easier to bear.

I'm sorry I've missed so much. I'll make it up to you, I promise sweetheart.

All my love and kisses,
Daddy.

Lucy offered the letter to Jim when she'd read it.

'Prisoner?' she said.

He nodded. 'Contact Portlaoise Prison and get his details. He says here he had months left and this was sent last summer. He must have got out fairly recently. Maybe he got out and the family reunion didn't go as planned.'

Lucy shook her head. 'He sounds like he loves her in his letter.'

'He wouldn't be the first father to let down his kids, now, would he?'

'Cynic,' Lucy said.

'Realist,' he replied. 'It looks like they packed up to go some-where. Toothbrushes gone, no sign of coats or shoes lying around.'

'Maybe they went to the father's house. Even if he did get out, he's obviously not been living here,' Lucy said.

'If he has been released, you should see if Portlaoise has an address for him,' Jim said.

'I was going to,' Lucy said, prickling a little at being told how to do her job.

'We'll need to put out an alert for the mother too. I'll bet you a ton he's got out, offed the missus and tried to do the kid too.'

'You're on,' Lucy said.

'Girls and their fathers,' he said. 'Tell you what. Leave the prisons to me.'

Lucy raised her eyebrows.

'We have good contacts with the Guards over the border,' Jim explained. 'They'll get info from them quicker than we will.'

An hour later, as Lucy pulled into the car park of the hospital, he called her back.

'Peter Kent was released a month ago from Portlaoise after serving five years. He was done in 2004 for planting a road-side bomb in Monaghan. He's a dissident, or at least he was. Apparently they'd set an explosive charge on the border to hit a checkpoint, then had stretched the detonator wires across into the South. The Guards came on him and another man, Kevin Mullan, hiding in a ditch. They charged them with membership, possession of a weapon and handling explosives. The two of them got twelve years, got out in half that with good behaviour.'

'Jesus,' Lucy said. 'That's great, Jim, thanks. Any luck with an address?'

He audibly inhaled. 'That's where our luck ran out. He had

given an address in Dublin, but apparently he never showed up there.'

'What about this character Mullan?'

'Well, you could be in luck there. He's a Derry man. You should have him on your files down there if he's involved with the dissidents.'

'Thanks for your help,' Lucy said. 'It was nice to meet you.'

'Likewise,' he replied. 'Maybe our paths will cross again sometime.'

CHAPTER 26

'Hello,' Lucy ventured, peeking her head around the door of Alice's room. She had glanced in through the glass pane in the door. The psychiatrist, Dr Matthews, had been sitting by Alice's bed, reading a book resting in her lap. Alice lay on her side, hunched away from the woman, facing the wall. When she heard Lucy's voice she turned and looked at her, her eyes expressionless.

'We're in the middle of something,' Matthews said irritably, standing up and laying her book face down on the seat. Lucy recognized the writer's name; it was not someone she would have thought of reading to Alice.

'I have something I thought Alice might want to see.'

Lucy reached into her bag and pulled out the teddy she had taken from Alice's bed. The girl stared open-mouthed, then stumbled from the bed and ran across to her. The movement, the first she had made since Lucy had found her, seemed too much and she staggered as she reached Lucy, grabbing the toy with one hand. She fell against Lucy, who instinctively reached and lifted her, hugging Alice's body tight against her own to stop the child falling.

Alice's arms snaked around her neck and tightened. The girl rested her face against Lucy's. The fur of the teddy bear Alice held against Lucy's back tickled the nape of her neck.

'Thank you,' Alice whispered.

Lucy felt the wetness of the child's tears against her skin and, despite herself, felt her own eyes begin to burn. She squeezed them shut to prevent the tears fully forming, but with little success.

'Shush,' Lucy said. 'It's OK.'

Matthews stood facing them, her arms by her sides. She smiled lightly at Lucy, nodding her head.

'Well done,' she mouthed.

'Her name's Alice Kent,' Lucy explained to Matthews and Robbie in the sister's room half an hour later. One of the nurses sat with Alice, trying to engage her with the toys. After her words to Lucy, she had not spoken again, though she seemed more lively, more interested in her surroundings.

'Any sign of her parents?' Robbie asked.

'None. The house is empty. It looks like they were planning on leaving; toothbrushes and that all gone. She lived with her mother.'

'What about the father?' Matthews asked, opening a folder she had brought into the office with her and beginning to make notes.

'He's an ex-con. He was released a while back, but doesn't seem to have been living with the mother and child.'

'What was he serving time for?' she asked.

Lucy glanced at her, unsure how much she should tell her.

'I need to know if there was a history of abuse, for example,' the doctor explained. 'Either of the child or the mother.'

'None,' Lucy said. 'He was caught planting a bomb on the border. He did time for weapons possession.'

'Do you think he killed the mother? Got out after a few years, maybe found the locks changed?'

'It's possible,' Lucy said. 'We did a fly-by of the woods but nothing showed. There've been no accidents reported. With the thaw I might ask for ground searches of the woods and the houses bordering it.'

Matthews nodded. 'It was a good idea to bring the toy,' she said. 'The girl clearly trusts you. You must have made an impression when you found her. She feels attached to you.'

'It's no bloody wonder,' Robbie said, jokingly. 'She apparently spends every night sleeping in the room with her and reading her fairy tales.'

Matthews glanced at Lucy in such a way she could not help but feel she was being assessed herself.

'Fairy tales. Which ones?'

Lucy shrugged. 'The usual. Goldilocks, Hansel and Gretel.'

'That might explain today's art work.' She flicked through the folder then selected a sheet, which she handed to Lucy. Alice had drawn two stick figures, holding hands, walking between black trees.

Lucy shrugged and handed it back. The two figures were both girls in the picture, but she was not sure the doctor would appreciate her pointing this out.

'Why those particular tales?' The woman was watching her more closely now.

'I like them, I guess.'

'You're reading stories about children lost in woods to her?' Robbie asked, smiling.

'They're my favourites,' Lucy said.

'Are they indeed?' Robbie said. 'What does that tell us about this patient, Dr Matthews?' he added, laughing.

'I'm not the one in need of attention,' Lucy replied.

'I don't know. All those stories of little girls lost,' Robbie said.

'Maybe Alice recognizes a kindred spirit,' Matthews said. 'A healthier work–life balance might not do any harm, you know, DS Black.'

'My balance is fine,' Lucy replied. 'Let me know if you need anything further brought down from the house.'

After Matthews had gone, Robbie stayed in the room with her. He rested his buttocks on the edge of the desk, his arms folded, smiling at Lucy.

'What?'

'Speaking of work–life balance,' he began. 'I was wondering if you fancied grabbing a bite to eat sometime.'

Lucy shifted uncomfortably in her seat. 'I'm kind of busy with my dad and that. I . . .'

'Fair enough,' he said. 'I just thought there'd be no harm in asking.'

'I'm not . . .' Lucy began.

'It's only a bite to eat, DS Black,' he said.

Lucy smiled. 'Maybe sometime,' she said finally. 'That might be nice.'

'Might be nice,' Robbie considered. 'That's good enough for me. It's a date. Or not. Your choice.'

Lucy raised her eyebrows, sighed heavily, but could not fully conceal her smile.

'I looked into that thing you asked, by the way,' Robbie said. He pulled a folded sheet of A4 paper from his pocket and handed it to her. 'Thought I'd ask you out before I gave it to you so you wouldn't feel obligated.'

'Thanks,' Lucy said, opening the sheet and being immediately disappointed by the lack of information on the page. There was no more than a few handwritten notes.

'Janet Houston,' Robbie said. 'She was in residential care until she turned seventeen. I can't give you any of the background, beyond the fact that she was removed from her family home.'

'Abuse or neglect?'

'Abuse,' he said grimly. 'We took her into care when she was ten. Shifted back and forth between care and her family home.'

'We?'

'They,' Robbie said. 'I was still at school myself back then. She vanished when she was seventeen. One of my colleagues did say that something surfaced about her, involving the Provos. But I don't know how accurate that is. Could just be rumour.'

Lucy scanned the information on the sheet: the name, DOB, a brief summary of the events he had just recounted.

'I'm not sure how much use it's going to be, to be honest,' Robbie said, shrugging apologetically.

'It's a start,' Lucy said. 'Thanks for getting it for me.'

Robbie held out his hands. 'I don't know what you're talking about,' he said.

Tom Fleming was sitting in the Interview Room with a child and a female officer when Lucy went into the unit. The child was being videoed, Fleming holding two dolls towards her, one of each sex, both anatomically correct. The child was gesturing towards one of them. Lucy didn't want to know the context, or which family relative the male doll represented in the child's mind.

She went up to her office and switched on the PC sitting on her desk. Charles Graham had said that Melanie Kent had booked her leave before she started with Clarendon Shirts. Perhaps what he had meant was that she had already booked a holiday before she started working for them. The state of the house and absence of toothbrushes and so on in the bathroom suggested that her absence was a planned one. Perhaps something had happened to her and Alice as they left for their break? Or perhaps Alice had been left behind with someone else? Her father?

Lucy phoned Belfast International Airport first and asked them to run a check for Melanie Kent, Peter Kent or Alice Kent as passengers booked to go out of the airport during the previous week. Having been given a promise that they would get back to her, she hung up and then immediately picked up again and phoned Dublin Airport, making the same request. Then she called the ferry companies and asked there. While she waited for them to return her call, she laid her notepad in front of the monitor. She had the names of Kent and Mullan circled on one page, Janet Houston's written in a different-coloured pen beneath it. While she waited for the new Police National Database to load, she prevaricated over which name to search first. In the end, it was Janet Houston's that she typed.

After leaving care, Houston had been arrested on and off numerous times over the years for public-order offences. The most recent arrest photograph, taken following her arrest for assaulting an officer, surprised Lucy: the woman should only have been in her early thirties but she appeared significantly older. Her features were bloated and ruddy, even under the harshness of the station lights. On her left temple a deep gash seemed to have festered, while one of her eyes was swollen shut above a thick bruise that yellowed her cheekbone. She appeared more the victim of an assault than the perpetrator.

155

Lucy scanned down through the woman's personal details and was dismayed to find her address listed as 'no fixed abode'. Regardless, she printed off Janet's record and the photograph of her. Then she ran a search on Peter Kent.

Kent's record was not quite as long as Janet's but significantly more serious. He had been arrested several times, in each instance on terrorist charges, stretching back to the mid-nineties. Considering the bulk of these had been post-ceasefire, in all probability it confirmed the Strabane inspector's assertion that he was probably a dissident Republican, dismayed with the Provos declaration that the war was over. Again, the address details were blank. Lucy enlarged the arrest photo of Kent, studied his face for some sign of Alice in the man. His face was thin and hard, his expression defiant. His eyes were narrowed, bright with a glint of arrogance. He sported a thin shadow of stubble. Like Alice, he had high cheekbones, which conferred his features with a degree of effeminacy. She also shared his mouth, his lips soft and full.

Lucy hit print and typed in Kevin Mullan's name. Mullan's record was the most interesting. He had been a bomber with the IRA during the later stages of the Troubles. He was believed to have led a break-away faction following the ceasefire which had been responsible for a spate of fire-bombings in shops and commercial premises around the town. At some stage, perhaps during one such attack, he must have burnt his face and required a skin graft. Lucy enlarged his photograph and involuntarily shuddered at the image. While the grafting may well have been successful, the man was still disfigured. The left-hand side of his face had the brittle shiny quality of plastic, the upper part of the cheek jutting slightly over the lower eyelid. The bottom part of the cheek looked as if it didn't quite fit the jawline, a tiny apron of skin overhanging the bone. Despite being unshaven on the right-hand side of his face, this grafted skin was unnaturally smooth. The skin was drawn back at the corner of the lip, revealing the edge of the man's teeth, giving the impression of a sneer.

Mullan's most recent arrest was not mentioned, though it was hardly surprising as the incident had occurred in the Republic. Promisingly, however, the database did list Mullan as living in Derry. If he still lived there, Lucy hoped, he might know Peter Kent's present location. While he might not want to help the police if he thought she was after Kent for a crime, he might be more forthcoming if he realized that it was a family crisis that had prompted her search. Still, glancing again at Mullan's photograph, Lucy was not entirely sure she wanted to face the man alone. In fact, even after she closed the database, she thought she could see the ghost of his features burned onto the screen.

CHAPTER 27

Lucy knocked on Fleming's door. He looked up at her from his desk when she opened it, his head resting in one hand as he completed the paperwork from his interview.

'Tough one?' she asked.

'Nightmare,' Fleming said. 'Any luck with the girl?'

Lucy came into the room and sat on the chair facing Fleming. 'I think I've found out who she is. Her mother's boss recognized her. She and the mother live in Strabane. I went up to the house but the place is empty.'

Fleming raised an eyebrow. 'Any signs of violence?'

'Nothing. It looks like they planned on leaving; no toothbrushes or the like.'

'Holidays?'

'I've contacted airports and ferries to see if any of them were booked to travel over the past week.'

'Good work. What about a father?' Fleming asked, closing the folder in front of him.

'He was doing time in Dublin for explosives. He was released a while back. No known address for him, but his partner in the bomb attempt got out at the same time; he has an address in Derry.'

Fleming nodded approvingly. 'How did you get all that?'

'The DI in Strabane got it.'

'So are you going to the friend's house?'

'If you'd accompany me,' Lucy said. 'He's a rough-looking character.'

Fleming slid the folder away from him and stood. 'I'd be delighted to,' he said.

As they left the unit, Lucy prevaricated, unsure whether or not Fleming would want to drive. However, he did nothing but look at her expectantly, glancing around the car park.

'Where's your car?' he asked.

'Over this way.'

As they strapped in their seat belts, Fleming, clearly feeling he needed to explain more fully, said, 'I was done for drink-driving, lost my licence.'

'I see,' Lucy said, not looking at the man.

'My wife left me. I took it badly.'

'I'm sorry to hear that, sir,' Lucy replied, shifting in her seat, exaggeratedly checking her mirrors as she moved off, anything but looking her commanding officer in the face during his display of collegial frankness. She could sense that he was looking at her, could sense his gaze. He was smiling mildly at her and she hoped he wasn't going to make a pass at her. Every time she moved to a new posting, she spent the first month making it clear that she was not looking for an office fling. For some reason, the older officers took longer to realize this.

'But that was before I found Jesus,' Fleming concluded. 'So, who are we looking for?'

Lucy suppressed an embarrassed laugh.

'I hope my telling you that didn't make you uncomfortable,'

Fleming added. 'People in the unit wonder why I don't drive. It's easier to be honest.'

'I appreciate your candour, sir,' Lucy said.

'So, who are we looking for?'

Lucy reached back into her bag and pulled out some folders then handed them across to Fleming.

He opened the first. 'Peter Kent,' he read.

'Alice's father, I think. There's no sign of him or the mother. He was released a while back; we've no address for him. His partner is the scarred man in the other folders – Kevin Mullan.'

Fleming opened the next folder and grunted softly as he saw the arrest shot.

'He's a bad boy,' Fleming said. 'He's a regular with the Response team. He burned himself, you know.'

Lucy nodded. 'Planting his own bomb?'

'Hoist with his own petard, apparently.'

'He's the one we're going to see. I'm hoping he'll know where Kent is.'

'He'll never cooperate with us; the likes of Mullan will never accept the law unless they're delivering it themselves with hurling bats and hammers.'

'I'm hoping that if he realizes we've found Kent's daughter, he might be more amenable.'

'Unless, of course, Kent is responsible for the blood on the girl's clothes,' Fleming suggested, scanning the information Lucy had printed from the Police National Database on Mullan. 'Mullan'll hardly hand him over.'

'He might contact him,' Lucy said, aware of the hint of desperation in her voice. 'We've a bulletin out on the mother too, in case this doesn't lead anywhere.'

Fleming nodded absent-mindedly, opening the final folder in his lap.

'Where does Janet fit into this?'

'She's something different I'm working on,' Lucy said, then regretted it. As her superior officer, Fleming would know every case she'd be working.

'Is Travers getting you tied into CID again?' Fleming asked, without lifting his gaze from the sheets in front of him. Lucy wondered whether she imagined a hurt tone in his voice.

'No, it's something personal.'

Fleming glanced at her quizzically, then shut the folder.

'You said "Janet" there, sir? Do you know her?'

'I know her fairly well,' he replied, looking out the passenger window.

'Where might I find her?' Lucy asked.

Fleming continued looking out the window, as if she had not spoken, though Lucy knew that he had heard. She guessed that his earlier display of honesty was about setting down a marker. She also suspected that, if he was to help her, he'd expect her to trust him enough to be honest.

'My father is suffering with Alzheimer's,' she explained. 'He has mentioned Janet a number of times. I discovered that this was the Janet he spoke about. He knew her when he was younger.'

'What did your father do?' Fleming asked, resting his hands on the folder. Lucy noticed that his nails were manicured and precise. He still wore a wedding ring too, despite telling her his wife had left him.

'He . . . he owned a shop in Derry.'

'What about your mother?'

'She worked there too,' Lucy said, more freely now, feeling

a little rankled by the lack of even a conversational tone to the questions. She suddenly regretted asking him to accompany her. She looked across at him, his features set, his mouth pursed. It struck Lucy that, by the nature of the questions and Fleming's response to her answers, he already knew the truth.

'They were both police too,' she admitted finally.

Fleming's expression softened.

'Your mother's secretary told me you had been up with her,' he said.

'What?' Lucy struggled to decide whether she was more angry with the secretary for telling Fleming, or Fleming himself for testing her the way he had.

Sensing her anger perhaps, he raised a hand from the folder in placation.

'I knew your father, Lucy,' he said. 'He was my inspector when I started in D District. He was a good man. Bill Travers took over from him.'

'You might have admitted as much, sir,' Lucy said. 'Before you asked me.'

'Perhaps,' Fleming agreed. 'I thought you didn't want people to know.'

'I don't,' Lucy said. 'If people know my mother's the ACC they'll . . .'

'Assume you got assigned to PPU through nepotism rather than merit?' Fleming said. 'There's not much fear that people will think your mother did you a favour when she put you in the PPU.'

Lucy had to agree with him on that.

'She has, however, asked me to look out for you,' Fleming said. 'Until you find your feet.'

'I can handle things on my own, thank you, sir,' Lucy said, making little effort now to hide her anger.

'I thought as much,' Fleming said. 'But if you're looking into Janet, I guessed you might like some help.'

'My mother suggested there was something between Janet and my father,' Lucy stated.

'She was his informant,' Fleming said.

'My father still talks about her.'

'That's because he probably still feels responsible,' Fleming said.

'What for?'

'You'll understand when you meet her,' he said. 'You've passed Mullan's house, by the way.'

CHAPTER 28

The woman's cursing continued unabated even while Lucy tried to explain the purpose for her visit.

'Leave him alone,' the woman, Kevin Mullan's partner presumably, screamed at her.

Lucy glanced around. At the houses opposite, two of the neighbours were standing at the respective sides of the fence running between their properties, watching across with open amusement.

It hadn't been surprising that she'd missed his house. The rows of terraces the whole way through the estate were identical, all crafted from red brick made in Lifford just over the border in Donegal, then shipped down to Derry. The whole city centre was a strange amalgam of ancient stone and red brick, often side by side. It was all red here, though.

'I'm not looking to question your partner. I need his help in a family matter.'

'You're lying,' the woman spat back, raising her voice for the benefit of the two across the street. 'Liar.'

'I'm not Miss—'

'You know a cop's lying, 'cause they open their mouths,' she added.

Lucy glanced back at Fleming who stood at the car, resting his buttocks against the bonnet. He shrugged his shoulders.

'Can we come in?' Lucy asked, already pushing forwards, keen to stop the public performance.

'You can't force your way in,' the woman screeched, even as she herself backed into the hallway. 'I'm calling the papers.'

Once inside, though, her demeanour seemed to soften. It was not the first time Lucy had encountered such a reaction on the doorstep – mostly so the neighbours wouldn't think the visited party was cooperating – for the party in question to become a little more amenable once inside.

Fleming took a last look across at the neighbours, then followed Lucy and the woman inside.

She was sitting on her sofa when they went into the living room, her legs clasped tight together to hold the ashtray which balanced on her lap. She lit the butt of an old cigarette, wrapped one arm around her chest, and looked up at the two officers standing in her lounge.

'You may sit down if you're here,' she said. 'Have you any fags? I'm all out.'

Lucy began to explain that she didn't smoke when Fleming stood and said he might have some in the car. She was a little surprised by this; she didn't think he smoked.

'I'm not actually looking for your partner, Miss . . .?' Lucy said, pausing for the woman to complete the sentence for her.

'Gallagher,' the woman said, dragging deeply on the butt, then twisting it out in the ashtray. She blew out the smoke low, towards the floor.

'I need to find an acquaintance of his – Peter Kent.'

'Don't know him,' Gallagher said, not quite looking Lucy in the eye.

'He served time with your partner,' Lucy said. 'We don't have an address for him.'

'Well, that's why I don't know him. Kevin didn't tell me who he did time with. Why would he?'

Fleming came back into the room, opening a box of cigarettes, one of which he offered to the woman. She took it with a nod of gratitude.

'You can smoke,' she said.

'I don't, thanks,' Fleming said, sitting down again, earning a quizzical glance from both women.

'What do you want with Peter anyway?' Gallagher asked, lighting the fresh cigarette.

So much for not knowing him, Lucy thought. 'We think we've—'

'It's a family matter,' Fleming said quickly. 'That's all we can say at the moment. It is important that we speak to him as soon as possible.'

Gallagher squinted at him appraisingly over the top of her cigarette, as if the smoke was bothering her eyes.

Lucy took out her card and passed it to the woman. 'He can call me any time, Miss Gallagher,' she said. 'I'm only interested in locating Mr Kent. He's not in any kind of trouble.'

'I'll mention it to Kevin when he gets back.'

'Where is Mr Mullan?' Lucy asked, but Gallagher had already stood up, signalling that, for her at least, their conversation was concluded.

Back in the car, Lucy looked across at Fleming as he strapped himself in.

'Why do you have cigarettes if you don't smoke?'

He shrugged as he put the box into his bag on the floor.

'I quit smoking when I went off the sauce,' he said. 'Someone told me that the best way to beat the craving was to carry an unopened packet with you all the time. It makes it easier to resist temptation.'

'Seems a bit sadomasochistic,' Lucy said.

'Every time I wanted to smoke, I looked at the box and prayed to the Lord to give me strength not to open the packet.'

'But you opened it there now.'

'A few months after I quit, I was questioning someone who wanted a smoke. I gave him my pack; made him much more cooperative. You never know when a cigarette helps someone become a little more helpful. I always carry a pack in my bag for just such an eventuality as today.'

'She didn't give us much for it,' Lucy observed.

'No,' Fleming agreed. 'But the next time I encounter her, she might be a little more forthcoming. Or the time after that. Or she may not. Either way, it only costs me a cigarette.'

Lucy lifted her mobile from the pocket beside her seat where she had left it. She realized there were a number of messages and she checked her voicemail. Both airports had checked passenger inventories: none of the Kents were on flights or booked to fly. One of the ferry companies left a similar message. She relayed this information to Fleming as she listened to each message. When she hung up he said, 'What about Derry Airport?'

'I forgot all about it,' Lucy admitted. The airport had been so small for so many years that it had never figured in her considerations. She dialled Enquiries, got the number and called.

The man who answered the phone was immediately suspicious of her enquiry. It was not usual to discuss passenger manifests, he said.

Lucy explained why she needed the information, but to no avail.

Sensing her frustration, Fleming reached for the phone and took it from her.

'Chief Superintendent Travers here. I believe there is an issue regarding passenger names, is that right?'

The man on the other end dithered in his response. It was most unusual, he said, for the request to be made in this manner. How did he know that Lucy was who she claimed; indeed, how did he know that Travers was who he said he was?

'We can come down there now, if you wish,' Fleming said. 'I can interrupt a kidnap inquiry to do that, if that's your choice. To get confirmation of whether or not a woman whose child is in hospital took a flight from there in the past week.'

There was a moment's silence on the other end of the line, then the man must have relented for Fleming said, 'I'll pass you back to my colleague.'

'What were the names?' the man asked when Lucy took the phone again.

'Melanie Kent,' Lucy said. 'And Alice Kent.'

She could hear the clatter of the keyboard as he typed. 'Melanie Kent flew out of here last Thursday,' the man said. 'To Majorca. She's booked on the return flight tonight. It's due in around eight thirty.'

'What about Alice Kent?'

'Nothing.'

'Peter Kent?'

'No.'

'Was Mrs Kent travelling alone?'

'She booked to travel with a Mr James Miller.'

'Thank you,' Lucy said, before hanging up. 'And thank you,' she repeated, to Fleming this time.

'It's the only chance I'll ever have at being a Chief Super,' he said.

Lucy had driven to the bottom of the street and indicated to turn at the corner to go back towards the station when Fleming spoke again.

'Do you want to speak to Janet?' he asked.

Lucy looked over at him. 'Of course,' she said.

'Keep going straight. We'll find her in the Foyle Street car park. With the street drinkers.'

CHAPTER 29

Turning right from the lower deck of the Craigavon Bridge, Fleming told Lucy to take an immediate second right, cutting into the car park along the river. She parked up, facing across at the ruins of the old printing factory that squatted at the end of Foyle Street. Lucy glanced around expectantly.

'Watch over there,' Fleming said, pointing towards the wooden boards nailed over the doorway into the building.

A moment or two later, just when Lucy was beginning to think Fleming had it wrong, the wooden board shifted backwards a foot or two and a man, dressed only in jeans and a T-shirt, squeezed out through the gap. The man loped his way along Foyle Street, seemingly impervious to the cold. He made his way up to the arched doorway of a kitchen design shop further along, the front doors shuttered at this time of the afternoon. There, Lucy saw two more figures, a man and woman, huddled together beneath the man's outspread parka jacket. They were holding cans in their hands. The man in the T-shirt approached them, his hand held out, presumably looking to cadge a drink. One of the figures on the ground lashed out with a sneaker-clad foot, catching the man below the knee, causing him to stumble backwards into the roadway, where a passing car swerved by him with blaring horn.

The man steadied himself as best he could, shuffling back onto the pavement. His assailant struggled up from beneath his coat and, approaching him, they embraced. The woman who had been huddled under the coat, also stood, a little shakily, and Lucy was shocked to see that she was, perhaps, seventeen years old.

'Let's go,' Fleming said, lifting his bag and opening the car door.

They crossed the road to where the three were gathered together, trying vainly to light a single cigarette, the wind blowing off the river extinguishing the flame of their lighter. The girl spotted Fleming approaching and nudged her partner.

Lucy assumed they would run, felt herself tensing in preparation for pursuit. Instead, the man turned towards Fleming, smiling broadly.

''Spector,' he slurred, raising his hands as if to embrace Fleming.

The girl moved forward and hugged into her partner as she smiled at Fleming. Close up, she still looked to be little more than a teenager. Her hair was blonde, unwashed, her face full, the scab of a wound across her left cheek ran as far as the bridge of her nose. When she smiled, Lucy could see that she had a number of teeth missing.

'Who's your friend?' the girl said.

'Flemin',' the second man said in greeting, staggering around to look at them, squinting as he did so, as if having difficulty focusing. He shivered, rubbing one bare arm with his hand. Lucy could see various purpled patches of bruising around the crook of his elbow.

'Folks,' Fleming said, opening his bag as he approached. 'We're looking for Janet.'

The first man shrugged theatrically, twisting around to the others to seek their response. The girl was watching Fleming's hand, which had paused halfway into the bag he held. She wet her lips with the tip of her tongue, tightened her grip on her partner's arm.

'She might be inside,' she said.

Fleming pulled out a pack of cigarettes from the bag and, removing a handful, offered them to the girl who was already approaching, palms outstretched, as if she had been expecting just this.

'Thanks, Steph,' he said. Then to Lucy, 'Come on.'

They left the three squabbling over the cigarettes, the girl holding them above her head in the mistaken belief that this might prevent the others taking them from her.

Fleming led Lucy back towards the building they had seen boarded up earlier. He rooted in his pockets and withdrew a pair of blue latex crime scene gloves. He looked at Lucy expectantly.

'I used mine,' she conceded. 'In Quigg's. I forgot to get a new set.'

He handed her the pair he held, then took out a second pair.

'Sometimes you have to double them up,' he explained.

He wrenched back the wooden board that served as a door then stepped back and removed a torch from his bag.

'Always be prepared?' Lucy ventured.

'You soon learn what you need,' he said, flicking on the light and leading the way in.

Inside, the lower floor of the building comprised what had once been the main factory floor, with a number of rooms and offices leading off from the central space. Now, of course, the entire place was dilapidated.

To the far left, in the corner, a fire blazed against the concrete wall, the scorch marks running almost to the ceiling. A number of figures sat nearby, their shadows stretching and dancing across the ceiling back towards where Fleming and Lucy stood. Some of the figures were seated, warming themselves; one was moving around, seemingly scavenging for something off the others.

To her immediate left, Lucy glanced into one of the smaller office areas. A couple lay covered with rags of blankets or coats, the woman's face turned towards Lucy, scowling at the interruption.

Someone at the fire had spotted them now, for a shout of 'Police' went up, and a few of the drinkers scampered away into the rooms to their right. One clambered onto the remains of the staircase in the right-hand corner, scaling the edges of the crumbled steps.

Then, another man, who had emerged from a room a little further along to the left, shouted to the others as he approached, his hand raised in salute. 'It's Fleming.'

'Martin,' Fleming said, by way of greeting. 'This is DS Black.'

'DS Black,' Martin said, offering his hand with a gapped smile.

Lucy was unsure whether to shake or not, then recalled the gloves Fleming had given her.

'Martin,' she said, returning both shake and smile.

Fleming palmed Martin a pack of cigarettes. 'We're looking for Janet,' he said.

Martin raised his eyebrows in enquiry.

'DS Black wants to speak to her; nothing criminal.'

Seemingly appeased, Martin nodded towards the uppermost room on the left-hand side.

'She's not well,' he said.

Fleming handed Martin the bag he had carried. Lucy was caught between wanting to go to Janet and wishing to see what Fleming had given the man.

'Bless you, Inspector,' Martin said, rummaging in the bag and pulling out a plastic-packaged sandwich. 'Tikka,' he added, winking at Lucy.

'Give the rest out would you, Martin?' Fleming said, his hand on Lucy's elbow, encouraging her to get moving. 'A member of my Christian fellowship runs a shop. He donates sandwiches he hasn't sold by the end of the day. I usually drop them off if I get a chance,' he explained.

'To keep the drinkers cooperative?' Lucy asked, smiling conspiratorially.

'To keep them alive,' Fleming replied, holding out his hand, gesturing that she should lead the way.

The room that Martin had indicated was in darkness save for the shifting of the shadows thrown by the fire outside. Against one wall, a body lay bundled in rags. She wore dirtied jeans and a man's sweater. Incongruously, on her feet she wore a pair of pink trainers more suited to a child than an adult.

'Janet?' Fleming whispered, entering the room. Lucy resisted the urge to cover her mouth, for the stench in the room, of sweat and decay, was almost unbearable.

The humped figure moved beneath the ragged coat someone had placed across her like a blanket.

Despite the darkness and the brief flickering illumination from the flames beyond, Lucy could see that this was the woman from the arrest photograph. She could also tell the woman was indeed not well. Her forehead glistened with a patina of sweat, and her body shuddered involuntarily.

'Janet?' Fleming repeated, moving over to the woman. He

laid a gloved hand across her forehead, his other hand moving back the coat that blanketed her. The unmistakable smell of infection wafted towards them. Angling his torch, Fleming called Lucy over.

On Janet's shoulder, running down the length of her upper arm, ran a gash, perhaps six inches long. The skin around the cut was livid, the wound itself green and slick with pus.

'Get an ambulance,' Fleming said. 'She's dying.'

CHAPTER 30

Lucy pulled into the parking bay at City of Derry Airport. She and Fleming had taken Janet to hospital, driving behind the ambulance. None of her drinking friends could tell when or how she had received the injury.

The doctor who treated her had not been hopeful about saving her arm. She concluded that the wound had grown gangrenous, the infection spreading in her blood. Almost immediately, they had hooked Janet to an IV drip, feeding antibiotics into her system. Even with that, she suggested, the arm would probably have to be removed.

Lucy wanted to stay with her, but had been warned that if Janet were taken to theatre, she would be in there for some hours. Besides, she knew that Alice's mother was booked on the flight back from Majorca landing at 8.30 p.m. Fleming argued that Lucy's priority was to Alice and returning her to her family.

The flight was fifteen minutes late. Lucy stood at the observation window in Arrivals with Fleming and watched it come up the approach along the river, watched the bounce as it hit the tarmac runway, its slipstream visible along the wings.

Mrs Kent was definitely on the plane; they'd got confirmation from Majorca that she had boarded. Lucy hoped that she would be able to pick her out.

She and Fleming made their way beyond the Arrivals area and were waved through to Baggage Reclamation. The airport was small anyway; once passengers disembarked, they walked the short distance to the terminal, entering through the door leading to the baggage carousel.

They heard the whine of the engines outside die, followed a few moments later by the first of the passengers coming through the doorway. The fifth person through, Lucy recognized as Alice's mother, her attention focused on her mobile phone, which she was clearly turning on after the flight. She was accompanied by a man.

Lucy prodded Fleming who was watching the passengers trailing into the building. 'That's her,' she whispered.

She moved from the wall where they were standing and approached the woman. She raised her head and smiled until she realized that Lucy was a police officer and her smile faltered.

'Mrs Kent?'

The woman nodded, swallowing. Her companion glanced nervously from Lucy to Fleming.

'I'm DS Black, ma'am. We'd like to speak with you.'

'Is anything wrong?' the woman asked as Fleming moved to her other side and began guiding her away from the other passengers who were watching the scene unfold.

'Let's find somewhere a little quieter,' he suggested.

'Mel,' her partner said. 'Is everything OK? I need to get back.'

Melanie Kent nodded nervously. 'I'll call you later. Go on.'

'You're sure?' The man glanced again at Fleming. 'You don't need me, do you?'

'We might, sir,' Fleming said. 'Don't leave until we've spoken with Mrs Kent.'

Melanie Kent sat in the small baggage-handling office, twisting one hand in the other.

'She was wandering in the snow?' Her accent was English; Midlands, Lucy thought.

Lucy nodded. 'In her pyjamas,' she added.

Melanie shook her head slowly, tears already breaking on her eyelashes. 'I warned him.'

'Warned who?' Fleming asked.

The woman sat back in the seat, lifted her chin as if counting on gravity to prevent her tears falling. She brushed the lower lid of her eyes with her index finger, sniffed deeply.

'My ex-husband. Peter.'

'Alice was left with Peter Kent?' Lucy asked.

Melanie nodded. 'My new partner was invited to a conference in Majorca. He booked tickets for the two of us, but they weren't inviting children. So we couldn't take Alice.'

'This is James Miller,' Lucy said.

Melanie looked at her sharply, then nodded. 'Where is he now?'

'He's waiting outside. He seems eager to leave,' Fleming said. 'Would you like me to bring him in here to be with you?'

Melanie shook her head.

'Is something wrong, Mrs Kent?' Fleming asked.

'Jim is . . . well, he's married himself. His wife doesn't know about us. I don't think he'd want to be stuck in the middle of something like this.'

Fleming nodded understandingly, glancing at Lucy. 'I'll pop out and tell him he's free to go then.'

When Fleming returned to the room, Lucy asked, 'Does your husband have much contact with Alice?'

Something in the tone of Lucy's voice prompted Melanie to pause a little before she answered. 'I'm guessing you already know that Peter has done time.' She waited a beat to see Lucy and Fleming nod again.

'Obviously, he hasn't been as big a part of Alice's life as he'd have liked. I wouldn't take her to see him in prison. When he got out a while back he asked to see her more often, maybe have her stay over with him. She'd stayed a few nights in his house. He seemed to have found his feet a bit. One of his mates from years back, Billy, had found him a job.'

'Billy?' Lucy asked.

'Quinn,' Melanie said. 'The two of them worked together in a bookies before Peter was sent down.'

Lucy nodded, glanced quickly at Fleming.

'So you left Alice with Peter?' he encouraged her to continue.

She nodded. 'I've no family over here. He wasn't best pleased either after crying about never seeing her, said it wasn't the best time. I figured he'd got himself a woman and didn't want a child hanging around the house.'

'What's your husband's address, Mrs Kent?'

'126B Woodside Road,' she said.

'That backs onto Prehen woods,' Fleming said to Lucy.

Melanie said, 'That's right; the woods run right up to the back of Peter's garden.' Then she added, delicately, 'Has Peter . . . hurt her?'

'No, ma'am, she's fine. She was a little cold, so the hospital have kept her in for a few days.'

'Did she not tell you she was staying with her father?' Melanie asked, laughing forcedly.

'She's barely spoken since we found her, ma'am. Hopefully now you're back she'll be able to tell us how she ended up in the woods.'

'Her bloody father was probably too busy at other things to even notice,' Melanie said. 'It'll be the last time she stays with him.'

Lucy considered that, if, as Tony Clarke claimed, the blood on Alice proved to belong to her father, this statement might be more accurate than the woman intended.

'You must think I'm a terrible mother,' Melanie said, glancing up at Lucy anxiously.

'Not at all, ma'am,' Fleming said in response. 'Shall we get you to the hospital?'

They sent Melanie Kent to the hospital in a squad car. After she left, Lucy called the duty social worker. The nasal twang of the woman who answered was familiar.

'Sylvia?'

'Yes?' The word was drawn out, non-committal.

'DS Lucy Black here. We've located Alice's mother and she's on her way to the hospital now with some of our officers. I thought someone should be there.'

'I'll be right up,' Sylvia said; then added brightly, 'I'll call Robbie and have him come up too.'

Before Lucy had a chance to respond, Sylvia hung up.

CHAPTER 31

Woodside Road, known locally as the Strabane Old Road, ran along the hill above the town, a few miles above Prehen. From this height, Lucy and Fleming could see right along the Foyle valley, could make out the flickering lights of the smaller villages and settlements between Derry and Donegal. There were no street lights along the road and the moon bathed the fields on both sides in lilac.

The only houses along the road were old farmhouses, dotted sporadically along the way between Derry and New Buildings. At times they drove a mile between buildings. Fleming called the station to run an owner check on the address Melanie Kent had given them. The database had not listed any address for Peter Kent.

'It belongs to someone called J.P. McCauley,' Fleming said. 'Kent must be renting.'

A few moments later, on the left-hand side of the road, they found the address. The black mass of Prehen woods loomed above the rear of the property. They drew up at the front gate, parking on the road.

Lights shone from the back of the house. Fleming approached

the front door and knocked three times, then stood back and waited. Lucy stood behind him a step, watching around them, aware of the absolute silence. No one answered. Fleming repeated the knock and waited a moment again.

'We'll try the back,' he said.

The house was probably late-nineteenth century with the brickwork rough, the pointing uneven. The windows were still old, wooden sash affairs, the guttering the original metal, rusted and gapped in places.

The snow in the driveway and around the rear of the house lay untouched. It looked as though no one had left the house in a few days.

To the side of the house they came upon the wooden doors of a coal chute lying open. Lucy shone her torch through the doorway; a step dropped down into a basement. In the weak light of her torch she could make out a room full of lumber, old kitchen units, half-used paint pots. Just at the edge of her torch-light, she discerned the metal frame of a camp bed, a thin white mattress on the top.

Past the opening, squatted a small concrete block, about four foot square. A flimsy metal chimney stood on the roof of it.

'Heating boiler,' Fleming said.

The boiler whined without the subsequent whoosh of the fuel igniting that one would expect.

'Sounds like he's run out of oil,' Lucy said.

'And hasn't realized it,' Fleming added.

They skirted around the perimeter of the house. Finally, at the rear, they found a pair of French doors ajar. Through the fabric of curtains pulled across the doorway shone the lights of the room beyond.

Fleming drew his gun and knocked once on the glass of the open door.

'Police,' he called.

Lucy drew her own weapon. She moved towards the door and took the edge of the curtain in her hand. Then, gently, she drew it back.

The first thing she saw, on the white tiled floor of the kitchen beyond, was a small, perfectly formed footprint, made in blood. A few pictures hung on the wall. Nothing else.

Drawing the curtain further back, they could see more of the prints, leading round the corner of what was an L-shaped room.

Lucy stepped into the house. It was as cold inside as out. Glancing back, to hold the curtain open for Fleming, she noticed a number of bloated bluebottles clinging to the fabric. She moved further into the kitchen, avoiding stepping on the prints on the floor. Even before she had rounded the corner she knew what to expect. The flies, the smell, the bloody prints. Peter Kent was dead.

Lucy wasn't prepared for the manner of his death, though. Kent was slumped in a chair, his legs splayed, his head hanging limply downwards. A thick rope crisscrossed his chest and was wrapped around the back of the chair, preventing him from slipping to the floor. His chest was encrusted with dried brown blood, his stomach distended and bulging at the gaps between the buttons of his shirt. More blood had congealed into a gelatinous skin on the floor around his chair. A blood-soaked cloth hung from his mouth where he must have been gagged.

One of his shoes had been removed and lay discarded against the far wall. The sock was balled in on itself and lay at the edge of the pool of blood. Kent's foot had clearly been beaten before he died; the skin was discoloured with bruising. The two outer-most toes hung at an angle from the rest of the foot. The arch of his foot was marked with round livid red circles.

'Sweet Jesus,' Fleming said, drawing level with Lucy. 'I'll call it in.'

As he took out his phone, Lucy edged around the pool of blood. Moving behind the body she found, in the sink, a hammer.

While they waited for back-up, Lucy and Fleming moved through the house, checking the rooms in case anyone else remained in the house. Lucy noticed as she climbed to the first floor that the step on the turn of the stairs offered a clear view of Kent's body in the kitchen, framed by the doorway.

Upstairs they found a small room where, presumably, Alice had been staying while with her father. A small inflatable airbed was pushed against one corner. A duvet was thrown back to one side. A nest of clothes lay on the floor. Beside the dresser a small pink case lay opened. A doll sat on top of the dresser. The decor of the room, though, was sparse and plain. Alice may have stayed in this room, but the room was not hers. Certainly that would square with Melanie Kent's comment that Peter had not been expecting Alice.

A second room was obviously Kent's own bedroom; the third was empty of all furniture.

'Fairly sparse existence,' Fleming said.

Lucy stood looking at the bare room.

'Strange that he didn't put the third bed up here,' she said.

'What bed?'

'There's a bed set up in the basement,' Lucy said, then realized the significance of it.

They found the stairs to the basement leading down from a

utility room to the side of the house. The door of the basement lay open. A new, heavy sliding bolt had been fitted to the outside of the door. Looking at the lock, Lucy was reminded of Mary Quigg's bedroom.

Inside the basement they used Lucy's torch to help locate the light switch. A fluorescent tube light sparked into life, then began flickering erratically. From the elliptical flashing of the light they could see the camp bed Lucy had spotted from outside. The mattress was covered in a sheet though it had bunched up on one side.

Strips of gaffer tape hung off the top of the bed frame. Each strip had been cut evenly. On the floor near the bed, a Stanley knife lay, bits of tape still stuck to the blade.

Lucy stepped over to the bed. Something small glinted in the light of her torch, sitting in the hollow of the pillow. She stopped and lifted it, placing it in the palm of her hand to examine it: a small golden teddy-bear charm.

'Looks like we've found where Kate McLaughlin was being held.'

Lucy glanced around the room. Through the open door of the coal chute in the far wall she heard the distant crying of sirens.

'The question remains,' Fleming continued, 'where is she now?'

CHAPTER 32

Tony Clarke shuffled up the driveway, lugging a case of equipment with him. The interior of the house had become too busy; SOCOs had set up arc lights in both the kitchen and the basement. Around Peter Kent's body, heavy-bodied flies flitted blue-green through the light's beam.

Lucy had come outside for a moment, to escape both the bustle and the smell in the house. Fleming stood beside her, his hands in his pockets.

'I'm going to have to start paying you commission,' Clarke said to Lucy as he drew abreast of them.

Lucy smiled. 'Good evening, Officer Clarke.'

'And a good evening to you too, DS Black. Always a pleasure.'

He glanced at Fleming and nodded lightly. 'Inspector,' he said.

'Any luck in the shed this afternoon?' Fleming asked, dispensing with the small talk.

'We found quite a lot, sir,' Clarke said, placing the case he carried gently by his feet. 'We know Kate was in there.'

'Fingerprints?'

Clarke nodded. 'I found hairs too. Plus, of course, the charm you found.'

Lucy nodded. 'There's one here too. It's as though she's leaving them for us like a trail.' Absurdly, Lucy recalled reading Hansel and Gretel to Alice, the trail of breadcrumbs leading through the woodland, the picture of the two girls in the wood Alice had drawn afterwards.

'We also found her prints all over the empty food cans in the shed in the quarry,' Clarke said.

'So she fed herself.'

'And tried to escape, I think.'

'How?' Lucy asked.

'There was a hole cut in the back wall. We found a knife lying beside it with her prints. We also found traces of blood on the edges of the metal where it had been cut.'

'Meaning?' Fleming asked.

'It's not my job to suggest, Inspector,' Clarke said. 'But if pushed, I'd say she was locked in the shed and couldn't get out. She tried cutting her way out, using the knife to cut through the metal sheeting of the wall. She pushed out the flap of metal she had cut, then put her hands under the edge to push it further out, cutting herself in the process. When she's found she'll have cuts on her hands.'

'Any indications of who put her in there?'

'The clasp at the front of the shed had too many prints on it to be useful. However, I did find a couple of prints on the padlock belonging to your friend.'

'Who?'

'Alice,' Clarke said. 'She'd probably locked the shed.'

'Is that where she met Kate?'

'Alice brought her there,' Lucy said suddenly. 'She drew a

picture for the shrink in the hospital of two girls walking hand in hand through the woods. Maybe Alice brought her to safety, then locked the shed.'

'Surely she'd have come back for her,' Fleming said.

'Maybe she tried,' Lucy said. 'Maybe that's why she went back into the woods when I found her.'

'Maybe,' Fleming said sceptically.

Clarke shrugged. 'I wouldn't know about any of that. It gets better though. The pieces of piping, jars, fertilizer? A bomb-making factory.'

'I suspected as much when I saw it,' Fleming said.

Clarke nodded. 'I lifted traces of Semtex off the worktop; old stuff but still traces there. It was part of the batch the Provos brought into the North in the early nineties.'

'That makes sense,' Lucy said. 'We know Kent was a bomb-maker for the Provos. Something like that hidden in the woods would be perfect for it.'

'There's more,' Clarke added. 'The batch was used in particular in one bombing in Derry.'

'Which one?'

'The Strand Inn on the docks. The bomb that killed McLaughlin's wife.'

While the SOCO unit worked through the house, Lucy headed back to the hospital with Tom Fleming. Travers suggested that they inform Melanie Kent of the death of her ex-husband before meeting at Strand Road for a CID briefing the following morning at 7.30 a.m.

Melanie Kent was in the office of the duty social worker when they arrived. Social Services were concerned about the circumstances surrounding the discovery of Alice in the woods and would not agree to Melanie being given custody of Alice again until they were satisfied that she had not been negligent in her care of the child.

Lucy and Fleming sat in the cafe while they waited for the interview to conclude.

'You have to feel sorry for the youngster,' Fleming said. 'Not even about the whole thing with seeing her father dead and that. But before that; her mother pissing about with a married man, her father doing time, her being shifted from pillar to post. It's no wonder the child doesn't want to speak. Maybe she knows that no one would listen anyway.'

Lucy looked at him quizzically.

'How many neglected kids are there looking for help and we don't give it? Take that wee girl from the other day, Mary Quigg. What hope does she have?'

Fleming nodded once, as if satisfied with his comment, then motioned towards where Robbie McManus stood at the door to his office, beckoning them over.

'We need to see Mrs Kent,' Fleming said. 'Her husband's been found.'

Robbie raised his eyebrows expectantly, though quickly gleaned from Lucy's expression that it was not good news.

'You'd best come in now.'

Melanie Kent was seated at the far side of the desk. Sylvia sat opposite her, a cup of coffee in front of her. A third, empty seat, beside Sylvia's was, presumably, where Robbie had been sitting.

Melanie stood when Lucy and Fleming came in.

'Did you find the bastard?' she snapped. 'It's his fault I'm in this bloody mess.'

Fleming glanced at Lucy, then spoke. 'We have some bad news, Mrs Kent.' There was no need for him to elaborate, for the woman was stopped short just as she seemed ready to launch into a further tirade.

'What hap— where is he?'

'We found him in his house, Mrs Kent,' Fleming said.

Lucy moved across to the woman and placed her hand on Kent's arm. She may have been separated from Peter Kent, but news of his death had still hit her.

'Might be best to sit, Mrs Kent,' Lucy said.

'What happened to him?'

'We'll be launching a murder inquiry, Mrs Kent,' Fleming said, clasping his hands in front of him.

Melanie Kent's expression crumpled momentarily, her tears coming quickly. She spluttered as she turned and sat, while Lucy squatted beside her, her arm around the woman's shoulders.

'We might not . . . but I still . . . you know,' the woman tried to explain as she wiped at her tears with the sleeve of her coat.

'We understand,' Fleming said.

Lucy found herself wondering if her own mother might feel the same way if she had heard similar news. Her mother had asked about her father when they spoke, though she had assumed it was out of politeness, out of a sense of what was expected. But then, her mother had never done what was expected of her, had seemed determined to ignore proprieties. In so doing she had broken the glass ceiling. And it was not all that she had broken.

'Perhaps you could be doing with a few moments alone,' Fleming said.

Lucy felt torn between the discomfort she always felt in delivering such news to a relative, and her desire to offer the woman some consolation, to remain beside her when she needed someone. In the end, Melanie Kent made the decision for her.

She nodded her head and turned away from her, seeking to be left alone.

Fleming suggested that they both go home for a few hours' sleep before the 7.30 briefing. The thought of going back to the empty house in Prehen did not appeal to her though, so Lucy said she would stay in the hospital, and perhaps visit her father. Fleming glanced at the clock in the foyer of the hospital, just edging towards 1.30 a.m.

'Try to get some rest, Lucy,' he said, before leaving.

Despite saying she would visit her father, Lucy found herself on the children's ward again.

Alice was lying awake in the bed when Lucy came in and rewarded her arrival with the gift of her smile.

'Hi, Alice,' Lucy said, but the child did not speak.

'Your mummy's downstairs,' Lucy explained. 'She'll be up soon, I expect.'

Alice yawned lightly, emitting a tiny squeak at the height of her stretch. She laid her hands back on the bedclothes and watched Lucy expectantly.

'I wish you would talk to us, Alice,' Lucy said, aware now of all that had forced the child into choosing not to speak. After all, what could she say? How could she vocalize what she must have seen? She was a child after all, Lucy reminded herself. An adult would have difficulty coming to terms with what she had witnessed.

She sat on the bed beside Alice and laid her hand on the girl's head. Her hair was shiny and smooth, her scalp warm to the touch.

'You poor, poor love,' she said.

Alice returned her stare, her eyes wide. Even now, they seemed to have lost their lustre, as if someone had stolen something from their centre.

191

'They took that too,' Lucy said. She felt her eyes grow warm, felt the first fat droplet fall onto her cheek, found herself thinking unbidden of the girl who had lain in the hallway of her house as eyes watched her through the letter box. She put her arm around Alice's shoulder and hugged her to her. Alice placed her hand on Lucy's chest, her other around her back and returned the affection.

They sat like that for some time, listening to the noises of the ward, the hushed movements of the nursing staff, the occasional clatter as patients shifted in their beds in the adjacent rooms on the ward.

Finally Lucy sat up and lifted the book that sat on the chair by the bed where she had left it the previous night. She flicked through to the index, mentally ticking off the tales she had read and those she had no wish to read. Finally she settled on one.

'Once upon a time, there was a young girl called Little Red Riding Hood . . .' she began.

CHAPTER 33

Alice's screams brought the nurses rushing into the room. They had not realized that Lucy was there and Margaret was surprised to find her standing by the bed, trying desperately to placate Alice. The child, on top of the bed, had backed against the wall and clenched the blankets in front of her face. Despite this, her screams echoed along the corridor, the cloth of the blanket doing nothing to diminish their strength.

'What happened?' Margaret demanded.

'I read her a story,' Lucy said, almost in tears herself as she stared at the child whose face was streaked with tears.

'She's wet the bed,' the nurse said to Margaret. 'We'll need to change the sheets.'

Margaret tried to lift Alice but the girl backed away from her and screamed all the harder. Her eyes though were vacant, as if she were looking at something beyond them all, as if she was not even aware of the room and the other people in it.

'She looks like she's having a night terror,' Margaret said.

At that moment, Melanie Kent rushed into the room.

'Alice,' she cried, running to the girl and gathering her in her arms. Robbie followed behind her into the room.

'What's wrong?' he asked.

'What did you do?' Melanie Kent snapped, turning to Lucy.

'Nothing,' she said. 'I came up and read her a story.'

She gestured to where the book lay discarded on the chair beside the bed, lying open at the page where she had been forced to stop. The image of the wolf, lithe and smiling, his fangs bared, stared back at them.

'You've terrified her!' Melanie Kent shouted. 'You stupid bitch, you've scared her half to death.'

'Mrs Kent . . .' Lucy began but Melanie Kent interrupted her, addressing Robbie instead.

'Get her away from my daughter.'

Lucy stopped off at the recovery ward on the way to her father only to be told by a harried nurse that Janet was sedated. The surgeons had managed to save the arm, though at the expense of the upper muscle, some of which had to be removed. Janet was not to be disturbed, she was told. In truth, Lucy had no intention of doing so; she wanted to see how she was because of her father.

Her father was listless when she called on him. The chill he'd received when out wandering in the snow had exacerbated an underlying chest infection. He was sitting up in the bed, a mound of pillows behind his head, forcing him to sleep with the upper half of his body at a 45-degree angle to the mattress. A small tube was connected to his nose and, in the silence of the room, Lucy could hear the constant hiss of the oxygen flowing through it.

He opened his eyes when she sat. He had not been shaved for a few days, his cheeks rough with jagged silvered stubble. His breath rasped softly in the silence as he watched her, his eyes swivelling in their sockets towards where she sat.

'Is that you?'

'It's me, Dad,' Lucy said, reaching over and switching on the bedside lamp, angling the shade so the light was directed at him. 'How are you feeling?'

'Sore chest,' he said, a cough grumbling through his lungs, building into a short bark. The effort seemed to exhaust him and he laid his head back on the nest of pillows.

'The doctors say you've a chest infection,' she said.

'I'll be fine,' he said, raising his arm an inch off the bed, then lowering it. His fingers bunched up the sheet where they rested. 'How's all at home?'

'Fine,' Lucy echoed, not wishing to admit that she hadn't really been home since he'd gone out into the snow.

'You've been talking about Janet,' Lucy said softly, laying her own hand on her father's as she leaned towards the bed.

'What?' His gaze flicked towards her.

'You've been talking about Janet,' she repeated.

He stared straight ahead, at the joint between the facing wall and ceiling. He mumbled something which Lucy couldn't catch.

'I know she was your informant, Dad,' she ventured, shifting forward slightly on the seat, edging closer to him.

He nodded wordlessly. His fingers found her hand, tightened lightly around hers.

'Do you want to see her?'

A sob shook his frame and he shook his head slowly back and forth. He rasped something.

'What did you say, Daddy?' Lucy asked gently.

'Forgiven me?' he managed.

Lucy released his hand, shifted back a little in the seat.

Her father struggled again to speak. 'Has she forgiven me?'

'Has who forgiven you? Mum?'

He shook his head. 'Janet?'

'Has Janet forgiven you?'

He nodded, his hand reaching for hers again.

'What for?'

He looked at her, his eyes glistening. He breathed deeply, then closed his eyes. He muttered softly to himself, over and over, but would not speak to Lucy again. Finally, she stood, leaned over and kissed her father on the forehead. His skin was dry and warm, though his breath carried the sour scent of illness.

CHAPTER 34

Lucy drove home as quickly as she could to shower and change ahead of the 7.30 briefing. She had forgotten to set the heating and changed quickly. After a quick breakfast she set off again. The heat in the car made her drowsy as she manoeuvred her way down the hill out of Prehen, the road bordered by the black expanse of the woodland.

Though the roads had been mostly cleared of snow now, and no fresh falls had come, despite more dire forecasts, she could still see the sparkling of ice off the road, could feel the steering wheel of her car light in her hand as she turned a corner. She opened the window in the hope that the cold air would keep her awake.

The traffic in town was light, the last of the late-night taxis slowly prowling the streets for a final fare before the dawn drivers started the work and school runs.

Lucy enjoyed the silence. For the past few days, she'd had little time to herself, despite being frequently alone. The silence suited her. Lights along the docks reflected off the river. Ice floes around the base of the pillars holding up the Craigavon Bridge had widened and joined together, running unbroken from one side of the river to the other. Staring downriver, she could make out the skeletal outline of the new footbridge being constructed to link symbolically the east and west banks of the city. The surface reflection was still, the river calm and beautiful, belying its reputation as one of the most deadly in Europe, claiming more suicides than any other in Ireland.

The station, by contrast, was a bustle of activity. Two big breaks in twenty-four hours in the Kate McLaughlin case had brought everyone in early. There was a positive mood at the sergeant's desk, a palpable sense that today was the day the case would be cracked.

Travers looked well rested as he strode into the CID suite. He wore the suit from the day of the press conference and a bright-green tie; clearly he felt that a further television appearance would be in order before day's end. Tony Clarke looked significantly less well rested as he trailed behind him.

Tom Fleming sat on a desk at the back of the room, studiously avoiding any of the CID team; they gladly reciprocated. He raised a mug of coffee in greeting when he saw Lucy. Just past him, Tara, her fellow detective sergeant, nodded at Lucy when she came in and shifted over in her seat to offer her room. Caught between the two, Lucy waved to Tara, indicating she would join her, then approached Tom and stood as they spoke. He slid across on the desk and patted the space beside him. 'Hop up,' he said. 'You look like you ignored my advice about getting some rest. I've made you coffee.'

Lucy took the proffered cup with thanks, then turned quickly to Tara, hoping she would read the situation. She returned Lucy's smile and nodded before shifting back in her seat again.

Travers raised his hand, waiting for silence. Clarke caught Lucy's eye and smiled a little embarrassedly. Then Travers began to speak.

'Morning all. Good to see so many fresh faces this morning after the excitement of last night.'

A few diehards glanced around; their bleary eyes an indication of their dedication to the job.

'SOCOs worked on Peter Kent's house through the night. They've confirmed that Kate McLaughlin was being held in the basement of the house and in a quarryman's shed in the middle of Prehen woods. I've asked Officer Clarke here to brief us on what he found.'

Clarke stepped forward and began to speak. His voice was lost among the crowd of people and someone at the back called to him to speak louder, prompting him to overcompensate by almost shouting his way through the presentation.

'We worked two scenes yesterday,' he said, his voice inflecting to show he was repeating himself. 'As best we can tell, Kate spent time in both places. I believe she was being held in the basement of the house on Strabane Old Road. I believe that Peter Kent's daughter, Alice, may have helped her to escape. We found a knife beside the bed Kate was bound to. It had been used to cut the bonds. Alice's prints were on the knife. In addition, the coal chute doors were lying open. Alice's prints were found on the hasp of the lock on the outside. I believe she opened those doors and, finding Kate inside, helped to release her. I think she took her into the woods to the shed we searched yesterday afternoon. Again, we found Alice's prints on the lock.'

He glanced at Lucy. 'We believe Alice took Kate into the woods and locked her in the shed to keep her safe. She must have been in the shed for some time for we found empty cans of food with her prints on them. She attempted to cut her way out of the shed, as we know from a broken blade found there, as well as a hole cut in the metal wall of the shed. The shed itself was probably used for bomb-making at some stage. There were traces of explosives that link to the bombing of the docks in the 1990s that resulted in Kate McLaughlin's mother being killed.'

The officers seated around watched Clarke intently, some of them jotting notes as he spoke.

Travers stepped forward again. 'Thank you, Officer Clarke. As you all can tell, Forensics has found quite a bit to get us going. They also found two charms that we believe to be Kate's in the two locations. A third charm was found the previous night by a civilian who contacted DS Black of the PPU.'

Several heads swivelled to look at Lucy. Fleming nudged her and raised a mocking eyebrow.

'So what's the story, sir?' a young detective sergeant at the front asked.

'We believe that Kent and Quinn abducted Kate and held her in Kent's house. A day after she was taken, Kent was landed with looking after his daughter when his ex went on holiday. His child, Alice, must have helped Kate McLaughlin escape, as Officer Clarke has explained. We can only assume that when Kent's partners arrived looking for her and found she had gone they assumed that he had let her go. As Alice was found in her pyjamas, we think that Kent didn't tell his partners about her and, presumably, they blamed him. There is evidence of torture on his body inflicted with a claw hammer. His associates must have been quizzing him over what had happened to Kate. The fact that Alice is still alive would suggest that he didn't tell them about her, or they would surely have used her to force him to speak. The blood misting on her clothes suggests she was in contact with him as he died, but we have to assume that she was hidden when his attackers killed him.'

'He died to protect her,' Lucy muttered to herself. Fleming

looked at her quizzically. 'And she probably saw who killed him, too.'

'Alice took Kate to the shed and someone found her again, we believe.'

'Might she not have escaped, sir?' someone to Lucy's left asked.

'Unlikely. The hole she made wasn't big enough for someone of her age and size to squeeze through. Plus the door of the shed was open. Police 44 did a fly-by the day before and in the images taken then, the door of the shed is clearly closed.'

'She was in the shed when they flew over,' Tara commented.

'It seems so,' Travers agreed. The admission was greeted with groans.

'So, as you know, we now have two of Kate's abductors dead; one of them as a result of being pursued by one of our officers.'

Someone near the back of the room let out a muffled cheer.

Travers smiled. 'I know. Still, had he been alive we might have got something useful from him. There must still be other members of the team on the loose and we still have to locate Kate herself. Thankfully, Mr McLaughlin's offer of a reward has brought out the vultures.'

The room buzzed as Travers pinned up photographs of two men on the noticeboard. Lucy thought she recognized one of them, the thinner of the two men, but could not immediately place him. His face was sharp, his hair lank, hanging across his face. The second man bore a familial resemblance to the first, though his face was rounder, his jowls sagging.

'Peter and Alan Cunningham,' Travers said. 'Our targets for today.'

When she heard the name, Lucy realized who the man was: the partner of Mary Quigg's mother.

'An informant tells us that these two men were involved in Kate's snatching. Both have form: the fat boy, Peter, did time for child sex offences in the eighties; he's still on the register. The younger one, Alan, has records for drugs offences and for a few domestic abuse reports, including those involving a child.'

'What's the connection here?' someone behind Lucy asked.

'Peter took up plumbing while inside; the two of them operate a plumbing service. Peter owns a red van matching a description of one spotted parked in the lay-by at Prehen woods yesterday.'

'Half the town owns red vans,' Fleming muttered to Lucy.

'Our CI gave the registration number of the van as being Cunningham's.'

It was a little more plausible, Lucy thought.

Then Travers turned to her. 'DS Black has encountered Alan Cunningham recently, isn't that right, Sergeant?'

'That's right, sir,' Lucy said.

'You didn't hear any screaming coming from Cunningham's basement or anything, no?'

'No, sir.'

'Didn't notice anything unusual?'

'No, sir,' Lucy said. 'I was following up a concern about a school child,' she explained. 'Cunningham is dating the girl's mother.'

'Despite his record,' Travers said, for the benefit of the whole room, 'Alan Cunningham is living with an eleven-year-old child. Our concern today is to take the two of them as cleanly as possible. We need the van for Forensics, obviously.'

'Is it a house raid, sir?' Tara asked.

Travers shook his head.

'It will be easier to get the two of them together, with the van. We've set checkpoints on both bridges, to try to pick them up. I'll be assigning teams to assist Uniforms for the lifts.'

Some people began to stand, ready to get going, but Travers had not finished.

'These two are scum, but they are unlikely to be armed. Be careful but there should be no reason for anyone to get hurt.'

Then he stared at Lucy directly. 'And do try not to kill anyone today, DS Black.'

As people began to filter away into their teams, Lucy stood to one side. Fleming excused himself, claiming he had paperwork to complete. As soon as he had left, Travers approached her.

'Inspector Fleming didn't hang around,' he observed. 'I hope you didn't mind the little joke.'

'It's fine, sir,' she said tersely, unwilling to show Travers that he had embarrassed her.

'Every newbie gets something. You have it light. When I started every new appointment got stamped.'

Lucy tried to be sincere as she shared his smile. She'd heard of stamping: new recruits having their trousers and pants pulled down and their buttocks stamped with the station rubber stamp. It was an initiation that had been reserved mostly for female recruits, strangely.

'It's fine, sir,' she repeated.

'I'll make it up to you,' he said. 'Go out with Team C.'

CHAPTER 35

Lucy went out to the car park and looked around for Team C. Finally, Tara approached her.

'You're with us,' she said. 'Come on.'

Lucy followed her across to the parking bays where five unmarked cars sat idling. Most were already filled and waiting to leave. Tara moved across to the furthest and climbed into the back seat. Lucy got in beside her.

The driver turned and smiled. 'All right, ladies,' he said. He was young, thin-faced, handsome.

Tara nudged Lucy. 'All right, Mickey,' she said.

The young man's smile vanished quickly. 'Shit,' he muttered, turning back in his seat.

Lucy looked beyond him and saw Travers crossing the yard towards them. He opened the front passenger seat and got in.

'Let's get going, Constable,' he said. 'We haven't got all day.'

Lucy caught Mickey's eye in the rear-view mirror, saw him raise his eyebrows. Then he shifted into gear and the car lurched forwards.

They drove up Strand Road behind four Response Land Rovers. At the rear of the Guildhall they split, two vehicles continuing on towards the Craigavon Bridge where they would set up a checkpoint on the upper and lower decks. The other two headed down the Quay towards the Foyle Bridge at the other end of the city; one would block the dual roads towards Derry, the other the two lanes leading to the Waterside.

The convoy continued up Culmore Road, the other cars slowing down to the thirty-mile-an-hour speed limit when they saw the PSNI cars approach. Mickey had the heating turned on in the car, making the atmosphere even stuffier than it already was with Travers's presence. Once or twice, Lucy and Tara attempted to engage in conversation but it fizzled out quickly as, with each attempt, Travers twisted in his seat, smiling in expectation of being involved. Finally, they settled into an uneasy silence.

At the Culmore roundabout, the convoy split, Travers issuing orders through the car's radio handset. Team C would park in the lay-by at the bottom of the Derry side of the bridge on the lanes leading towards Waterside. Team D would be in the lay-by on the opposite side of the road, the lanes separated by a low metal fence. Teams A and B would take up similar positions at the Waterside end of the bridge. If any team spotted the van, they were to close in behind it. When it was stopped by the Uniform checkpoint at the apex of the bridge, they could close in on it and lift the two Cunninghams.

They sat in the car for half an hour, watching the cars speed past, many disregarding the 50 mph limit. The large orange windsock attached to a lamp post just past the lay-by managed an occasional desultory flutter. A few snowflakes drifted onto the windscreen. Lucy glanced down to her left, to the fields below the bridge. Standing out amongst the trees near the river's edge, she saw the crumbling outline of Boom Hall. She remembered seeing this place when she was younger; it was an eighteenth-century mansion, built on the spot where the Jacobean army had erected a wooden boom across the River Foyle to prevent relief ships bringing supplies upstream to the Williamites during the Siege of Derry in 1689. Despite its significance, it had fallen into disrepair.

Eventually, Travers seemingly tired of the silence in the car.

'Mickey, cut over to the van there and get a few teas, would you?'

Mickey, in reply, glanced towards the back seat, clearly hoping Travers would give the task to one of the women. Instead, Travers handed him a ten-pound note. 'Milk and one sugar. What about you girls?'

'No sugar,' Tara said, smiling. 'Milk though. Thank you, sir.'

'Milk and one as well, please,' Lucy said.

Mickey took the money and, getting out, slammed the door a little harder than necessary.

'No point in having a DC if he can't get the tea, isn't that right?' Travers said, turning in the seat to face them. 'Benefits of promotion.'

They watched Mickey wait for a break in the traffic before running across the two lanes to the central partition. He clambered over the wooden fence and similarly waited for a chance to run across the opposite side of the bridge to the lay-by where Team D sat. A white chip van was parked at the edge of the bay. A moment after Mickey took up position outside it, someone was dispatched from Team D's car on the same mission.

Mickey had made it back to the central partition with the four polystyrene cups balancing on a piece of card as a makeshift tray when Lucy noticed the red van pass him, heading across towards Waterside. Travers spotted it at the same time.

'That's us,' he said, climbing across into the driver's seat.

Mickey dropped the tea and, dodging a car, scampered across to them. Travers pointed for him to get into the passenger seat, and, when he had done so, took off.

They pulled out into the left-hand lane and headed up the gradient of the bridge to where they could see the van's brake lights flash as it began to slow. Clearly the Cunninghams had spotted the checkpoint further along the bridge, although it was still some distance away, and were slowing.

'They're thinking of cutting across,' Travers said.

'Except they can't,' Mickey said. 'The middle partition runs the whole way up.'

The van sat in the outer lane. To their left was another lane of traffic going in the same direction as them. To turn they would have to cross the central partition which was impossible because of the buffer fencing. They were trapped, with no choice but to continue along the bridge towards the checkpoint. The driver of the car behind the van sounded his horn in enquiry, for they had now stopped dead in the middle of the road.

Lucy thought for a second that they might make a run for it, abandon the van and try to escape on foot. Instead the van suddenly lurched left.

'He's doing a U-turn,' Mickey said.

Sure enough, ignoring the blaring horns of the other cars in its path, the van executed a three-point turn and began driving the wrong way down the road again, causing the cars climbing the bridge to pull in tight on the inner lane to let it past.

Travers hit the siren and flasher. 'Get D across here,' he snapped flinging the handset to Mickey.

'Team D assist. Suspects driving back down the bridge on the wrong side towards Culmore roundabout.'

Lucy glanced back and, as the radio crackled with a click of static in response, she saw Team D's car pull out of the roundabout and head towards the Culmore roundabout to come onto their side of the bridge.

The Cunninghams had spotted Lucy's car now and were swerving on the road, the slushy conditions making it hard for them to retain control of their vehicle.

Travers pulled across the road diagonally, trying to block their path. Whoever was driving the van sped up in response and mounted the edge of the central partition so that the fencing dragged alongside the side of the van. One section of it twisted off the wooden poles cemented into the road and unravelled like ribbon, dragging along the ground behind the van.

'Brace yourselves!' Travers shouted as the van approached. The driver was hoping to squeeze past the rear end of the car but had underestimated the width of his own vehicle.

Lucy felt the car shift, felt herself being flung in the opposite direction to that of the car, heard the dull thud as the van clipped the back of the car, then the screech as it pulled off their bumper.

The force of the impact caused their car to turn so that, in fact, they ended up facing the direction in which the van was travelling. Further down the road, ahead of them both, Team D had adopted a similar position, cutting diagonally across the lanes. This time, perhaps seeing the fate of C's car, they parked tight against the central reservation.

The red van slid to a stop. Travers slammed the car into gear and set off after them.

'Everyone OK?' he called, glancing in the mirror at the two women.

Ahead, the Cunninghams had pulled across the road into the lay-by where Team C had been parked moments earlier and came to a halt. Instantly two men alighted from the van and set off on foot, down the embankment from the lay-by. Lucy recognized the thinner of the two as Alan Cunningham. He carried a bag in his hand as he ran.

Travers pulled in behind them, as Team D pulled in at the other entrance to the lay-by. Both cars emptied and the teams set off on foot after the Cunninghams.

At the top of the bank, they could see instantly the wide disturbances in the snow where the two men had slid down to the field at the bottom. Peter Cunningham was caught on a barbed-wire fence leading into a field behind Boom Hall. Alan Cunningham had abandoned his brother and was running towards the old dilapidated building.

'He's dumped the bag!' Lucy shouted.

'Secure the van!' Travers shouted, then set off down the embankment after them, sliding on his buttocks to the bottom.

Peter Cunningham was twisting now, pulling at his jacket where it was caught on the barbs. Finally, he unzipped the coat and, leaving it hanging off the fence, set off across the snow, wearing only a T-shirt.

Lucy followed Alan Cunningham who was running towards the ruins of Boom Hall, every so often seeming to lose his footing on the snow that still lay on the uneven ground. He finally reached the building and disappeared around the corner.

Lucy sprinted after him, only slowing as she reached the front of the building. The ground-floor windows had been blocked up to prevent local children climbing inside and injuring themselves in the ruins. Only the uppermost windows remained open, their glass long since gone. Thick tendrils of ivy scarred across the face of the building, twisting round the brickwork and in through the open apertures of the upper windows.

At first Lucy could not see Alan Cunningham anywhere. Then she heard a soft scraping and, looking up, realized he had used a set of thick vines growing up the wall to help scale the side of the building. He had almost reached the top. Pulling himself up to an upper window ledge, he heaved himself over and dropped from view.

Lucy stood back and gauged the height of the wall. Then she took hold of the vines to pull herself up. She knew that if the vines had taken Cunningham's weight they should take hers, but still she was a little concerned that he might have dislodged their hold on the crumbling brickwork. Putting one hand in front of the other and leaning her weight on her legs, she climbed slowly and steadily. In places she found that the cement had been weathered away from between the bricks of the wall, the gaps providing good footholds. As she neared the window ledge she felt her arms beginning to ache. Finding a suitable foothold in the brickwork, she used her legs to push herself upwards, her hand clawing for purchase on the upper ledge.

Glancing back, she saw Travers standing below her, reaching for the first vine. Then she heaved herself the final few feet onto the window ledge and found herself staring into the belly of the ruined building. Apart from a few surviving rafters, the roof was completely absent meaning that she could see the ruins clearly, even in the weakening winter light. The interior walls were in varying states of disrepair, the floors of the rooms littered with pieces of timber and lumps of rubble.

Gripping the window ledge, she swung her legs over and, lowering herself halfway down the interior wall, dropped to the ground. She reckoned she was standing in what had once been the main living room for the crumbled remains of a huge fireplace dominated the wall opposite. The floor under her feet was uneven below the coating of snow, which had not melted, the interior of the building being enshadowed by the surrounding walls.

She stumbled across the floor, trying to follow the disturbed snow where Cunningham had moved. She became aware of the number of internal walls, all of them potential hiding places. She began to regret her haste in following him and considered for a moment waiting for Travers to catch up. But she also knew Travers was older than her, less fit, and would struggle to scale the wall easily.

Somewhere to the rear of the building she heard scuffling, then a bird exploded into the sky, disturbed by something. Lucy followed its path, a crow, grey-capped, its wings thudding against the chill wind.

She moved towards the spot where she had seen it appear. Rounding the corner of a wall, she guessed she was in the hallway of the house, a long thin corridor, along which two walls ran almost the entire length of the house, a number of doorways giving off from each side.

She continued moving towards the rear of the building. Because the floor was so uneven, the snow did not lie smoothly and she could not be sure if Cunningham had caused the marks in the snow. Still, at one doorway further ahead and to her right, there did seem to be definite footprints. She approached the doorway, her gun drawn, and paused for a moment, listening for the sound of breathing, holding her own breath as she did so.

Finally, she peered around the edge of the doorway, cautiously, with no more than a snatched glance.

Still, the rock caught her full on the forehead. Cunningham was standing just inside the doorway, pressed against the wall, the rock clasped in his hand, rising again for another strike. Lucy stumbled backwards, losing her footing and falling onto her back. Her vision seemed to twist and distort and she could feel the heat of the blood trickling down her forehead.

She looked up at Cunningham, stepping into the doorway, following her. She realized that he looked terrified, almost as if he took no pleasure in what he was doing. He stared down at her, his face drawn and pale, then he flung the rock to one side and sped past her, running back along the corridor she had just come down. Lucy tried to grab at his foot to stop him, but he kicked backwards, connecting with her shoulder and forcing her to let him go. She lay on the ground, struggling to get up, watching him make his escape. He was drawing near the final doorway at the far end of the corridor when Travers stepped through it, his baton raised. With a deft flick of the baton, he caught Cunningham on the throat. The man dropped to his knees instantly. Travers raised the stick a second time and struck again, this time at the lower part of the back of Cunningham's neck. The sharp crack of the wood on bone carried down to Lucy who watched helplessly as Cunningham flopped forward onto his face.

CHAPTER 36

Lucy waited inside the building with Travers while the team outside began breaking down the blocks that had been cemented into one of the ground-floor windows. Travers made her sit against the wall and rest, his coat wrapped around her to keep her warm. Neither of them paid much heed to Cunningham who, once Travers had cuffed him, had lain face down on the rubble without moving.

Finally, they saw a glimpse of light in the wall as the middle block was pushed in. After that, the surrounding blocks came out easily enough. Outside, Peter Cunningham sat against the fencing at the bottom of the bank leading up to where the cars had been abandoned. He already sported a black eye, a gash on his cheek livid against the pallor of his face. He still wore only his T-shirt, none of the officers seeming minded to give him his jacket.

Mickey helped Lucy and Travers through the window. When Cunningham had been lifted through, he was taken over and placed beside his brother. Glancing up through the fields, Lucy could see a Land Rover making painfully slow progress along the narrow roadway that led down to Boom Hall from beneath the bridge. Mickey approached Travers with the bag they had seen Cunningham carrying when he first ran from the van.

Travers opened the bag. Inside were a number of small food bags. Each contained twists of paper around small brown blocks, no larger than an Oxo cube.

'Heroin?'

'Looks like, sir.'

'Anything else?'

Mickey shrugged. 'They're searching the van now, sir.'

A moment later an officer slid down the embankment towards them, calling for Travers. He held out his hand in offering. Lucy followed Travers over and he took the object the man offered him. As he held it up, Lucy could see the small golden figure of a ballerina.

'Bingo,' Travers said.

Lucy spent the rest of the day in hospital. Her cut required stitching, then the doctor had insisted on keeping her in in case of concussion. The nurse wouldn't even let her go down to see her father, telling her that she had to stay in bed. If she was being honest, it suited her. After the local anaesthetic had worn off, the cut had begun to sting madly, added to which she had developed a thumping headache.

She asked for and was finally given a heavy painkiller and slept fitfully through the afternoon. Just before five, when the shift had changed, she asked the nurse who had taken over if she might be able to see Dr Matthews.

'You might have concussion,' the nurse said, glancing at her chart.

'That's right,' Lucy said.

'I'm not sure that requires a psychiatrist,' the girl continued, deadpan.

'We share a mutual friend. Could you tell her I want to speak to her about Alice?'

Matthews arrived just before six. She wore her overcoat as they spoke, despite the heat of the ward and made it clear that she was leaving for the day.

'You wanted to see me,' she said.

Having asked to speak to her, Lucy now realized she had no real reason for doing so. 'I was wondering if you had spoken to Alice recently.'

Matthews demurred for a moment. 'I've seen her once.'

'How is she?'

'Why?'

'I upset her,' Lucy said quietly. 'The last time I saw her. I didn't mean to but . . .'

The woman put down her bag and sat heavily on the seat beside Lucy. 'How?'

'I was reading to her and she started screaming.'

'What were you reading?'

Lucy thought. 'Little Red Riding Hood.'

Matthews smiled grimly. 'More fairy tales.'

'I was just reading to her. I thought fairy tales would be safe.'

Matthews unbuttoned her coat as she shifted in the seat, aiming to get more comfortable. 'Fairy tales reflect innate fears: separation; the darkness; evil; being lost in woods. Many children who have gone through trauma will associate themselves with a fairy-tale character. It could be that Alice sees herself in the Little Red Riding Hood story that you told her.'

'Why?'

215

'I'm not sure yet. Each child sees a different element of them-selves or their story in the tales. Just look at some of the pictures she drew and you'll see children in woods, straight out of the fairy tales.'

Lucy considered the response. She herself had drawn the par-allel between one of the pictures and Hansel and Gretel. 'What about the one with the red rectangle?' she added.

Matthews shrugged. 'Which one?'

'The red rectangle with the black animal in the middle.'

'I know the one. Based on her reaction to your story, the black animal may be a wolf.'

'She saw who killed her father, didn't she?' Lucy asked, shift-ing herself up straighter in the bed.

Matthews nodded. 'Possibly. But at the minute, the only thing she'll see or remember is a symbol of the act rather than having a clear sense of the individuals involved in it.'

'A wolf?' Lucy guessed.

'A wolf,' Matthews agreed, standing to button her coat once more.

Lucy watched the late evening news in her room. Travers was interviewed about the breakthrough in the kidnapping case. Two men were assisting police with their investigation. He was sure they would have Kate safely home soon, he assured the reporter.

The story had just finished when her mobile rang. She hoped it was someone from her work, calling to see how she was doing, Instead, when she answered it, she did not immediately place the voice.

'I need your help.' The voice was a girl's, timid, broken.

'Kate?' Lucy asked, immediately aware of the absurdity of the question. How would Kate McLaughlin have her number?

'It's Mary. You said to call you if I needed help. I need your help.'

Lucy turned on the flashers on the car as she crossed over the Foyle Bridge, though she deliberately kept the siren off in consideration of the time of night. As she pulled into the estate where Mary lived, a group of youths on their way home from a night out staggered onto the road in front of her. One of them yelled abuse at the car, grabbing at his crotch and leering in the windscreen at her. She pulled on the handbrake and opened the door without cutting the engine. Sure enough, the Dutch courage left him and he turned and, half falling onto the pavement, sprinted away from her while his friends scattered among the warren of alleyways.

She drew up outside the Quigg house. The living-room light was visible through the thin fabric of the curtains in the main window. Then Lucy realized a small figure was standing between the curtains and the window, watching out at her. A small white hand rose in salute, then the curtains were pushed aside and Mary disappeared back into the room again.

After a few seconds, the front door swung open, spilling light onto the snow-covered driveway. Lucy trudged her way up, scanning the surroundings while she did so, remembering the attack on the car they had suffered on her previous visit.

Mary stood in the hallway waiting for her. She wore a vest which simply served to accentuate the thinness of her body; her shoulders were narrow, the bones protruded through her skin, her arms gangly and pale. She wore a pair of pyjama bottoms and no socks or slippers. Lucy felt a pang when she noticed that the girl's tiny toenails were painted with pink nail varnish, the normality of the application so at odds with the circumstances in which the child lived.

'What's wrong, Mary?' she asked. 'Has someone hurt you?'

The child shook her head, her small front teeth worrying her lower lip as she struggled to hold back her tears.

Lucy crouched before her and outstretched her arms. 'It's OK, honey. What's wrong?'

But the child would not allow the tears to fall. She took Lucy by the hand and pulled at her to force her to stand and follow her.

They went up the stairs to the first floor. As they climbed the stairs, Lucy gradually became aware of a low moaning coming from one of the rooms. They stopped at the door, which was closed.

'Mummy won't stop crying,' Mary said. 'I need you to help her.'

The directness of the request caught Lucy a little off guard. 'Are you OK?' she asked.

Mary nodded sharply and pointed to the door of her mother's room. 'Mummy's been crying all day and I can't get her to stop. I made her dinner but she didn't eat it.'

Lucy stared at the child a moment, revisiting the urge to lift her, wrap her in her coat and carry her away from this house. Finally, she turned and thumped on the door with her gloved fist.

'Mrs Quigg, is everything all right?'

The only response was an increase in the groaning, a clearer sound of crying, and the thudding of something off the door.

Lucy tried the handle; it depressed but did not open.

'Mum's boyfriend put a lock inside. He said it was to stop me coming into her bed at night.'

Lucy pushed gently at the door. While the bottom opened slightly, she could feel the resistance at the top and decided that there must be some sort of small sliding bolt there similar to the one on Mary's door. She knocked once more, lightly, without response.

'What's your mum's name?' she asked Mary.

'Catherine.'

'Catherine?' Lucy called, knocking again.

Inside the room, she heard the woman muttering something, the words indistinct through the wall. Lucy placed her weight against the door and felt the upper half begin to creak as the pressure worked against the screws holding the bolt in place.

'Where's your little brother?' she asked Mary.

'In his cot in my room. I put him to bed.'

'Of course you did, honey,' Lucy said. 'Check on him a moment, would you?'

As Mary turned to go, Lucy shoved against the door again and heard the crack as the wood splintered around the bolt. She half fell into the room, still holding on to the door handle as she did so.

Catherine Quigg lay on the bed. She wore only her under-wear. An empty bottle clattered at Lucy's feet as she approached the woman, and Lucy guessed that this had been the source of the thud on the door when she had first knocked.

Catherine Quigg shifted on the bed and stared at her, bleary-eyed. Her make-up had run down her cheeks and dried into black streaks. Her face was puffy with tears, her cheeks and nose red with crying and alcohol. The heady smell of vodka hung in the room. A waste-paper basket in the corner overflowed with crushed beer cans. On the bedside cabinet, the twisted empty paper of a cigarette lay discarded like a shed skin beside an unused filter of a cigarette and a few flakes of tobacco. They must have been there for some time, for Lucy could not discern the smell of marijuana in the room.

'Piss off!' Catherine Quigg spat, lashing out with her foot as she did so.

Lucy stepped out of the way, instinctively reaching to her belt for her baton.

'Catherine, can you sit up and talk to me?'

The woman tried to spit at Lucy but the gesture lacked force and the spittle dribbled onto her chin. She pushed herself up on her elbow and smeared it away with the back of her arm.

Lucy bent and lifted a white T-shirt that was lying on the floor and offered it to her.

'Would you put something on?'

The woman stared at her, her red-rimmed eyes narrowed and scornful. Then her vision slipped beyond Lucy. Lucy turned to see Mary Quigg standing in the doorway.

'Are you OK, Mummy?' she asked.

'You little bitch, calling the pigs.' She lashed out with her fist ineffectually. Nevertheless the gesture made Mary step back in fear.

'Run down and put the kettle on, Mary,' Lucy said, forcing a smile. 'I'll help your mother up.' Despite her efforts, the child did not seem wholly reassured, though she did leave the room. Lucy listened as her light footfalls padded downstairs and across the floor below.

Lucy sat on the bed beside Catherine Quigg who shifted away from her, reaching for the T-shirt to cover her chest.

'That child phoned a police officer in the middle of the night because she was worried about her mother. She made dinner and tended to a baby while you lay here on your bed. I'd mind how I spoke to her if I were you.'

'Don't lecture me about my kids,' the woman slurred. 'What do you know?'

'I know that I should take that child and her brother with me and leave you here to stew in your own shit.'

The woman stared at her in horror. 'You can't speak to . . .'

'I'll speak how I like, Mrs Quigg. You should be ashamed of yourself.'

Catherine Quigg's mouth opened and shut. 'I'll be on to my solicitor.'

'And I'll be on to Social Services. Now get dressed.'

Catherine Quigg held her stare a second, then lowered her head and began to blubber into the T-shirt she still clasped in her hands. 'Your crowd arrested my Alan.'

Immediately Lucy realized what she meant and understood the woman's state.

Catherine Quigg began to shudder as her crying intensified. 'He's all I have.'

Biting back the urge to point out that she had two children, Lucy laid her hand on the woman's shoulder. Her bra strap was twisted and Lucy untangled it.

'I understand how you feel, Mrs Quigg,' Lucy said. 'But we've connected him with Kate McLaughlin's abduction.'

'He'd nothing to do with that child going missing.'

Lucy demurred from continuing the discussion further, for Catherine Quigg would not be convinced regardless of what Lucy said.

Catherine shifted herself quickly on the bed, sitting up and placing her hand on Lucy's free hand. 'You could get him out,' she said.

'What?' Lucy straightened herself up and stood.

The woman scrambled off the bed and stood too, swaying as she did so. Lucy had to hold her by the shoulder to steady her.

'You could help him get out. You know he had nothing to do

221

with it, don't you?' The woman's tone was desperate, pleading. 'I can give him an alibi. What night did the wee girl go missing?'

'Wednesday.'

'He was here all night.'

'From what time?'

'What time did she go missing?' Catherine Quigg moved towards Lucy pressing some mysterious advantage she had convinced herself she held over her. 'He's been here non-stop since that girl disappeared. I can vouch for him.'

'If you can provide your partner with an alibi, you need to sober up and come to the station.'

Catherine Quigg narrowed her eyes and sneered. 'You're just looking to take my Mary off me,' she said, waggling her finger. The strap of her bra slipped off her shoulder but the woman did not fix it.

'Please put on some clothes, Mrs Quigg,' Lucy said. 'Mary is making tea. We can talk then.'

Reluctantly, the woman lifted the balled-up T-shirt from the bed and pulled it on over her head. Lucy lifted a pair of jeans from the floor and held them out to the woman.

'Do you want a photograph?' Catherine Quigg said, her mood shifting again.

Lucy stooped and lifted the empty vodka bottle from the floor and went downstairs.

Mary stood in the kitchen, two mugs of tea in her hands, her face pale, her expression one of total loss.

'You should get to bed, Mary,' Lucy said. 'You need your sleep.'

'Someone needs to keep an eye on Mummy.'

Above them, Lucy heard the creaking of springs as the

woman lowered herself onto her bed again. Lucy glanced at her watch. It was edging 4 a.m.

'Your mum says that Alan has been here since Wednesday night, Mary,' she said, taking one of the mugs from the girl. 'Is that right?'

Mary raised her head to the right and squeezed her eyes shut as she tried to recall the night. Finally she nodded. 'He hasn't left since the snow started. Mum's happy when he's here.'

'You're too good, Mary,' Lucy said. 'Your mum's lucky to have you.'

Mary smiled lightly, the gesture almost reaching her eyes.

'Can you get Mummy's boyfriend home?' Mary said. 'She'll stop crying then. She'll be OK.'

CHAPTER 37

Fleming met her on Strand Road at eight the following morning.

'Shouldn't you be in hospital?' he said.

'I discharged myself last night,' Lucy said.

'I had hoped to get up to see you,' Fleming began. Lucy waved away the comment.

'I was fine,' she said. 'I slept most of the time anyway,' she lied.

'I got caught up in something,' Fleming added by way of explanation. This too was a lie, for Lucy could smell, beneath the sweet scent of breath mints, the ketone smell of alcohol from the previous evening. For all his protestations about finding God and getting off the sauce, she thought, he had obviously fallen off the wagon.

'So what's up?'

'I need to see Travers, sir. I have concerns about the arrests yesterday. I spoke with Cunningham's partner last night. She says he's not been out of the house in days.'

Fleming grimaced.

'He'll not be happy to hear that,' Fleming said. 'They did find one of Kate's charms in the van. You said yourself, she seems to be laying a trail for us to follow.'

'I promised Mary Quigg I'd see what I could find out,' Lucy explained.

'On your head be it,' Fleming said. 'But I'll gladly sit with you. Anything that raises Inspector Travers's blood pressure does my own heart good.'

'Explain this to me again,' Travers snapped. 'Start from where you were meant to be in hospital having taken a knock on the head,' he added sarcastically.

'I know, sir,' Lucy said. 'The child says that Cunningham hasn't left the house in days. His brother may well be involved but he has an alibi.'

'Given by a child.'

'And her mother.'

'Oh, that's right. The reliable testimony of his drunken partner. I'm glad you mentioned that.'

'I'm not saying that they're both innocent.'

'Neither of them are innocent. In addition to whatever Alan Cunningham has to do with Kate McLaughlin, he's also carrying drugs. He's scum and he's going to serve time for this.'

'Has he even said anything about Kate?' Lucy asked, then immediately realized she had overstepped the mark when Fleming laid a placatory hand on her arm.

'That's enough, Sergeant,' Fleming said.

'Now you get involved, Inspector,' Travers said. 'Were you aware of this interview?'

Fleming paused, clearly trying to work out how best to respond without incriminating anyone, but that in itself told Travers all he needed to know. 'I thought so.'

He turned again to Lucy. 'I appreciate your keenness to get

back to CID, Lucy,' he said glancing pointedly at Fleming. 'But this is not the way to do it.'

'It's just . . . I think there's something not right about the whole thing, sir,' Lucy said.

Beside her Fleming bowed his head, covering his brow with his hand.

'I mean, there's been no ransom. Yet I was told that Michael McLaughlin was trying to source almost ten million through his accountant the other day. Doesn't it seem strange that someone took the daughter of such a wealthy man and didn't make a demand for money? Especially when his own driver, Billy Quinn, and the bomber who killed his wife were part of the kidnapping gang.'

'What are you trying to say, Sergeant?' Travers said impatiently. 'McLaughlin kidnapped his own daughter.'

'No, sir,' Lucy said, struggling to remain unflustered. 'He was looking for ten million though. Maybe he's had a ransom demand already and hasn't said. I don't think he's been straight with us, sir. I think he knows who has his daughter.'

Fleming raised his head and glanced at her.

'Who told you he was looking for ten million?' Travers asked.

Lucy was caught between wanting to give the name of her source to be able to verify her suspicions by basing it on authority, and an awareness that the comments had constituted little more than teatime gossip.

'A reliable source, sir.'

'That you've cultivated in the month you've been here.'

'Her husband works for McLaughlin's accountants.'

'You know how that sounds, Lucy, don't you?' Travers said, taking a seat behind his desk.

Lucy swallowed back her answer.

'It might be best if you go home for the day, Lucy. I'm going to pretend that all that happened here this morning is a result of the knock on the head you got yesterday. Come back in when your head's clear and we'll forget this conversation.'

Fleming stood to leave alongside her.

'As for you, Inspector,' Travers added as Fleming made to leave, 'you need to keep your team in check.'

As Lucy crossed the bridge to go home, she realized with embarrassment that she had not been in to see her father the previous day when she was in the hospital herself. She decided to take a quick run up now and, if possible, planned to call on Alice too, in the hope that her lasting memory of Lucy might be a positive one.

Her father was sitting up in bed, eating breakfast when she went in. He had been left a bowl of porridge, which he was attempting to spoon into his mouth with little success judging by the globules of congealed oats lying on the blanket.

Lucy took the spoon from him and, carefully scraping excess food from round his mouth, helped him to eat.

'How are you today, Daddy?'

He chewed slowly and swallowed. 'Fine,' he said. 'You look tired, sweetheart. Are you not sleeping?'

The normality of the statement took her by surprise. 'I had a busy night,' she explained. She leaned over and kissed him on the cheek, the silver stubble of his face scraping against her skin. His breath carried the staleness of sleep. 'It's good to see you, Daddy,' she said.

His eyes glistened and he grasped her hand awkwardly in his and squeezed. 'You too, love.'

The swish of the curtain being pulled back from around the bed heralded the arrival of the doctor.

'How are we today, Mr Black?' he asked, lifting the clipboard from the end of the bed and flicking through the pages, offering an 'Uh-uh' during each gap in her father's response.

'A little sore. Tired of being in this place.'

'And the prime minister's name?'

Lucy suppressed a smile as her father winked at her. 'David Cameron. Unless they've got rid of him since I came in here.'

The doctor returned his smile. 'No, he's still there for now. That all seems fine. I think you can go home today.' He spoke slowly and loudly, as if to a child.

Lucy felt her hand being squeezed again, more tightly.

'I'll have a quick word with your daughter, if I may,' the doctor said, moving away from the bed. Lucy followed him out towards the corridor.

'Your father does seem to be improving Miss Black. We have concerns about his general mental health though. You're aware I'm sure that he has something a little more severe than usual dementia for his age. We suspect he's in mid-stage Alzheimer's. It's going to get increasingly difficult to look after him, so you may want to start looking for somewhere that can provide more specialized care.'

Lucy nodded, having expected the news since her father's arrival. Still, it did not mean she would necessarily follow the advice just yet.

'Thanks for looking after him,' she said.

She helped dress her father and, carrying his bag, walked beside him while one of the porters pushed him in a wheelchair down to the car park. The man helped to lift him into the car.

'Don't want you slipping and having to be wheeled straight back in again now, do we?' he said.

The old man looked blankly at him as he spoke and, though he shared his smile, he did not seem to understand the source of his humour.

Lucy phoned Sarah on the way home and told her that her father was out of hospital and would require her help again. The woman promised to be at the house by lunchtime.

It was only as she passed Prehen woods on the way home that Lucy remembered she had meant to call in on Alice.

CHAPTER 38

Just as she had got her father settled into the house again, Robbie called her. Social Services were satisfied that Melanie Kent had acted appropriately with regards to Alice. The doctor had felt that being back home with her mother would be best for her; the girl had been discharged before 11 a.m. Lucy thanked him for calling, trying hard to disguise the sense of hurt she felt that, after all she had done, she was no longer a part of Alice's life. She would have liked to see her once more, if only to say goodbye. Despite her best efforts, Robbie still sensed her disappointment.

'It stings, doesn't it?'

'What?'

'Knowing you did so much, and getting no thanks for it.'

Lucy coughed away the emotion. 'You don't do it for thanks.'

'True. But you still make a connection with some of these kids and then they're gone. It's hard to get used to.'

'I'm happy she's home with her mother,' Lucy said honestly.

'I don't doubt it,' Robbie said. 'Any luck with Janet?'

Lucy realized that she had not seen her either since she had

gone into hospital. Having the day off might give her the opportunity to do so.

'We found her sleeping rough. She was very ill,' Lucy said.
'Thanks again for your help with her.'

'No problem. I passed on the name of that child you mentioned, Mary Quigg. Someone will visit the home as soon as we
can and see what can be done for her.'

'Thanks, Robbie,' Lucy said. She felt a sudden lethargy,
could not face the thought of explaining to him about Cunningham. Instead she said, 'It was good to work with you.'

'You too, Lucy. Maybe I'll be in touch about getting that bite
to eat sometime.'

'I'd like that,' Lucy said.

She made tea while her father got himself comfortable in the
living room. When she went in, he had one of his boxes opened
and was working his way through a notebook.

'What are you doing, Daddy?' Lucy asked, handing him
the mug.

He muttered to himself, half closing the notebook, so that
Lucy could not see what he was reading.

Sarah arrived just as she had finished clearing up the dishes.
She was effusive in her greeting for Lucy's father despite the
fact that the old man's reception of her was rather more muted.
Lucy explained that she had a short visit to make and would be
back later.

When she went up to the ward, Janet was sitting up in bed. Her
hair was brushed back severely from her face, though it still hung
in straggles across her shoulders. She had been washed since
Lucy saw her last and wore a hospital gown, which was open

at the side revealing the withered skin of her side and haunches. A long, thick scar traversed her chest, ending just below her left breast. Lucy glanced quickly, then looked away, mentally having to remind herself that this woman would be no more than in her early thirties.

Her face was heart-shaped, her features small, her eyes wide. Small patches of old scar tissue on her face shone under the fluorescence of the hospital lighting.

She turned in the bed and stared at Lucy accusingly when she entered. The IV feed connected to her hand restricted her movement, as did the bandage on her arm further above the drip. A darkish fluid had seeped through the dressing slightly and, as Lucy approached, the smell of infection caught in her throat, causing her to breathe through her mouth.

'What?' Janet snapped.

'I wanted to . . . my name's Lucy Black.' She waited to see if the name elicited any reaction, then realized that it would not.

'My father is Jim Black.'

If she had expected some instant response, she was disappointed.

'So what?'

'I believe you knew my father. He's sick at the moment and he's been talking about you.'

A laugh rattled deep in the woman's chest, building to a spluttering crescendo which caused her shoulders to shudder, then dissolved into a cough.

'What was his name?'

'Jim Black.'

The woman squinted slightly as if struggling to remember.

'I'm not sure I know him,' she decided finally.

Lucy tried to hide her disappointment. She was not entirely

sure what she had been hoping for anyway. She had set out looking for Janet telling herself it was for her father. Now she realized it was for herself, first and foremost. She wanted to understand what made this woman so important she should feature in her father's addled thoughts for almost two decades – so far as Lucy knew, since he last saw her.

Janet smacked her lips several times and Lucy suspected she was beginning to feel the effects of her enforced drying out. She leaned across for a glass of water on the side cabinet and, in so doing, her gown fell open further, revealing the full extent of the scarring Lucy had seen. The scar was almost six inches long, running across her breasts. The skin was puckered and livid red.

'Was you the one that brought me in?'

Lucy nodded.

The woman leaned towards her. 'You wouldn't have a few pound on you, would you, love, for when I get out again?'

Lucy rummaged in her pocket and produced a twenty-pound note.

'God bless you, love.'

'Is there anyone you'd like me to call? Have you any relatives that might be wondering about you?' Lucy asked.

'None that want to know me,' Janet said, sipping again from the water glass, spilling water down her front as she did so.

Lucy was about to excuse herself and leave when the woman put down the glass and began to speak.

'I saw you looking,' she said. 'At me scars.'

Lucy began to protest, but Janet continued.

'The Provos burnt me,' she said.

'What?'

'I was sixteen. Three men came to my house one evening. I'd only been home a few weeks. I was upstairs doing my homework. I heard them downstairs, talking with my da. I heard their thuds on the stairs. One of them came into my room; I was still in my uniform. He grabbed me by the hair and pulled me off the bed. The other one grabbed my legs and they carried me downstairs. My ma and da stood in the doorway of the living room, watching. They did nothing.'

Lucy felt she should offer some words of comfort to the woman but could think of no adequate expression.

'They took me out into the street. A lot of the local boys were standing around, laughing. They took me over to one of the lamp posts and, before they tied me up, they took off my clothes. Everything. One of them laid them in a neat pile on the kerb, like he was careful not to get them dirty. They stripped me right down in front of all those boys, standing sniggering and pointing at me. Then my hands were tied; I couldn't cover myself.'

Lucy sat by the bed, listening.

'One of them had scissors and they cut clumps of my hair off. I had such nice hair then; long blonde hair. "Goldilocks" he called me as he cut. The second wrote a sign on a piece of card. "Brit loving slut." He hung it round my neck. He stopped long enough to roll up the bottom of his mask, just up to here.'

She pointed to the base of her nose. Her voice had softened and dropped in tone.

'Then the third man went down the alley by our house and came back with a bucket. They'd been heating tar. I could smell it. It was so hot he had to hold the bucket with two bits of wood. Someone put a milk crate beside me so he could stand up on it. Then he poured it over my chest. He'd promised my ma he'd not do my face, he said. "We'll burn your tits instead" he said. "See how the Brits like them then." He went back for a second bucket to do down there too.' She gestured towards her crotch and Lucy was struck at the dignity she attempted to retain in describing such a violation.

Lucy sat in silence for a moment. She placed her hand on the woman's arm. 'Why?'

The woman stared at her grimly. 'I was a Brit-loving slut.'

'My God, Janet. That's terrible. I'm so sorry.'

'I should have known someone would find out. They were right. I went into the barracks at the top of Bishop Street every week, played around with some of the Brits. A cop too.'

Her comments caused Lucy to draw back. 'A cop?'

Janet nodded as she took another sip of water.

'When was this?'

'8th June, 1994. I was studying for my GCSEs.'

'The cop that got involved? Do you remember his name.'

The woman shook her head. 'He was an inspector.'

'Do you remember anything about him?'

'He had a kid. He talked about his daughter.'

Lucy felt herself unsteady, had to grip the edge of the seat on which she sat to hold herself upright. She felt a burning in her throat and the growing taste of bile.

'What age were you?'

Janet stared at her. 'Fourteen when it started,' she said. 'Sixteen when they burned me.'

Lucy groaned, and lowered her head. The floor seemed to move beneath her and she had to place her hand against the cold plastic seat of the chair to steady herself.

'There was a Land Rover sat at the end of the street while the Provos did me,' Janet continued. 'They sat and watched.'

'I'm sorry,' Lucy mumbled. 'I have to go. I'm really sorry.'

Numbed, Lucy wandered up the corridor towards the entrance of the ward. To her immediate left she saw the Ladies' toilet and rushed in, just making it before her stomach twisted and she vomited noisily into the bowl. She knelt, resting her head against the seat, and began to cry.

She stayed that way for some time, until someone began knocking on the door, looking to use the toilet. Rinsing her face with cold water, Lucy studied herself in the small, rust-dappled mirror screwed to the wall. Her eyes were shadowed with lack of sleep, her skin red and raw.

She unlocked the door and uttered an apology, keeping her head down until she was out of the ward. She stood waiting for the lift, looking out of the windows. The height of the hospital afforded a wide view of the city. From here, the river was hidden, the separation between east and west bank invisible.

The pinging of the lift door opening roused her from her reveries and forced her to consider where she was going next. She dared not go home yet, dared not face her father. What could she say to him? How could she look at him again? Instead she took out her phone and called Sarah, explained that she'd been held up at work and would be home as soon as she could.

She felt the urge to talk to someone, to feel some form of connection with another adult. She couldn't speak to her mother, couldn't face the thought of the pleasure her mother would take in her vindication. 'Don't deify him just because he's sick,' she'd said. Had she known all along? Was that the cause of their separation, of the end of Lucy's childhood? Her father started drinking after that, lost his sense of who he was.

Finally, because she had nowhere else to go, she pressed for the lift again and, when it arrived, travelled up to the children's ward.

CHAPTER 39

'I'm sorry for bothering you,' she said as Margaret filled the kettle and switched it on.

'It's no bother, love,' she said. 'It's a bit early for my tea, but that's the perk of being boss.'

Lucy smiled quickly, glanced at her hands, twisting one around the other. Having felt like talking, she now found she had nothing to say, couldn't think where to start.

'So what's up?'

'Nothing,' she said.

Margaret looked at her sceptically.

'Alice has gone home,' she said.

Lucy nodded.

'You did a great job with her, you know.'

Lucy nodded again.

'How is work?'

'Fine. We found a shed where Kate McLaughlin was being held. The police helicopter actually did a fly-by when she was in there, but she'd gone by the time we got there.'

Margaret tutted as she set out the cups.

'God, I shouldn't have told you that. You'll not tell anyone will you?' Lucy said, then regretted doing so, in case the woman should think she didn't trust her.

'Who would I tell?' she replied. 'Besides, God love him, but that man McLaughlin's never had to look far for misfortune.'

'You mean his wife?'

'Everything. He bought a bar and his wife is killed in it. By the time the land gets out of the courts, the value of the place has collapsed. He has no luck.'

'Why was it in court?'

'The buildings were all listed; that's why he got so much of the land so cheap. If he'd wanted to renovate, he'd have needed to work within the existing structure apparently and it would have cost a fortune to do. The Planning Department wouldn't authorize him to raze the place after the bombing, even though the buildings were unsound. It's been going through the courts for the best part of a decade. He got the all clear last year and got planning permission and everything, but by that stage the value of the land dropped with the recession. Then all this happens with his daughter.'

Lucy nodded, took the proffered cup of tea with thanks.

'So what really brings you up here, then?'

'I . . . you . . . you're one of the few people I can talk to. Isn't that weird?'

Lucy could tell she was disarmed by her frankness.

'I'm sorry for landing on you like this. I . . . my dad talked about a woman he knew when he was younger. I found her.'

Margaret grimaced. 'Not a good idea?'

Lucy shook her head. 'I think I've found out something about him.'

'An affair?'

Lucy nodded, unable to look her fully in the face in case she could read that there was more to it than that.

'When he was still with your mother?'

'Yes.'

Margaret laid her hand on her shoulder, kneaded gently. 'You must be feeling awful.'

Lucy looked up at her. 'I brought him home today. The doctor says he has Alzheimer's. He suggested I put him in a home. The way I feel at the moment, I'd do it tonight if I could find somewhere.'

Margaret nodded silently.

'I am sorry for landing this on you,' Lucy said again, putting down the tea and standing. 'I wanted to thank you for being so good to me when Alice was here.'

'It was nothing,' Margaret said. 'You helped us out, keeping an eye on her. Are you going to visit her?'

'I don't know. I'd like to, in one way, but it's not really appropriate.'

Margaret pushed back from her desk and opened the drawer. 'She left this here,' she said, removing the teddy bear Lucy had brought down to Alice from her home. 'Someone would need to return it to her, at some stage.'

Lucy took the toy, felt its softness give to her touch.

'Thank you, Margaret,' she managed. 'You're a good friend.'

'Well, one's a start,' the woman said, standing. 'Good luck whatever you decide. Maybe we'll see you again.'

Lucy was leaving the ward when she felt her mobile vibrate in her pocket. It was Sarah King.

'I'm on my way home, Sarah,' she said on answering.

'You need to hurry,' Sarah said. 'There's been an incident.'

One of the street lamps outside the house had blown, leaving the entire street subdued and dull. Consequently, she didn't see the writing until she pulled into the driveway of her house and the headlamps raked across the gable wall.

'Lucy Black. PSNI Scum' was written in red letters, each a foot high, along the side of the wall. Below it was the registration number of her car. On entering the house, she saw where the congealed yolks of the eggs thrown at the house had slid halfway down the PVC door.

Sarah King stood in the hallway, her coat already on.

'They done it when we were in the house and I didn't hear anything.'

'Is everyone all right? Is Dad OK?'

'He's fine. I'm more shocked than he is.'

'I'm sorry for being late, Sarah. I really appreciate your help. I'll get someone to clean it off tomorrow.'

'I need to think things through, Lucy,' the woman said, her voice shaken, the wattles of skin at her throat trembling slightly as she spoke. 'What if they did something worse to the house when I was in here with your father?'

Lucy nodded. 'That's understandable, Sarah,' she said. 'I really appreciate what you do for Dad, but whatever you think is for the best.'

The woman nodded curtly. 'I don't want to cause you problems, Lucy. I'll not see you stuck. But at the same time . . .'

The thought hung unfinished between them. Lucy pulled out a few crumpled notes from her pocket and gathered together enough to cover the woman's daily wage.

'That should cover today,' she said. 'You can let me know what your plans are tomorrow.'

The woman took the money with mumbled thanks and shuffled past Lucy and out of the house.

Lucy went upstairs and glanced in quickly at her father, who seemed to be asleep. Closing his door gently, she padded into her own room. Boxes of her father's old notebooks and files were still piled against the far wall. Lucy had had to move them when she first moved in, just to make room for her bed. She placed Alice's teddy bear on top of one of the boxes, then changed her clothes, grateful for the comfort of a hoodie and tracksuit bottoms.

She heard a thudding echo from her father's room, and his voice. 'Lucy? Is that you?'

Lucy prevaricated, reluctant to face him and yet aware that she had no choice.

She knocked lightly on his door and went in. The room was in darkness, the curtains already drawn, dulling further the weak light that filtered into the room from the distant street lamps.

'Is that you?'

'Yes,' Lucy said. 'I'm back.'

As her eyes adjusted to the gloom, she saw his hand extending from the bed, grasping in the air for her hand.

She moved over and sat on his bed, deliberately keeping her hands in the long centre pocket of her hooded top.

'Are you OK, love?' he asked.

She looked at his face in the shadows, at the movements of his lips. Against her wishes, she imagined him forcing himself on a fourteen-year-old girl, imagined the hand now flailing in the air looking for hers, tugging at the young girl's clothes. She placed her hand over her mouth, turned her face from him.

'Where were you, love?'

'Out,' Lucy said. 'I was at the hospital.'

'Are you OK? Were you hurt?'

'Yes,' Lucy said. 'I found Janet. She told me.'

Only the irregular rasping of her father's breath, as he

processed all the meanings in what she had said, broke the silence of the room.

'She was fourteen,' Lucy stated. 'She said she was fourteen. Is that true?'

Even the breathing had stopped now. Lucy held her nerve as long as she could, but eventually turned to look at him, to see if he was still with her.

A tear ran down from the corner of his eye to his temple, then onto the cloth of his pillowcase.

She felt his hand moving across the bedclothes, taking hers. She pulled away sharply. 'Don't touch me,' she snapped.

She got up quickly and went next door to her room. The sounds of her father sobbing could be heard through the wall.

However, he did not call for her again that evening.

CHAPTER 40

She was aware of a pounding on the door. She glanced at her clock; it was not yet 7 a.m. The light seeping in through the high window of her room was grey and still. Again she heard the thudding and the rattle of the letter box.

Lucy jumped out of bed and moved to the top of the stairs. Through the frosted glass of the panel in the front door, she could see a bulky figure. His face seemed to be partially covered, as if a scarf covered his mouth.

Keeping to the sides of the stairs, she crept down. She'd left her personal protection weapon in the sitting room. She was just crossing the hallway when she heard the rattle of the letter box again. She turned to see two eyes staring at her through the gap.

'Miss Black,' the voice said. 'I'm going to fix your wall. I didn't want to scare you.'

Lucy picked up her coat and put it on over the T-shirt she had worn to bed. She opened the door as far as the safety chain would allow.

A middle-aged man stood on the step. What she had taken for a scarf through the frosted glass was, in fact, a beard. He held a bottle of white spirits in his hand. A tin of whitewash sat on the ground beside him.

'I'm Dermot. I live across the street.'

Lucy followed the direction he was pointing in. The third house up on the left, an MPV in the drive, and an assortment of children's toys scattered around the front lawn.

'The missus sent me over to fix your wall. We were talking last night – the neighbours and all – and we're disgusted at what they wrote. I'll get it off for you before too many people see it.'

Lucy widened her eyes to prevent them filling. 'I don't . . . I mean, that's really kind of you.'

'No bother. Go in or you'll catch your death. If the writing won't come off, I'll have to whitewash the whole gable. Is that all right with you?'

'Fine,' Lucy said. 'Look, thank you so much.'

'It's no problem,' he said. 'Just so you know none of us around here hold with this nonsense. And the wife said to tell you to call over for a cuppa if you've ever got an hour to kill.'

And with those words he conferred on her a sense of belonging she had not felt since she was a child.

She was making Dermot a cup of tea when she heard thudding from above. Her father frequently did this in the morning when she was up and he still in bed, thumping on the floor of his room with a walking stick to summon her. Despite understanding the necessity for it, she could not help being irritated by it, more than ever this morning.

'What?' she called up.

She heard the soft mumbling of her father's response, but could not discern the words.

'I'll be up in a minute,' she said, not caring if he heard.

When she'd finished making tea for herself and Dermot, she

carried it out to him. He had given up trying to clean off the paint and instead had begun a first coat of whitewash on the gable end.

'Sorry about that,' he said as he explained it to her.

'I'm sorry you're being put to this hassle. Your wife is very kind. You both are,' she added quickly. 'I'm sorry I haven't made more of an effort to meet my neighbours.'

The man nodded towards the upper storey of the house. 'You have your hands full. Everyone understands that.' He placed the tea on the windowsill and dipped the roller into the tray again. 'Besides, it means I'm missing feeding time at the zoo over there. Given the choice . . .' He laughed, then set to painting again.

Lucy went back into the house and mounted the stairs slowly to her father's room. She was dreading this morning more than last night, knowing she would have to face him in daylight. Worse still, she would have to do so with them both aware of the shared knowledge of her father's crime.

She pushed the door open, recognized the familiar warm smell of her father's room. She moved across and drew the curtains, opening the window on tilt to let in some fresh air.

'Morning, love,' her father said, watching her motionless from the pillow, following her progress around the room only with his eyes.

'Daddy,' she said, busying herself with lifting his clothes and sorting out clean from dirty.

'Who was at the door?'

'The man across the street.' She hesitated, unsure whether to remind him of the events of the previous night. However, she knew that if he saw the man working on their wall, he'd demand to know why. 'Someone painted on the wall last night. He's covering it.'

'Who?' he asked loudly.

'Dermot somebody.'

'Oh, him!' her father commented, his mouth pinched.

'He's fixing the wall for us,' she said, stopping what she was doing and looking at him for the first time. 'You should be thanking him.'

He stared at her, guilelessly. 'I didn't mean anything by it.'

Of all the responses she had expected, this was the one she had not counted on. Her father was behaving as if nothing had happened, as if she had not told him that she knew about Janet.

'What are you doing today?' he asked, pushing back the covers as if to get up. He stopped suddenly and blushed, quickly pulling the duvet back over himself.

'Will you give me a minute, love?'

Lucy glanced at him suspiciously. 'What's wrong?'

'I . . . I've had an accident.'

Lucy moved across to him and pulled back the covers again. His pyjama trousers were sodden, the sheets almost transparent with damp, the pattern of the mattress beneath visible.

'Get up and I'll change it,' Lucy said irritably, pulling up the lower edge of the sheet from beneath the bottom end of the mattress. She heard a subdued sob and looked up at her father. He sat, staring at the patch on the bed, his face smeared with tears.

'I'm sorry about that, love,' he said. 'I . . . I'm sorry.'

He pushed at his legs ineffectually with his hands, as if trying to peel off the trousers.

Lucy struggled to stop herself from offering him words of comfort. 'Get up and I'll change it.'

He shifted off the bed and stood looking at her. 'Are you angry at me for this?' he asked, placing his hand lightly on her back.

She shuddered at the touch and moved away from him to the other side of the bed to remove the sheet.

'What do you think I'm angry about?'

She stared at him standing slumped before her. His pyjama jacket hung open, the fine wisps of grey hair visible above his shirt, the shapes of the bones of his neck and upper chest protruding through his pale skin.

'I . . . I don't know.'

'You don't know?' she repeated quietly, aware that Dermot was still outside and the window open.

Her father shook his head, his mouth hanging slightly open.

'Janet,' she said, balling the sheet up on top of the bed. She looked up at him expecting to see a flinch, some acknowledgement of his guilt or remorse.

'Who's Janet?'

She stopped what she was doing, placed her hands on her hips. 'Don't give me that, Daddy. We talked about her last night.'

His mouth opened and closed wordlessly. 'Last night? I . . . did we talk last night?'

'Yes,' Lucy said in exasperation.

'What about?'

'Janet.'

'Oh,' he said, simply, more in acceptance than recognition.

'Do you remember Janet?'

The old man stared at the floor. Finally he shook his head. 'Is she a friend of yours?'

Lucy moved towards him, holding his stare, trying to read the sincerity of his responses.

'Who's the prime minister, Daddy?' she asked.

His eyes glazed, the reflected light from the windows

sparkling across their surface. Finally his gaze lowered. 'Prime minister,' he repeated to himself over and over. 'I can't . . . I don't . . . I don't.' He sat on the bed, his arms hanging by his sides, the tears running freely down his cheeks. He stared up at her bewildered. 'Where's Lucy?' he asked.

The doorbell rang downstairs.

'Get out of your pyjamas,' Lucy said. 'I'll be up again in a second.'

She went down and opened the door, expecting it to be Dermot saying he was finished. Instead, Sarah King stood on the doorstep.

'I've slept on it,' she said. 'I'm here to work.'

CHAPTER 41

The mid-morning traffic on the road to Strabane was quiet. She had called Fleming and explained that her father had taken a turn for the worse. She needed to find a care home for him. He had told her to take as long as she needed. Neither of them mentioned the discussion in Travers's office the previous day.

If she were honest, she felt a degree of relief in her father's deterioration. Even if he did not recall Janet, she could not forget her or what she had said. This way, she was putting her father into care because he needed it, rather than because she could not countenance living in the same house as him. She considered telling Fleming what he had done; he was a child abuser after all. But if his state that morning were any indication, it would be a futile exercise. He would never face trial, would probably not understand what was happening to him anyway. What justice would that serve? she reasoned. She even half convinced herself that she was right in that assessment.

The first place she contacted had given her an appointment for one o'clock. It gave her time to return Alice's teddy bear first.

She switched on the radio and caught the start of the ten o'clock news. Travers was speaking at a press conference, updating the media on the state of the Kate McLaughlin case. They were, he insisted, very close to finding her and had indeed located two different spots where she had been held. He named Peter and Alan Cunningham as the two men in custody who were helping police with their inquiries, which Lucy read as a euphemism for them knowing nothing but were being held to convince the public that the police were on the job.

She was able to find her way to the house unaided this time, though she did take a few wrong turns along the way. Melanie Kent opened the door, still dressed in her bedclothes, her hair hanging in wet straggles as if she had just showered.

'Yes?' she asked, her head held sideways, clearing her ear of water. Then she recognized Lucy. 'Oh. It's you.'

Lucy held out the teddy bear in offering. 'The hospital asked me to return this.'

Melanie Kent took it, muttered a thank you. 'You'd best come in,' she said, standing back to allow Lucy past.

Alice was sitting cross-legged on the floor in front of the TV when she went in. The girl looked at her when she entered and, for a moment, Lucy feared that her memory of her was a bad one. Instantly though, the child beamed and ran across to her, hugging her legs lightly, then resumed her position on the floor. A blue character on the TV, speaking in squeaks and grunts, waved a red blanket at the viewer. Alice returned the wave.

'Will you have tea?' Melanie Kent asked.

'Only if you're making it,' Lucy replied. 'How has she been?'

'Fine.' The woman stood with her back to Lucy, filling the kettle. 'She still isn't saying anything. The psychiatrist has seen her since. She says your story must have triggered some memories of the night her fath . . . Peter died.'

'I'm sorry.'

She dismissed the apology with a light wave of her hand. 'She said it would be good. It might help her begin to process what she saw. Help her deal with it.'

'I was so annoyed with myself,' Lucy said. 'I didn't want to do anything which might hurt Alice.'

Melanie nodded with understanding. 'I never thanked you for saving her in the wood,' she said awkwardly. 'Milk or sugar?'

'Both,' Lucy answered. She glanced in again at Alice. The programme had ended, the blue man sailing into the darkness in a small boat.

Melanie handed her a mug of tea, laid a plate of biscuits on the table.

'It is hard to know what it must have done to her to find that girl in his basement, isn't it?'

Lucy nodded, her mouth was dry when she spoke. 'We think Alice let Kate McLaughlin out of the basement, into the woods. I think your husband died because his associates thought he was trying to cheat them. Kate was missing and he didn't know where she was. The only way he could have saved himself was to blame Alice . . .'

Melanie Kent placed her tea on the table. 'And to save her, he needed to take the blame himself.'

Lucy nodded. 'I don't know if that helps.'

Melanie smiled sadly. 'I think it makes me feel worse.'

Lucy was about to apologize when she noticed that the children's programme had ended. A news bulletin was showing the press conference. Two pictures, one of each of the Cunninghams, were displayed on the screen. Alice was watching the two, without reaction. Considering how she had reacted to the story of Little Red Riding Hood, Lucy considered it strange that the child should show no reaction to the images of the two men believed to have been involved with her father.

'Do you know those men, Melanie?' she asked.

The woman leaned forward in her chair to get a clearer view of the television. She shook her head. 'Should I?'

'They weren't friends of Peter's, were they?'

Again she shook her head.

Lucy had a thought and excused herself. She went out to the car and, opening the passenger door, found the files Fleming had been looking at the day they had found Janet. She shuffled through them until she found a picture of Kevin Mullan. She took it back into the house. Melanie Kent stared at her suspiciously.

'Do you recognize this man?'

She laid the picture on the table. Melanie Kent glanced at it once, then shuddered.

'Kevin Mullan,' she said. 'A bad animal.'

'Do you know where I might find him?' Lucy asked.

Melanie did not get a chance to answer, for they were interrupted by a stifled cry from Alice. She was standing to Lucy's left, looking at the picture of Mullan, shuddering.

'What's wrong, love?' Melanie Kent said, moving to comfort her.

Alice stared at the image of Mullan's face.

'Are you OK, love?' Melanie Kent repeated.

'Do you know this man, Alice?' Lucy asked.

The girl stared up at her, then nodded, once.

'Did you see him with your daddy? At the house?'

Alice nodded again.

Lucy put the picture away, then hunkered down to Alice's level. 'Was he the wolf, Alice?'

Alice glanced across at where the folder lay, then returned her gaze to Lucy.

'Is he the wolf?' Lucy repeated.

Another nod.

'It pretty much confirms that she saw Mullan killing her father,' Lucy said.

'It doesn't actually,' Fleming countered, taking a seat behind his desk. 'It confirms that she saw him at some stage during her time in her father's house, not that he killed Kent himself.'

'We know she saw her father before he died. She had expirated blood on her clothes,' Lucy said. 'That means he was alive when she was with him.'

'I can read evidence, Lucy,' Fleming commented.

'Sorry, sir,' Lucy said. 'The shrink in the hospital showed me a picture Alice drew. It looks like a doorway and inside was blood red and at the centre was an animal. A wolf.'

'And?'

'I think Alice arrived back from hiding Kate and saw what happened to her father. When we were in the house, I could see clearly into the kitchen from the turn on the stairs. I think Alice was in her bed and heard what was happening. I think she came down and saw her father being tortured. I'll bet if you ask Tony Clarke he'll find her prints around that section of the staircase. Then I think she went into him as he died.'

'And?' he repeated.

'It's just that, if she saw the killer and he learns Alice was there, he'll go after her. She didn't know either of the Cunninghams. Mary Quigg gave Alan Cunningham an alibi. They don't have Kate.'

'Her charm was in their van,' Fleming countered.

'They didn't kill Peter Kent. I believe that Mullan did.'

'And you might be right,' Fleming agreed. 'But Travers won't listen to anything you have to say after yesterday.'

'I know,' Lucy said. She had hoped Fleming would argue on her behalf, but he had not offered any such thing.

'Which means we need to find him without telling Travers,' Fleming added.

Lucy stared at him, unsure she had heard properly. 'Travers will claim it as a CID success unless PPU put their stamp on it. We can claim we were following it up in terms of Alice instead of Kate.'

'Thank you, sir,' Lucy said. 'I appreciate it.'

Fleming lightly waved away her thanks. 'You need to dig out his files now, though, to see where to look.'

CHAPTER 42

Their first action was to call Mullan's partner Gallagher. She did not know where he was, hadn't seen him in days, she said. Then, over coffee, they pored over his records again in Lucy's office in the PPU block at Maydown. Mullan had been lifted with Kent for the roadside bomb that had not gone off. The arrest had been made over the border, in Monaghan. But the PSNI and the RUC before them had known of Mullan. He was arrested a number of times in connection with other attacks, including, they noticed, the docks bombing which had brought down the riverside building Michael McLaughlin owned. In each case, there had been insufficient evidence to charge him. Even his arrest in Monaghan had been more luck than police work. A Garda patrol setting up a checkpoint on the border had literally come upon them where they had hidden. They'd had the detonators on them.

Fleming and Lucy split the intelligence reports on Mullan, and scanned through them for mention of any locations where he might have set up his operations. It was Lucy who made a connection first.

'He was lifted four times on Trench Road,' she commented. 'Coming in from Donemana.'

Fleming glanced up from his own sheaf of notes.

'He claimed to have been coming from a local farm; said he helped out the owner, John McCauley, with his cattle.'

'Maybe he was.'

'Kent's house, on Strabane Old Road, was registered to someone called McCauley too.'

'Which means it's worth taking a closer look at, I think,' Fleming said, closing the file he held.

'Should we contact Travers first?' Lucy suggested.

'We're not going to do anything,' Fleming said. 'We're just taking a look.'

The narrow country tracks on the back road to Donemana were slow to travel. The snow had melted off most of the houses out in the open now, but the fields and road, in the shadow of the hedgerows, still held a thin crust of ice.

The slower speed of travel suited them anyhow, for it gave them both a chance to examine each property as they passed. At one stage, they had to pull in tight against the hedge as a tractor trundled down the road towards them. Even with that, there was little gap between the vehicles.

Fleming rolled down his window and flagged down the driver. The man, an old toothless figure wrapped in a blanket over his clothes as he drove, glared down from his seat.

'We're looking for John McCauley!' Fleming shouted, striving to be heard above the rumble of the tractor engine.

'Wha'?' the man called, his hand behind his ear to emphasize his inability to hear.

'John McCauley!' Fleming shouted a second time. Mouthing the words exaggeratedly in the hope that, if the man didn't hear him, he'd at least be able to read his lips.

'Ma'Cauley?' he called back.

Fleming nodded.

The old man spluttered, twisting in his seat and pointing backwards. 'Mile or two up on the left. Wasting your time, though,' he added, flashing his gums as he smiled.

Fleming raised his arms in bewilderment rather than shouting again.

'JP's dead this past eight month. Farm's empty.'

Fleming waved his thanks. The old man snapped down the window flap and the tractor spluttered into action again, narrowly missing removing Lucy's bumper as it passed. She pulled back out onto the road and continued towards where the old man had pointed.

Sure enough, just over a mile further up the road, they came to a dilapidated farm building. The five-barred gate across the main entrance was closed and chained. A For Sale sign swung on one chain from a post fixed to the gate frame. Selling such property in a recession would be difficult, Lucy thought, remembering the problems Margaret had claimed McLaughlin was having in shifting his land.

They stared in at the place, which looked abandoned. There was a barn, its large metal door lying open showing a bare interior. An old rusted car was parked in front of the house, the tyres absent, the bonnet removed exposing the innards of the engine block, which protruded in places through a coat of snow.

The house was in a similar state of disrepair, the glass panel in the front door smashed, the window on the left-hand side boarded up. It was a small, two-storey affair, shaded by a semicircle of large oaks whose thick boughs cast long shadows across the yard and on up the brickwork. Lucy followed their path. Two bedrooms upstairs, perhaps, Lucy thought. Most of the roof was covered with snow, save for a small patch to the front right.

'Look at the roof,' she commented, pointing.

Fleming leaned across and she could feel the pressure of his body against hers as he placed his cheek close to her arm to follow the direction she was pointing.

'The melted spot?'

Lucy nodded, lowering her hand, but Fleming did not sit back.

'Could be the sun,' he commented, glancing across at the trees.

'The patch is still in shadow,' Lucy said.

Fleming sat back. 'Drive on,' he said. 'As if we're leaving. Then park the next chance you get.'

Lucy did as she was instructed, pulling into a lay-by about a hundred yards further along the road. They got out of the car, both checking their weapons. The air was fresh, the cover of the trees keeping it well chilled.

Fleming moved across to the side of the road and climbed down into the ditch bordering it. Lucy followed him down, along the ditch, then up and out the other side, picking their way through the trees lining the road and finally into the field adjacent to the property. From this position, they could see the rear end of a red van parked inside the barn, but angled in such a way that it could not be seen from the main road.

'Someone's here,' Fleming commented. 'Call for back-up.'

'Travers claimed someone tipped them off about a red van near Prehen woods. He said it was Cunningham's,' Lucy said as she took out her phone, having to remove her gloves to be able to press the buttons.

Meanwhile, Fleming kept moving up the field towards the

house. There were no windows facing them which meant that their approach would be unlikely to be seen, unless the watcher were outside the house.

She put through the request with the 999 operator and hung up, following Fleming who was crouching as he moved, staying close to the cover offered by the line of trees separating the road from the field.

As they edged nearer the barn, they could see the red van parked inside. The bodywork was coated in the white dust of road salt, suggesting that the vehicle had been used recently. Certainly it had not been lying here since McCauley's death if he had died eight months previously as they had been told.

They were moving towards the front of the house when Lucy's phone began to ring. Cursing, she fumbled in her pocket for it while Fleming swore at her. She opened the phone and recognized the number as Travers's.

'Stay where you are, do you hear me?' he snapped. 'We're on our way.'

'Yes, sir,' Lucy managed, even as Fleming reached the front door and, twisting the handle, pushed it open.

'He said to wait,' Lucy hissed to Fleming as she closed the phone.

'If Mullan's here and heard your phone, Kate'll be dead by the time they get here,' he snapped. 'Take the back door. I'll go in the front.'

He moved against the wall of the house, leaving Lucy to sprint around the back as quickly as possible while trying not to slip on the patches of ice still packed on the path.

Passing a low window into the kitchen she risked a quick glimpse in, seeing only that the room was empty. She moved to the back door and placed her hand on the handle. She depressed the handle and, pushing open the door, entered the kitchen. Then, holding her gun in front of her, she scanned the room.

The kitchen was empty. A stained mug and a few crusts of bread lay on top of a small wooden table in one corner. Lucy was struck by the disconcerting heat in the room and realized that the stove in the corner was turned on – two rings burned with intense blue flames. Mullan must be near.

She moved out of the kitchen into the hallway to see Fleming emerge from the room to the front left of the house. He gestured that he had checked both rooms and they were clear. Then he pointed upstairs. Lucy nodded and pointed her gun upwards.

Fleming took the first step slowly, placing his foot lightly to ensure creaking stairs did not betray his movements.

Lucy moved behind him slowly, her gun trained up the stairs, in case someone tried to shoot down at them. Fleming picked his way carefully, each tread of his foot placed as softly as possible. A thick flowered carpet on the stairs helped cushion both the pressure and the noise of his ascent as Lucy followed behind, trying to place her steps in the wake of his.

They reached the turn in the stairs. Three doors led off from the landing above, all closed. Lucy recognized the sweet smell of a gas heater, felt the contradictory sensations of heat from above and the chill of the house below. The heat at least accounted for the snow melting off the roof.

'They must be in that room,' Lucy whispered, pointing over Fleming's shoulder towards the room beneath where the snow had melted, off to their left.

Fleming nodded in acknowledgement, then raised his index finger to silence her. They moved again upwards, in unison, their bodies so close together that Lucy could feel each movement of Fleming's back with each slow breath he took.

At the top of the stairs, they reached the door she had indi-cated. Fleming lowered his head near the door, straining to hear any movement inside. He reached out and gripped the handle. Then, mouthing a count of three to Lucy, he shoved open the door and rushed into the room. Lucy followed, aiming her gun over his shoulder.

Kate McLaughlin lay on a mattress against the wall. Her mouth was covered with black duct tape, her hands bound in front of her, her ankles taped together. She was blindfolded with black cloth that accentuated the pallor of her skin. She made no response to their entrance into the room, made no indication that she had heard them. Lucy moved to her quickly. Fleming tapped Lucy on the shoulder.

'I'll check the other rooms,' he whispered.

The air in the room was heavy with the smell of the gas burner in the corner, its hiss so loud Lucy could not hear if Kate McLaughlin was breathing. She felt for her pulse and, for a moment, thought the girl was dead. Her skin was cold, her pulse so faint, Lucy had to clasp her wrist for over a minute to be sure she had felt anything at all.

Lucy heard the creaking tread of Fleming's footfalls in the room next to her, then heard him again on the landing. She tugged lightly at the tape on Kate's mouth, felt the tug of the girl's skin against the glue, and heard her moan softly in reaction. Then, pulling out her keys, she used the edge of her front-door key to begin sawing through the tape binding her legs.

Outside she heard Fleming push open the door of the final room. Instantly, the place shook with the low reverberation of a gunshot. She heard a thud of something falling heavily, then the further thumping of someone tumbling down the stairs. Leaving Kate, she lifted her gun and ran out to check on Fleming.

He lay on the landing, blood oozing from between his fingers as he clasped his hand against a wound on his shoulder, trying to stem the flow. Fleming must have tripped Mullan as he made for the stairs, for the man's gun lay on a step halfway down where he must have dropped it.

'He's gone down,' Fleming hissed. Sweat popped on his forehead, his own skin pale and clammy-looking.

Lucy took the stairs two at a time, twisting on the turn and aiming her gun downwards, scanning the hallway. She heard the slamming of the rear door and guessed that Mullan was making for his van. She took the rest of the stairs as quickly as she could. She moved quietly down the hallway. She could see both the front and rear doors from where she stood and both were closed, so Mullan was still in the house.

Lucy steadied herself, crouching slightly, holding her gun in both hands. She edged closer to the kitchen. She heard a creak from above and glanced up quickly, training her gun on the area where the noise had come from. Fleming was struggling to his knees, using the banisters for support. She had just turned again to the kitchen when Mullan rushed out at her.

He carried her down with his weight, pinning her against the floor, knocking the gun from her grip, the weapon discharging harmlessly. His face was twisted, his eyes glistening with the adrenalin rush propelling him. He grappled with her until he managed to get his hands to her throat, then banged her head against the floor twice, in quick succession.

She felt herself weaken, felt her head go light. For a moment she thought he had released his hold, but when she tried to move his weight still pinned her.

Then the whole room reverberated with a sharp crack and Mullan fell sideways across her. She twisted, trying to push him off. He was crawling himself now, reaching out for her gun, just beyond his reach.

Just above him, on the bottom step, Fleming held his gun in his uninjured arm. 'Stop, or I will shoot,' he called.

Mullan scrabbled for the gun, but Fleming shot twice more, in quick succession. Mullan was dead with the first shot.

CHAPTER 43

Some of the press arrived while Kate was still receiving attention in the rear of one of the ambulances that had arrived shortly after the police. Lucy and Fleming sat in the back of another, while Fleming's wound was tended.

Travers was talking to the press, about a job well done, the successful end of an operation. Lucy silently laughed at the word 'operation'; it suggested something planned, clinical, precise. But while Travers was the main speaker, the press seemed more interested in her and Fleming. She could tell from the angle of the cameras that they weren't filming Travers; they were filming past him. Through the open front door of the house, Mullan's body could be seen lying, covered in a blanket.

Travers had been furious with both Lucy and Fleming for going into the house without him. She sensed that he felt cheated, that it was not enough to have the case solved; he needed to be the one solving it. Still, he could not argue with the fact that Kate McLaughlin had been recovered and was still alive.

The girl herself had said little since being rescued. The medics suggested that the gas fumes in the room, with the door closed, would have left her groggy and uncommunicative for the first few hours. That wasn't taking into account the ordeal she had endured for the guts of a week.

The first ambulance had already left with Tom Fleming, the medics tending to the wound on his shoulder. Despite his protests that it was only a flesh wound, they were taking no chances.

The press pack shifted suddenly as a car sped up the country road and slid to a halt at the five-barred gate. Michael McLaughlin was out of the car and across the lane, pushing through the reporters who pressed their questions and microphones ever more forcibly in front of him.

He placed his foot on the middle bar of the gate and hoisted himself over, looking desperately for his daughter. When he saw her shape in the rear of the ambulance he let out a low cry and rushed towards the vehicle.

The girl had obviously seen him too for she stood, her silver heat blanket wrapped around her shoulders like a shawl, and opened her arms. Her father embraced her, gathering her in against his chest as he began to weep.

Lucy found herself welling up just watching them. She thought of her own father, her own sense of disappointment at what she had learned about him.

A second car pulled up on the road beyond and the press scrimmage was repeated when the door opened and ACC Wilson stepped out. Ignoring the reporters, she crossed to the gate and waited for one of the Uniforms standing there to open it for her. She entered the yard and came straight across to the ambulance where Lucy sat.

'Lucy?' she began. 'How are you doing?'

'I'm fine, Mum,' Lucy said.

If her mother heard the final word, she did not react. 'You shot the suspect, is that right?'

Lucy shook her head. 'My gun discharged in the struggle but it was Inspector Fleming who actually shot him.'

Her mother raised her hand. 'Better him than you. How are you feeling?'

Lucy felt her voice quiver slightly. 'Fine.'

Her mother stared at her appraisingly. 'You'll be suspended pending an investigation. I need you to write up your report now while the events are fresh in your mind. I need you to surrender your weapon when you get back to the station.'

'I didn't do anything wrong, did I?'

Her mother shook her head. 'Those are all formalities, Lucy, standard procedures in any shooting. You know that. You'll be back in action within a day or two if I can push this through. Let me speak with the Chief Super, then I'll take you back to the station.'

She turned to go, then thought better of it and turned to face her again. 'And well done on rescuing Kate McLaughlin.'

Lucy sat in her office while she compiled her version of events. She wrote it simply, without embellishment. She wondered if Kate McLaughlin had spoken yet, if she had revealed anything about Alice and the role the child had played in her escape from Kent's house. She also felt the urge to see Alice again, to explain that the wolf was dead, that she need no longer be afraid.

The story had already broken on TV. She had seen herself in grainy footage, sitting in the back of the ambulance. The press had already decided the angle they would report, calling herself and Fleming heroes. Fleming, in particular, was praised for being wounded in the rescue of the girl.

Lucy was finishing her statement when her phone rang. It

was the desk sergeant in Strand Road. Chief Superintendent Travers wanted to see her to debrief her about the events.

Despite the breaking of the case, and the positive press attention he had received in the aftermath, he was still angry at what had happened.

'I'm not blaming you, Lucy,' he said. 'But Tom Fleming should know better. He took you into a house without proper support. If he'd been killed or incapacitated more severely, you'd have been on your own.'

'Inspector Fleming was afraid that Mullan would kill Kate if he realized he was surrounded; that he would have nothing to lose.'

'It's admirable to see you sticking up for him, Lucy,' he began.

Lucy looked down at her hands, clasped together in her lap.

'Still, I'd say you've earned your way back into CID if you want it. I don't think anyone would argue with me on that one.'

'Thank you, sir,' she said.

'Though, obviously, when you get back from suspension. Take the few days, spend time with your father,' he added generously, as if gifting her the time off.

'Yes, sir,' she said.

The hospital was quiet, visiting hours long since over. She visited the post-surgery ward first, to see Tom Fleming, though was told that he was only just coming round from his surgery. The doctor suggested she call back in an hour for a brief visit. Without fully intending it, five minutes later, Lucy found herself back on Janet's ward. The nurse on the ward would have refused to allow her in, were it not for the fact that Janet was causing so much trouble, she was glad of something to distract her, even gladder when Lucy revealed she was a policewoman.

'I want to leave!' Janet shouted when she entered the room. 'Those bitches won't let me out.'

'The doctor wants to see you first,' the nurse said. 'To check everything.'

Lucy looked at the woman, could imagine the worms wriggling under her skin as she endured another day of sobriety.

'Janet, you can go any time,' she said. 'You know that. You're not a prisoner. But the doctor wants to make sure you're OK, first. If he thinks your arm is healing well, he'll let you go.'

Janet stared at her, teasing out whether there was any ulterior meaning in what she had said.

'What are you doing here?'

Lucy glanced at the nurse, hoping that the woman would understand that she wanted some privacy. For her part, the woman seemed grateful for the relief and excused herself before leaving the two of them alone.

Lucy approached Janet. 'I wanted to see you before you left,' she said. 'I wanted to say sorry.'

'What for?'

'For my father. For what happened to you.'

'Why?'

Lucy swallowed hard. 'I think . . . I believe my father was the policeman you knew.'

'Why?'

'You were his informant.'

The woman regarded her coolly.

'Do you know who I mean?' Lucy asked.

'Yes!' she snapped.

'He wants to be forgiven. I think he's truly sorry for what happened.'

'Sorry?'

Lucy nodded, embarrassed herself.

'Kevin Mullan,' Janet said suddenly.

The shift in conversation disconcerted Lucy, and she immediately felt herself on guard.

'What?'

'I saw you on the news,' Janet explained, pointing towards the TV in the corner. 'You were there with Kevin Mullan. How did he die?'

'I can't tell you that,' Lucy said, shifting back in her seat, away from the woman.

'You asked what you could do. I want to know who killed Kevin Mullan.'

'What difference does it make?'

'Did you see his face? The burns.'

Lucy nodded, uncertainly.

'I'm not the only one who got burned that day.'

The comment shocked Lucy. She had assumed Mullan was burned planting one of his devices.

'Mullan blew up the Strand Inn,' Janet said. 'The one the woman died in.'

'Michael McLaughlin's wife?'

Janet nodded.

'How do you know?'

She laughed scornfully. 'Everyone knew. The whole town knew. The word was that it was an insurance scam; that McLaughlin was in on it with them. He didn't know his wife would be there that night.'

'It wouldn't have just been town gossip?' Lucy suggested softly.

'My cousin was in on it. He told me.'

'Who was your cousin?' Lucy asked.

'Billy Quinn,' Janet said, raising her chin slightly.

'Why are you telling me this now?'

'I told then too. That's why I really got this,' she said, gesturing towards her chest where the scar tissue could be seen above the dropping neckline of her gown. 'They said it was about the Brits, but Billy told me it was 'cause they knew I was a tout. Mullan knew. He was the one who stripped me.'

Lucy felt her face flush, felt as if the air around her was being sucked from the room. Her chest hurt when she tried to breathe.

'Why didn't you come forward? Tell somebody.'

'Tell somebody? That's what got me punished.'

'Who did you tell about Mullan doing the Strand Inn?' she finally asked, dreading the answer, already knowing what the woman would say.

'My handler. Your da. That's why he wants forgiven. Because of what happened to me. Because he let it happen.'

The complaint sounded absurd, yet clearly Janet felt its sting. Lucy could not explain it, could not offer any justification for her father's arguments, though she sensed that Janet wanted some explanation for her abandonment.

'So. Who killed Kevin Mullan? Did you do it?'

Lucy straightened herself up. 'I'm sorry for all that happened to you, Janet. And for my father's role in it, in particular. And I understand your feelings. Kevin Mullan died. That's all I'll tell you.'

She turned and walked down the corridor towards the door, Janet's shouts echoing in her wake.

CHAPTER 44

Fleming was lying up on raised pillows when she went up to his room. His shoulder was heavily bandaged, his arm in a sling despite his claim that the wounding was superficial.

'Hit the bone apparently,' he said sheepishly, raising the other arm in greeting. 'Shattered it.'

Lucy placed the bottle of lemonade she had bought on the bedside cabinet. 'Thank you for saving my life, sir,' she said.

'No problem, Lucy,' Fleming said, attempting a shrug, which caused him to wince. 'How's it falling out?'

'Kate is back safely. The kidnappers are dead. Travers is glad of the result, I think.'

'And you?'

'Suspended until the shooting is investigated.'

Fleming nodded. 'A formality. It was me that killed him.'

'I went to see Janet. She mentioned Mullan to me too,' she said. 'She said that Mullan was connected with the Strand Inn bombing that killed Kate's mother. And that McLaughlin had arranged the bombing for an insurance claim on the building. The wife's death was an accident.'

'That's news to me,' Fleming said. 'And I worked the bloody case. She's about twenty years too late with the information.'

'She claimed she told my father. Is that true?'

Fleming looked upwards, as if visually sifting through his memories. 'Certainly it was never mentioned to me. We never looked at McLaughlin.'

'Why did my father not tell anyone?'

Fleming started to shrug again, then thought better of it. 'Maybe he thought she was unreliable? I don't know.'

By the time she got home, her father was lying curled on the sofa in the living room, having clearly decided against trying to climb the stairs. His coat was spread over his upper body.

Lucy went and gathered blankets, covering the man up to his chin. That done, she gathered together her notes and sat at the table to work. She reconsidered Janet's story again, recalled the date of her being tarred and feathered in June 1994. Lucy recognized it as being the day after the attack on her own family home. Her parents' marriage, and to a degree her childhood, were both in tatters by Christmas of that year.

She needed to check the veracity of Janet's claim that she had told her father about Mullan and nothing had been done. She considered waking her father and asking him why he hadn't passed on the information, but knew that, given his condition, any response he could give would be unreliable. Finally, she recalled his boxes of notebooks upstairs, lining the wall of her room, arranged in order in a futile attempt by her father to hold back the progress of his own senility.

She went up, a mug of tea in hand, and settled down to begin picking through the folders. One set of boxes in particular looked sun-faded, the labels peeling and yellowed. She was able to work out that the notebooks at the bottom of those boxes were the oldest, dating back to the mid-seventies.

She began working through the boxes, one by one. Lucy recognized some of the place names from cases she remembered from her own childhood. Coshquinn, Greysteel, The Rising Sun. The passing years were marked only by the changing names of the dead.

The final box of notebooks ended midway through 1992. She had not seen mention of Janet in any of the books she'd checked despite the fact that she had been an informant for him. Lucy wondered if she had missed a box but checked through a second time with no further success. She began to wonder if her father might have destroyed the notebooks relating to Janet.

She hefted the boxes back into the corner, lifted the mug of cold tea and carried it downstairs. The tips of her fingers were red with flicking through the pages, her hands dusty with the grime the books had gathered in storage. As she passed the living room she glanced in at her father's sleeping form. He had only begun speaking of Janet over the past week. Had it been prompted by his sorting out the notebooks? He'd been work- ing on a box in the living room. She went in and checked. Sure enough, the edge of a box showed from beneath the sofa where her father lay sleeping.

She lifted the box without disturbing him and took it to the table. She knew immediately that this one was different. There were more notebooks in this box than the others, ranging from 1992 to 1994.

She opened the first one and began thumbing through each page slowly, scanning through the notes line by line, looking for mention of Janet. Her name first appeared after about ten pages of the first book. She was mentioned infrequently over the course

273

of a few weeks. Then her name began to appear every few pages. Increasingly her father had used a form of shorthand and her presence was denoted with a single J. Sometimes he had written reminders to himself to consult her: 'Ask J if she's heard?' appeared a number of times.

Three pages into the final notebook, she saw mention of Kevin Mullan's name. It was circled in red, with J printed in black ink at the top of the page. Below Mullan were the words: *Strand Inn. Orchestrated. McLaughlin Insurance scam??*

'What are you doing?'

She looked up. Her father was sitting up on the sofa now, the blanket she had put on him gathered in a pile on the floor.

'Those are mine,' he said. 'Put them back.'

'I need to see them, Dad,' Lucy said, embarrassed at having been caught reading her father's notes.

He struggled to his feet, holding the arm of the sofa to keep himself steady. 'Put those back!' he snapped.

Lucy glanced down at the page again. 'I'm nearly finished. I need to know about Janet and Kevin Mullan.'

Her father lunged at her then, grabbing his arm in hers.

'Give me my bloody books!' he shouted, raising his hand.

Lucy tried to pull herself away from him, dropping the book she held on the floor.

'Look what you've done. Pick that up.'

Lucy stood. 'Daddy, I'm . . .'

Her father lashed out with his open palm, smacking her hard on the side of the face. She felt her teeth cut her lip, tasted the coppery taste of blood in her mouth.

Her father stopped what he was doing and his gaze shifted, as if he was seeing her for the first time.

'Oh, sweet Jesus, love. I'm sorry,' he said, his eyes already weeping. He placed his hand to his mouth, his fingers, thin and feminine, covering his quivering lips.

Then he reached out to her. Determined not to cry, she pushed his hand away.

'You're not my father,' she said. 'I don't know you any more.'

She pushed past him, out of the room and went to the bathroom. She stood under the fluorescent glare and stared at herself, her reflection pale, save for the red of her bleeding lip. She turned on the tap, stared into the water as one drip of blood after another fell from her mouth into the water, diffusing in clouds at the centre of widening concentric rings.

Only when she was sure that the noise of the running water would cover her sobbing, did she allow herself to cry. She sat at the edge of the bath, her arms wrapped around herself and cried for her mother.

She stayed there until she heard the creaking of her father's footfalls outside the door. He knocked softly, whispered her name so quietly it was little more than a dull murmur through the wood. When she did not answer he padded into his room.

After waiting for another twenty minutes, she quietly unlocked the door and went downstairs. She felt the urge to pack her bag and leave, but had no idea where she could go.

In the living room, the notebook she had been reading when her father struck her still lay on the floor. She lifted it to put it on the table. Then she saw at the bottom of the page the words: *Passed to IO.*

She knew that *IO* meant Investigating Officer. She assumed that that meant Tom Fleming. He had been working on the case. If so, he had lied to her about not knowing about this.

She called Strand Road station and asked the desk sergeant if it would be possible to double check who the IO was on the

Strand Inn case. She could tell from his tone that he was not particularly pleased with the task; nevertheless, he told her he would phone her back as soon as he knew.

Ten minutes later her mobile rang. She recognized the Strand Road station number on the display.

'DS Black,' she said.

'This is Travers.'

At first Lucy assumed he was calling to see how she was doing. Then he said, 'You've been asking about the Strand Inn case. Why?'

'I'm following up on something, sir,' she said, trying to keep the details vague.

'What exactly? You are meant to be on suspension.'

'An old informant of my father's mentioned the case in connection with recent events.'

'What events, Lucy?'

'The kidnapping, sir. Mullan. She told my father that Mullan was connected to the Strand Inn case. My father's notes say he passed on the information to the IO on the case. I think it was Inspector Fleming, sir.'

'How did you get your father's notes?'

'I . . . he has them at home,' Lucy said, then cursed herself for revealing this.

'The McLaughlin case is over, Lucy. Mullan is dead. Enjoy your days off.'

'Thank you, sir,' she said. 'But, just as a matter of interest, who was the IO?'

There was the briefest pause on the other end.

'I was, DS Black. Your father never mentioned Mullan to me.'

CHAPTER 45

The ACC half opened the front door, peering out through the gap allowed by a thick security chain. Lucy wondered why she bothered; she had already announced herself at the intercom embedded in the pillar at the front of the house.

Above them, the rumble of a low-flying jet heading towards the airport a few miles further down the road shook the windows of the house.

'Is everything all right?' her mother asked, opening the door fully and ushering her inside. She wore a dressing gown over her night clothes.

'I'm sorry for coming here so late,' Lucy said. 'I've no one else.'

Her mother peered at her. 'What happened to your lip?'

Lucy gnawed at the wound. 'He hit me.'

'Who?'

'Dad.'

Her expression softened. 'Oh, Lucy,' she said. Lucy sensed that her mother wanted to embrace her, to comfort her. Instead, she laid her hand lightly on her shoulder for a moment.

She heard the creak of floorboards and turned to see a man standing at the top of the staircase staring down.

'Is everything all right?' he called down.

'Fine. Go back to bed,' her mother said, raising her eyebrows in exasperation and leading Lucy down the hallway to the kitchen.

Lucy allowed herself to be directed to a seat and waited while her mother poured them two glasses of wine. The glasses were large, heavy crystal affairs, and they were filled to the brim.

'What happened?'

'I was looking through some of his old notebooks,' Lucy said. 'He lost his temper.'

Her mother looked aghast at her. 'That's not like your father.'

'I don't know what he is like any more,' Lucy said. 'I found Janet.'

Her mother's features sharpened, her lips tightening to a white line. 'Why?'

'He was speaking about her. I needed to know.'

As Lucy spoke the shaking of her mother's head increased in intensity. 'No. No you didn't. I deliberately didn't tell you. What would've been the point in you knowing?'

Lucy drank half a glassful of the wine in one go, felt the bite of the aftertaste in her mouth.

'Did you know she was a child?'

Her mother looked into her own glass, drained a mouthful before nodding.

'And you left me with him. I was a child myself.'

'It wasn't like that, Lucy,' she said. 'Your father loved you, whatever else about him. We discussed it. He had to leave anyway when he was threatened. If it had become common knowledge, he'd have been finished. I . . . I had worked hard to get as far as I had got. It wasn't fair for me to give that up because of what he had done. And I couldn't have done it with a child.' She looked at Lucy, allowing a note of pleading in her voice. 'Things were different for a woman then. It wasn't easy for me, Lucy.'

'Nor for me,' Lucy retorted. 'Nor for the girl, Janet. She was tarred and feathered the day after we left Derry.'

Her mother groaned softly. 'You shouldn't have brought this back up, Lucy. The past is past.'

'No, it's not,' Lucy said. 'It's still infecting the present. Janet says Kevin Mullan was the one who tarred her. Because she was a grass. She told Dad that Mullan bombed the Strand Inn.'

'McLaughlin's bar?'

Lucy nodded. 'According to her, it was an insurance scam on the building. Dad passed the information on, but it was never investigated. Now, twenty years on, Mullan and Kent are involved in kidnapping McLaughlin's daughter. The Semtex found in Kent's shed was from the same batch used to blow up the bar.'

'That was a terrorist attack, Lucy. I remember it happening.'

'It was a listed building. McLaughlin bought it for next to nothing because the land couldn't be developed. The bomb cleared the field for him. Once the wrangling was over in the courts, the land was worth a fortune. He had offers near forty-five million for it. Then, just when he could sell it, the recession hit and the arse fell out of the market. The land's not worth more than he bought it for.'

Her mother had stopped arguing with her now, was considering all she said.

'The people who planted the bomb were lifted doing something else. When they get out they take McLaughlin's child and don't demand a ransom? Yet he was trying to source ten million the day before he made the reward offer.'

'How do you know this?' Her tone had changed, had assumed the coldness more associated with the ACC.

'I spoke with the wife of his accountant. He was trying to shift the land on the quiet and couldn't do it. He leaked news of a fake deal for £25 million to try to push up the price. Instead it attracted his old partners, looking for their cut.'

'So McLaughlin had a deal with the bombers? He'd pay them a cut of the profit on the land if they took care of the restrictions on the listed building.'

Lucy nodded. 'But by the time they got out, the land wasn't worth what they had been promised. Then they heard he was on the verge of this great deal. They still wanted what they were owed.'

'Kate McLaughlin told us that one of the kidnappers said that's what they wanted – "what they were owed".'

'What else did she have to say?'

Her mother shook her head. 'She was held in Kent's house, bound and blindfolded. They kept her in the dark. She heard the girl arriving in the house, said she overheard a row between Kent and a woman over his daughter. The others weren't there at that stage. She guessed that they didn't know that the girl was in the house. Maybe Kent was afraid they might hurt her. The child, Alice, found Kate in the basement. She had been playing outside and came down through the coal doors to explore. Kate convinced her to cut her ties. She took her into the woods. The snow came, she hid out in the shed you found till it passed.'

'But Mullan found her first.'

She nodded.

'Did she know that Kent was killed?'

'No.'

'Did she see any of the kidnappers?'

Her mother drained her glass of wine and refilled it. She topped up Lucy's to finish the bottle.

'No. She heard voices. Four male voices.'

'But we've only got three kidnappers. Quinn, Mullan and Kent.'

'She was adamant that she heard four.'

'Dad wrote in his notebook that he passed on Janet's tip-off about Mullan to Bill Travers.'

She noticed the tightening around her mother's lips.

'He was the one who told you about Janet too, wasn't he?'

Her mother nodded.

'Dad names Mullan to Travers and our house is attacked and Janet is the victim of a punishment squad. And the day I mentioned to Travers my suspicions about McLaughlin's involvement, a threat was daubed on the gable wall of the house.'

'You need to be careful what you're suggesting, Lucy.'

'Travers led the Strand Inn investigation. Now he's leading the investigation of the kidnapping. It would be a handy way for the gang to be sure they'd never be caught. An inside man.'

Her mother nodded slowly, as she followed the circumference of the ring of wine left by the bottom of her glass on the table with her index finger. Finally she stood, took her glass to the sink, rinsed it and placed the glass upside down on the draining board.

'What do you want me to do, Lucy? Arrest Travers and McLaughlin?'

Lucy twisted in her chair to watch her mother. She could see already that the woman was considering the angles, looking for a way to minimize the damage. She was an ACC. It was her station, her district. It would be her mess.

'If they did these things.'

'That's a big "if", Lucy,' she said, suddenly speaking in an even, reasoning tone Lucy recognized from so many arguments with the woman. 'You know how it feels to find out something about your father that you didn't need to know. Will Kate McLaughlin thank you for taking her father from her? Her mother's dead. Do you think that would be a good way for this to end?'

'He has to pay for what he's done.'

'Jesus, Lucy, you don't think he's paid already? You don't think all that has happened this past few weeks isn't enough? His wife is gone, his daughter was abducted. By your own admission, his property is worthless to him. If we arrest him, that child may as well be an orphan.'

'She deserves to know the truth.'

Her mother sat down opposite her again. 'But now? You didn't need to know the truth when you were a child. No one would benefit from it.'

'And Travers? What if he is the fourth gang member? What if he thinks Alice saw him at the house? She'll talk eventually. He's not secure while she's alive. And she'll not be safe so long as he is free.'

Her mother lifted her glass without asking her if she had finished.

'Go to the girl in the morning. Take photographs. If she identifies Travers, I'll deal with it. Until that, everything else is circumstantial, Lucy. You have nothing concrete on him.'

She stood again. 'I'm going to bed. There's a spare room at the back, or you can sleep on the couch. I'll leave out blankets and night clothes for you. My partner's name is Mark, in case he's still here for breakfast when you wake.'

Lucy watched her pad across the kitchen towards the door. She stopped at the door and turned to face her.

'You know your father hitting you was the disease acting, don't you? It wasn't him. He wouldn't hurt you, Lucy. I hated him for what he did to that girl, but I knew he loved you too much to ever hurt you.'

Lucy stared at her but said nothing.

'What are you going to do about him?'

'I don't know,' Lucy replied.

CHAPTER 46

Lucy had just lain down on the sofa and drawn the blanket around her when her phone rang.

'Hello.'

'Where are you, Lucy?' It was Travers. His voice was quiet, soothing.

'Ah, I'm home, sir. In my bed.'

'No you're not.'

Lucy felt her skin go to goosebumps. She shivered as she rubbed them on her arm.

'Excuse me?'

'There's just me and your father here at the moment,' Travers continued.

Lucy felt her innards lurch. Her instinct was to run up to her mother, but she could not face the strange man in her mother's bed.

'Is everything all right, sir?' Lucy said. 'Is there something wrong at my home?'

'Not at all,' he said. 'I called to see these notebooks your father kept, to see if I can work out who he gave the name of Mullan to all those years ago.'

'My father's not well, sir,' Lucy said, standing now and lifting her jacket.

'I've noticed that. In fact, I think he may have gone out looking for you in the woods, but I'm not sure.'

Lucy clicked off the phone and ran out of the house, slamming the door behind her.

It took twenty minutes to make it to her house. When she got there, the front door lay open. She parked haphazardly in front of the drive and ran into the house, shouting for her father as she did. The place was in darkness, her shouts gaining only echoing silence in response.

She checked each room quickly but there was no sign of either her father or Travers. She ran to the locked unit beneath the sink for her father's gun as her own had been taken from her pending the results of the shooting investigation. She had kept the key after locking the gun away the night he had fallen in the snow. Despite this, however, the door to the cabinet lay open, the gun missing; her father must have had more than one key. The box of ammunition spilled bullets onto the floor of the cabinet.

She ran out to the hallway. Suddenly, a figure stumbled through the doorway, lumbering towards her, causing her to tense, ready to fight. It was Dermot, the neighbour.

'Jesus, you gave me a fright,' Lucy said.

'I saw you arrive,' he explained. 'Your father headed up the street a few minutes ago. His visitor followed after him. They've not come back.'

Lucy nodded. 'Where did they go?'

Dermot pointed to the far end of the street where the darkened edge of the woods ran adjacent to the street.

'I think they went in the woods,' he said. 'Do you need a hand? I'll get a torch.'

He ran back towards his house while Lucy jogged on to the end of the road. She reached the edge of the woods and scanned as far in as she could. The snow had mostly melted now, which, in fact, made the woods all the more dark. The air was chilled and sharp.

She pushed through the gate at the entrance and stepped into the woods proper. She took a moment to stand, her eyes closed, allowing herself to acclimatize to the darkness here, beneath the ancient oaks.

Finally, taking a deep, slow breath, she opened her eyes and began moving through the trees. Using the illumination of her mobile phone display as a torch, she picked her way along, glanced constantly from left to right, always alert for a flash of her father's white shirt against the black trunks.

Above her, something moved in the branches, causing her to start. Branches thrashed and rattled, then she heard something take to the sky.

As she walked, she kept her head down, watching the ground for roots or branches lying in the way. The wood was alive with movement now, creatures skittering across the dead leaves of the woodland floor, always just beyond the weakening ring of light thrown out by her phone.

After some time she realized she was nearing the upper lip of the quarry. She angled the phone to gauge how close to the edge she was. Just at that moment, the woods were plunged into darkness as her battery died.

Suddenly she heard a crack from behind her and a heavy movement. Before she could turn, a hand gripped her shoulder, causing her to flinch.

'Hello, Lucy,' Travers said.

'Sir,' she replied, failing to control the stammering of her voice as she turned to face him. 'What are you doing here?'

'Looking for your father,' he replied. He was dressed in black, one hand in his pocket where, she assumed, he had his gun.

'Some of the neighbours are coming behind me, sir,' she said.

'We'd best be quick then.' As he stepped closer to her, Lucy recalled that the upper edge of the quarry lay only a few feet behind her and she had to resist the urge to step back from him.

'So, who is this tout your father got his information from?'

'I'm not sure of her name, sir.'

'It was that schoolgirl, wasn't it?'

'I'm not sure,' Lucy repeated.

'Who else have you mentioned it to?'

'My mother,' she said quickly. 'That's where I was when you phoned.'

He nodded, as if this confirmed what he had suspected all along.

'Good. Your mother will not want this coming out,' Travers said. 'She'll not want to admit that her husband abused a schoolgirl and she did nothing about it. Christ, she left you with him and you were only a schoolgirl yourself.' He shook his head. 'That doesn't say much for what she thought of you, does it, Lucy?'

'No, sir,' Lucy agreed, if only to keep him talking. He moved towards her, forcing her to step back nearer to the edge of the quarry.

He reached out his free hand and touched her cheek. 'But you'll not keep quiet, will you?'

Lucy glanced to her side, desperately trying to see how near she was to the edge.

'I could, sir.'

'You'd have done very well in CID, Lucy,' Travers said. 'Such a promising officer.'

Lucy could not speak. Travers moved a step closer, causing her to inch nearer the quarry edge.

'You can't just kill me, sir,' Lucy said, desperately looking out for any sign of her neighbour following behind.

'It was very brave of you to come into the woods in the dark after your father. But accidents happen. Maybe you lost your footing in the dark, stepped too close to the quarry edge.'

'No one will believe you.'

Travers laughed, edged closer. 'Everyone will believe me, Lucy. That's the point.'

'Janet!'

Lucy looked up to her right, quickly, to see the spectral figure of her father moving through the trees.

'Run, Dad. Get help!' she shouted.

Instead, at the sound of her voice, her father moved closer to them. Lucy realized that he was holding his gun in his hand. Travers must have noticed at the same instant for he shifted suddenly, lurching at him, grabbing his shirt and pulling him backwards. He reached for the gun, clawing at her father's arm, pulling him onto the woodland floor while the old man fought back.

In the struggle, the gun spun from her father's grip and landed in the undergrowth. Lucy scrabbled across to where it landed, feeling through the low-lying bushes with her hands until she felt the cold solidity of the metal.

She straightened up and pointed the gun. Travers stood above where her father still lay, using him to shield the lower half of his body. He struggled in vain to pull the old man to his feet to protect himself more fully.

'Leave him, sir.'

'Lucy?' Travers stopped suddenly and raised his hands. 'I'm unarmed. What are you going to do? Shoot me?'

'I know you.' The old man was squinting up at Travers, desperate to place him. 'I know your voice.'

'Help is coming,' Lucy said. 'You're under arrest.'

Travers laughed hollowly. 'What for?'

'The murder of Peter Kent. The kidnapping of Kate McLaughlin.'

'Prove it.'

'Alice saw the killing. She must have been upstairs in bed. Why did you kill him?'

Travers moved a step closer to Lucy, prompting her to raise the gun further, warning him to stay back.

'We thought he'd done a deal with McLaughlin himself. The girl was gone and he wouldn't say where.'

'He died to protect his child. You killed him for that.'

Travers laughed. 'You make it sound so chivalrous. Kent was an animal. So was Quinn. You took care of him though, didn't you?'

'Were you involved with them all along? Right back to 1994. Janet told Dad about Mullan bombing the docks and he told you. Were you part of the gang from the start or did McLaughlin pay you off to say nothing after the bombing went wrong?'

Travers began to edge towards her again.

'Don't,' she hissed. 'Step back.'

'I know you,' her father said, his voice firmer now. 'I know you.'

'Did you set Mullan on Janet? And the attack on our home? Did you do that?'

'So many questions, Lucy.'

Her father struggled to stand without success. 'I remember you,' he said, looking up at Travers.

Travers glanced at him. 'He was shagging a schoolgirl,' he said. 'She was not much older than you. Does that not make you think?'

'Shut up,' Lucy said. 'You didn't want me in CID. You knew I had a case in the woods bordering Kent's house and you wanted to keep an eye on what I found out.'

'A fourteen-year-old girl,' he added, moving towards her again.

'Don't,' Lucy said. 'You thought you could control me.'

Travers shook his head. 'Is that why you still live with him now?'

'Don't,' Lucy hissed, struggling to stay in control.

'Keeping it in the family? That explains so much,' Travers added, stepping deliberately towards her.

'I will shoot,' Lucy said, keeping her aim steady.

'No, you won't.' Travers lunged for her, his hand grabbing for the gun, gripping the barrel.

Lucy fired once, low, the echo of the shot reverberating down off the rock face of the quarry below them.

Travers immediately stopped short, his expression drawn in surprise. He looked down at where his hand prodded his stomach, moaned as he pulled his hand away from the wound slick with blood.

'You bitch,' he spat, lunging for her again.

Her father had stood up by now and suddenly moved forwards, grappled with Travers, taking him by his coat.

'I remember you,' he said.

He swung Travers sideways towards the quarry edge, causing him to stumble. Travers struggled to keep his footing at the quarry edge, flailing his arms to retain balance. He seemed to remain suspended in air for a second, then shifted suddenly to the left and disappeared from view.

Lucy grabbed her father before the momentum of his movement pulled him over the edge too. They fell to the ground. She lay there, clinging to him, as in the distance she saw the bobbing of torchlight through the trees, heard her neighbour's voice calling her name.

CHAPTER 47

The dawn had torn a red gash across the horizon to the east. Dermot helped her bring her father back home, then, plugging in her mobile, she called for help. She had thought of climbing down to check if Travers had survived the fall, but a quick glance over the edge rendered this unnecessary. His final resting position was all the confirmation she needed that his body was broken beyond repair.

It took the Response teams the best part of an hour to arrive. When she heard the sirens approaching, she had walked back to the entrance to the wood and waited, then had led the first team through the woods, the journey made easier now by the lightening dawn.

'There's been a house fire on the city side,' one of the officers offered by way of explanation for the slowness of their response as they picked their way through the trees.

She stood at the top of the quarry and watched as the team worked their way down to where Travers lay. They were still erecting the small SOCO tent over his body when Lucy's mother arrived.

'Are you OK?' she asked, laying her hand on Lucy's arm.

Lucy nodded. 'He brought Dad into the woods. I came in after him.'

'What did he want?'

'He was looking for Dad's notebooks. And the name of his informant. He was trying to cover his tracks, I think.'

'What will the SOCO find?'

'I shot him. Once. Then he scuffled with Dad and fell over.'

'Was he armed?'

Lucy shook her head. 'I don't know. I thought he was, but then I never actually saw anything.'

Her mother's mouth tightened. 'You shot an unarmed chief superintendent,' she said softly.

Lucy swallowed and nodded.

'Where did you get the gun?'

Lucy shook her head. 'Dad's.'

'Where is it now?'

Lucy took it from her pocket. Her mother glanced around, then took the gun from her.

'Go home,' her mother said. 'I'll be up with you as soon as I can.'

As dawn broke through the trees, softening the edges of the shadows, she moved back towards her house.

Her father was sitting in the living room when she came in, sorting through his final box of notebooks. He raised his head and smiled at Lucy when he saw her.

'Nearly done,' he said.

She heard her phone ringing in the kitchen where she had left it charging. Lifting it, she saw that it was Robbie and could see from the display that she already had three missed calls.

Robbie's voice seemed muted when she answered. 'Lucy? I've been trying to contact you.'

'Robbie, can I ring you later? Now's not really a good time to talk.'

Robbie cut her short. 'Something's happened,' he said. 'I'll collect you in ten minutes.'

CHAPTER 48

By the time Lucy and Robbie pulled into the estate in Foyle Springs, the fire brigade had managed to bring the blaze under control, but even with that the house was no more than a blackened shell, the walls glistening in the growing light.

One of the firemen sat on the kerb at the side of the road, the streaks of his sweat marked in rivulets on the grime of his face.

'What happened?' Lucy asked.

The fireman stared up at her, perhaps suspecting she was a journalist.

'She's with the PPU,' Robbie said.

'Arson,' the man said. 'The stink of petrol in the place is desperate.'

One of the firemen came out of the house, his breathing apparatus over his face. He pulled it off and moved to the side of the house. He stood, facing the wall, his head resting on his forearm against the brickwork. One of his colleagues patted him on the back as he passed.

'There were two children living there,' Lucy managed, the acrid taste of the smoke burning in her throat and causing her to struggle to breathe.

The man shook his head dejectedly.

'Where are they?'

He glanced at the house. 'They were in the bedroom together – one curled round the other. The wee girl had wrapped the baby in wet towels. Hadn't kept any for herself, just for the baby. He'd not have survived otherwise.'

'Where are they now?'

'The wee boy's in the hospital. He took in a lot of smoke. The girl . . . we couldn't help her . . . she'd already . . .' He hung his head, staring between his knees at the ground. 'She used all the towels on the baby.'

Lucy felt a sob shudder through her body.

'What about the mother and her partner?' Robbie asked.

'We found the mother. She was in the living room. There is no one else.'

'Did she do it?'

'We don't know yet. The pathologist will have to examine her first.'

'Her partner got out on bail yesterday,' Robbie said. 'One of our workers was out here with them when he arrived. He was in the house last night.'

Lucy felt the ground shift beneath her. She sat on the kerb beside the fireman.

'We found a phone still in the wee girl's hand. She must have tried calling for help,' the man said. 'Can you imagine that?'

Lucy suddenly felt her innards twist. She began to retch, had to turn her head away from the man beside her.

With trembling fingers, she took out her phone. She dialled voicemail, retrieved the message she would have received when she'd been in the woods with Travers and her father had her battery not died.

Mary Quigg's voice was hushed, her words slurring, as if she was crying.

'I need help. You said you'd help. He's hurt Mummy. He's going to hurt us. I'm in my room with Joe. Please come and get me.'

Lucy allowed her tears to run freely, lowering the phone from her ear. Mary's voice could still be heard. Robbie sat beside her and listened, his arm around her.

'He's going to kill us. Mummy. Mummy!' The word was a scream, pleading, desperate.

Robbie reached across to take the phone from Lucy but she would not let him. She had to hear the message.

And so they sat and listened. Mary's speech became more broken over the course of the next two minutes, her words more slurred, punctuated by her screams. In the background they could hear the baby's crying become more muffled, could hear Mary occasionally hushing him. Over and over she said, 'Is there anybody there?'

After those few minutes, they heard only the gasping of her breaths. Then those too stopped.

CHAPTER 49

By the time she got home, the house was empty. A note on the table from her mother told her to call the station when she was ready. Robbie dropped her off, promised to call on her later to check how she was doing.

When she went into the PPU suite, Lucy's mother and Tom Fleming were questioning Kate McLaughlin. Michael McLaughlin sat next to her on the sofa, her hand clasped in his. The interview had been going on for some time, for they were discussing Alice.

'She said she knew somewhere safe, in the woods. A hut her daddy used for camping,' Kate said. 'She led me there through the snow, then said she had to go back, in case her father found out she'd let me out.'

Lucy's mother glanced up and, seeing her, excused herself from the interview.

'I thought you spoke to Kate yesterday,' Lucy observed when her mother came out.

'We're softening up the father. I'm going to put a few of your accusations to him and see what he has to say for himself.'

'You're making him listen to Kate's ordeal again to make him feel guilty,' Lucy said.

Her mother smiled briefly. 'Something like that,' she said. 'I want you to know that your father has been charged with Bill Travers's killing.'

'What?'

'I spoke to him in the house. I showed him the gun that was used and he said it was his. He says that Travers tried to attack you and so he shot him. They fought and he threw him over the quarry edge.'

'But that's not true,' Lucy said. 'He can't take the blame. He didn't do it.'

Her mother stared at her steadily. 'He says he did.'

'He's senile!' Lucy snapped.

'He seemed sensible enough this morning. He'll claim diminished responsibility and be put in a secure unit in Gransha Hospital.'

'That's not fair, Mum,' Lucy said. 'I can't let him take the blame.'

'It's best all round, Lucy. He has signed a statement already. The case is closed.'

'You're just punishing him for Janet,' Lucy said angrily.

'He's punishing himself,' she replied. 'I'm just letting him do it. It should have been done years ago.'

Lucy knew her mother well enough to know that she would not change her mind on this.

'I heard about the young girl, Quigg,' her mother said. 'I'm sorry. Tom said she had connected with you.'

Lucy struggled to remain composed. 'For all the good it did her.'

'She called you, is that right? As she died.'

Lucy nodded, but could not trust herself to speak.

'You need to make a real impact on someone to have them think of you at the moment of their death.'

'I let her down,' Lucy said. 'She called me and I wasn't there.'

'That wasn't your fault, Lucy, and you can't blame yourself for it.'

'That's easier said than done,' Lucy said.

'If you want someone to blame, go for Alan Cunningham. The case is open. Cunningham has fled over the border apparently. I'm sure whoever takes over CID from Travers will be glad to have PPU input. Especially from someone with such an affinity for the vulnerable, Lucy. Don't waste that.'

'Are you saying this as my mother?'

'And as your commanding officer. I've already left the preliminary case notes on your desk.'

Lucy stared at the woman, then quickly embraced her. Her mother seemed surprised by the gesture.

'Do we have an understanding?'

Lucy managed a brief smiled. 'Yes, ma'am.'

Her mother nodded, then turned and went back into the Interview Room.

'Let's talk about property deals, Mr McLaughlin,' Lucy heard her say, as she passed on the way to her office.

Through the high window in her room she could see the sun had crested the rusted fence beyond; its light refracting through the drops of meltwater hanging from the barbs on the wire. A thin folder lay on her desk with the initial reports on the fire in the Quigg house. Photographs of Catherine and Mary were attached to the cover sheet.

She sat and stared at the picture of Mary, rubbed her finger along the girl's cheek.

'I'm sorry, Mary,' she whispered.

Lifting the photograph, she went over to the old noticeboard and pulled down the poster on the need to destroy ragwort. In the centre of the board she pinned Mary's picture so that, whenever she sat at her desk, Mary would be facing her, reminding her.

During the rest of the afternoon, as the sun moved across the sky, the small square of light from the window shifted incrementally across the far wall until it seemed to Lucy that, just before dusk, it settled on the picture of Mary, framing her in its dying light.

CHAPTER 50

It did not take long for McLaughlin to confess. By the following morning, the story was already featuring on the front pages of the papers. Fleming relayed the details of the interview to her over coffee in the PPU kitchen.

McLaughlin had bought the land to build on, knowing that the listed buildings would have to be razed if he was to make a profit. Billy Quinn had worked for him even then and suggested he knew someone who could help him out for a cut of the profits. Little did they realize when they planted the bomb that McLaughlin's wife, who knew nothing of the scam, was in the building.

Travers had been investigating her killing. When he got the tip-off from Lucy's father, he'd challenged McLaughlin. McLaughlin claimed he felt relief that it was out in the open, was glad to accept the punishment for what he had done. But then Travers offered him an alternative. He too would take a slice of the profits and, in return, take care of the source of the tip-off, and her handler.

McLaughlin heard nothing further until he leaked the story about the £25 million bid for the site weeks earlier. He hadn't realized that Kent and Mullan were out. He'd paid off Billy Quinn in dribs and drabs, keeping him on a full salary for driving a car for him once or twice a month. It was Billy who told him what had happened to Kate. He knew he'd no chance of getting her back when Travers took over the case of her disappearance. But by that stage, he was so deeply enmeshed with the gang, he could tell no one.

The papers ran a slimmed-down version of the story, focusing on the tragedy of the husband's actions in killing his own wife, drawing comparisons with Ancient Greek drama. The Director of Public Prosecutions was compiling a file. McLaughlin could serve time. His daughter, Lucy reflected, would be alone again.

Two smaller stories featured on the front pages too. The first concerned the fire that had claimed the lives of Catherine and Mary Quigg. Police confirmed that it had been started deliberately. The partner of the children's mother was being sought as part of ongoing inquiries. Latest reports suggested he had made for the border and was hiding out in Donegal. A hospital spokesman said the young boy rescued from the fire was making promising progress.

The second, smaller sidebar story mentioned, in passing, the events in Prehen. A serving PSNI officer had died in tragic circumstances after going into the woods to search for a retired RUC officer who had got lost. Travers had not been mentioned in the McLaughlin story either. Travers had been right in one respect. Lucy's mother would not want her own reputation besmirched by the truth of her father's crime against Janet coming out. As a consequence, Travers's own reputation, publicly, remained unblemished.

*

After leaving Fleming, she visited her father in Gransha. A psychiatric nurse led her down the corridor to the secure room where her father was being held. It was a basic affair: a metal-framed bed, a hard chair, a sink.

Her father looked older than she had ever seen him before. He sat on the edge of his bed, one arm strapped to the frame. His eyes were glazed as if he were having difficulty in focusing. His head was bowed, his mouth hanging slightly open.

'Daddy?'

He made an effort to glance up at her, then lowered his head again.

'It's me, Daddy. Lucy.'

He nodded lightly.

'Mum told me what you said. You should have told the truth.'

He angled his head to one side, rubbed at his cheek with the back of his hand.

'You should have told them what really happened. In the woods.'

'The woods,' he repeated.

'You remember we were in the woods,' she said, sitting beside him on the bed. She laid her hand on his back, felt the frail movements of his ribs as he breathed.

'I found the grave.'

'What grave?'

He smiled a narcotic-induced grin.

'Where the elephant was buried? Do you remember I told you that?'

Lucy placed her hand on top of his.

'I'm talking about Bill Travers, Dad. Do you remember?'

Her father held her hand lightly. 'For years I could never find it, but I knew it was there. But I found it again last night.'

'Travers, Daddy,' Lucy said with desperation. 'Do you remember?'

Her father shook his head. 'Remember, remember,' he repeated. 'Things get lost and things get found,' he cooed, rocking lightly to a rhythm only he could hear.

Lucy sat with him a moment longer, then got up to leave. 'I'm meeting someone for lunch, Daddy. I have to go.'

When she was at the door, he spoke a final time to her.

'I'm sorry, Lucy. For everything. For all you lost because of me.'

Lucy nodded, but did not look back at him.

It was bright outside, the air carrying the new-found heat of the early spring sunshine. Robbie was waiting for her in the car.

'How did it go?'

'Fine,' she said. 'It went fine.'

'Are you OK?'

Lucy inhaled deeply, held it, then released, feeling herself relax.

'I am,' she said.

Robbie shifted into gear.

'Good. So, where do you want to go for lunch?'

'Wherever you like. I want to visit Mary's baby brother afterwards. See how he's doing. Would you mind?'

'So that's a visit to a psychiatric hospital, some lunch, and then a trip to the children's ward. Has anyone ever told you, you're quite the date, Lucy Black?'

'So, you think this is a date, do you?' Lucy said.

'Or not,' Robbie replied, his hands raised in surrender. 'You choose.'

'I already have,' Lucy said, with a smile.

Acknowledgements

Thanks to all who helped in bringing *Little Girl Lost* to life. Thanks to my friends and colleagues in St Columb's for their support. Thanks, too, to Bob McKimm for his help and support.

I received very useful advice from a number of individuals regarding various aspects of this story, particularly Alex Mullan, Jody Kirby, Susan Montgomery, Tara Vance and James Johnston.

Thanks to Peter Straus and Jennifer Hewson of RCW and Emily Hickman of The Agency for their incredible encouragement, advice and support.

Special thanks to all the team at Pan Macmillan: Cormac, Liz, Jon, Sophie, Ellen, David, Helen and particularly Will.

My family continue to be hugely supportive of my writing; thanks to all the McGilloways, Dohertys, O'Neills and Kerlins. Particular thanks, and love, to Carmel, Joe and Dermot and to my parents, Laurence and Katrina for all they have done and continue to do.

Finally, I could not write without the support and love of my wife, Tanya, and our children, Ben, Tom, David and Lucy. For that, and for everything else too, I'm extremely grateful.